The Glass House

Also by Beatrice Colin

To Capture What We Cannot Keep

The Songwriter

The Glimmer Palace

Disappearing Act

Nude Untitled

The Glass House

Beatrice Colin

FLATIRON
BOOKS
NEW YORK

THE GLASS HOUSE. Copyright © 2020 by Beatrice Colin. All rights reserved. Printed in the United States of America. For information, address Flatiron Books, 120 Broadway, New York, NY 10271.

www.flatironbooks.com

Designed by Donna Sinisgalli Noetzel

Library of Congress Cataloging-in-Publication Data

Names: Colin, Beatrice, author.
Title: The glass house / Beatrice Colin.
Description: First Edition. | New York : Flatiron Books, 2020.
Identifiers: LCCN 2020017249 | ISBN 9781250152503
    (hardcover) | ISBN 9781250152497 (ebook)
Subjects: GSAFD: Mystery fiction.
Classification: LCC PR6103.O443 G53 2020 |
    DDC 823/.92—dc23
LC record available at https://lccn.loc.gov/2020017249

Our books may be purchased in bulk for promotional, educational, or business use. Please contact your local bookseller or the Macmillan Corporate and Premium Sales Department at 1-800-221-7945, extension 5442, or by email at MacmillanSpecialMarkets@macmillan.com.

First Edition: 2020

10 9 8 7 6 5 4 3 2 1

The Glass House

Prologue

Argyll, Scotland. June 1911

It was so still on the day of the funeral that you could hear the church bell echo back from the other side of the loch. The light was soft, diffuse, as if the sun itself had been wrapped in a white mourning veil. While fields of wheat whispered consolation to themselves, the hedgerows were filled with the bright shout of buttercups and campion, bluebells and cow parsley. Even in the shade the air was warm. It would be a good year for honey.

Edward Pick was buried in the plot he had reserved, at the edge of the graveyard with a view over the water. His coffin was unadorned, his committal brief; he had paid in advance for sandwiches and beer for anyone who came. Not many did. Afterward they walked back to the estate, to Balmarra, the small group of mourners, mainly employees, a calligraphy of indigo dashes against the great ocher mountains beyond. Most of them had been expecting—some hoping—that he would die months, even years, earlier. Although his family had made their fortune in sugar, the truth was that prosperity had turned him sour. He was stubborn, too, determined that he would not be finished off by freezing temperatures or influenza or inertia, and he clung to life until it suited him to leave.

Pick was a man, as so many are, of contradictions. The mourners fell silent as they headed up the driveway to the main house. Here were gardens first dug seven hundred years ago by monks from Burgundy, France. But the beds of dill, shallots, and chervil, the apple and pear orchards beneath which so many of the order had been interred, were long gone. Now late rhododendrons, their flowers circus pirouettes of pink or lilac or purple or apricot, bloomed with abandon. The scent of azaleas lingered in the air like perfume on a woman's wrist, while the tiny petals of a Japanese wisteria shivered modestly as they passed.

The glass house lay to the left of the drive, a vast wheel of glazing and decorative ironwork that housed the most precious of Pick's plants: palms, orchids, orange trees, and roses. And when the wind changed that night and the clouds burst, the sound of rain hitting the glazed roof was louder than thunder. The noise, the temporary opacity, the water streaming down the panes to flood the gravel paths seemed to suggest a curtain call, a final flourish, perhaps, with an explosion of rose petals. But that, as only Edward Pick knew, was yet to come.

1

Glasgow, June 1912

At the taxi rank on Gordon Street there was a small queue: three old ladies who fussed over a cat in a basket, a man with a wooden cane that he tapped on the curb to some music he alone could hear, and a woman and a young girl with a trolley stacked high with bags and suitcases.

"Won't be too long now," a porter told the woman as a taxi drew up and the three old ladies with the cat climbed inside.

The man with the cane turned and gave them a curious look. The woman closed her eyes, hoping to avert any attempt at conversation. London the night before had been dark, rain-soaked, and chaotic. They had almost missed their connection, and the memory of their hands clutched tight as she pulled her daughter through crowds of people all pushing in the opposite direction still filled her with a sense of swallowed panic. On the journey north in their compartment in the first-class sleeping car, the feeling didn't subside: She had the overwhelming sense that something had been forgotten and had to resist the urge to check, for what could she do if it had?

The train from London had arrived in Glasgow after seeming to meander around northern Britain, skirting small mountains, chugging across sluggish black rivers, and stopping at remote stations where no one climbed on or off. As they stood on the empty platform, Cicely Pick looked around for assistance. What on earth was one to do, where should one start, who was there to ask? All she had was an address with no idea how far away their destination was or how they should get there. And then she noticed the conductor, collecting his belongings from the mail van.

"Excuse me," she called out. "We are in need of a little advice."

After he had frowned at her piece of paper, the conductor blew his whistle, summoned a porter, and instructed him to take them to the taxi rank. Now the porter stood staring into the middle distance, his watch frequently checked. How much did one tip?

A fine rain began to fall, beading their hair, their faces, their coats with tiny droplets. The umbrella had been left on the train, of course. She turned her face skyward. Travel made one feel so dirty, so squalid. Her clothes were stiff with coal smoke and crumpled with sleep, the skin on her ankles itching with bites from fleas or mosquitoes or maybe both. She hoped they had not picked anything up, she prayed they would not be sick, she wished she had not fought with her husband the day before they left.

The man with the cane was squinting to read the shipping address on their luggage tag. She had written it herself in blue ink, which was beginning to run in the rain: "Mrs. George Pick Esquire, Darjeeling, India."

"Nice weather for ducks," he said.

She cocked her head. Was he talking to her?

"I said, *Nice weather for ducks,*" the man said louder and more slowly. "Speak English?"

"I do indeed," Cicely Pick replied with a smile. "And I'm not hard of hearing either, in case you were wondering."

He opened his mouth as if to reply and then closed it again. Thankfully at just that moment another cab drew up. He climbed in without a backward glance. Even without the luggage tag it was obvious that they were not local. She was sure he could tell from a single glance at their clothes, their manner, their skin. Almost every single person she had seen since they arrived in Britain had been pale, so pale their skin looked almost blue. It was probably the light. There was barely any of it. She checked her watch. Despite the gloom it was already 11:15 a.m.

The city smelled of coffee grounds underlined by the faint whiff of drains. An omnibus passed on the road in front, a horse and cart close behind. From somewhere nearby a church bell struck a single note. Finally another taxi drew up. The porter gave the destination, and the driver quoted a price. At least she guessed he did. His words were incomprehensible. Maybe the man with the cane had asked her the right question, maybe the English she spoke wasn't the right kind of English. The driver glanced at the porter and repeated the price louder this time, his voice raised above the noise of the traffic. She gave a decisive nod of agreement even though she did not know what she was actually agreeing to. The driver looked pleased and helped the porter stack their luggage in the taxi's boot. Cicely handed the latter a coin—more than enough, judging by the upturn of his mouth—and climbed in after her daughter. Once they had both settled into the sagging leather, the doors were slammed, the engine cranked, and with a puff of gray smoke and a grind of the gears, they were off.

Almost immediately Kitty yawned and rubbed her eyes.

"Tired?" Cicely asked.

"Not really," the child replied.

She blinked several times and sat up straight, as she had been taught. Within moments, however, her head nodded forward and she had fallen asleep. A folded blanket lay on a rack for cold days and drafty journeys. Cicely removed her daughter's straw hat, undid the buttons of her coat, and tucked the blanket carefully around her lap. But even while sleeping Kitty threw it off.

"Leave me be, Mother," she murmured.

Cicely's eyes burned. If only she could doze as easily as her daughter, if only she could throw off complications as easily as a rug. It seemed as if she hadn't slept for days, lying wide awake all night in her bunk on the train and in her cabin on the boat before that, her blood thickening, her mind a tangle of what-ifs and how-coulds and should-nots. And even now her ears roared with the rumble and grind of the steamship and the rhythm and clang of the train, and she longed to be still, to be quiet, to be clean again, but most of all finally to sink into the careless oblivion of sleep.

They passed along a canyon of masonry, deep red, pale gray, and charry black, the left side of the street lit by the morning sun, the right still in shadow. In India, she calculated, it would already be late afternoon. She pictured their house on the side of the mountain, the empty rooms, the furniture swathed in dust sheets, and the daylight falling in stripes through the locked shutters. It would all be the same when she returned, she told herself, nothing changed but the season. And yet she imagined cracks in the plasterwork and doors banging in the wind, an absence, a shift, that manifested itself in fallen slates and cracked tiles, a profusion of weeds and the blocking of sinks, the house punishing her for leaving.

She hoped she had labeled their trunks correctly; she willed that the railway company's delivery system was efficient but not overly so. It would be embarrassing if the trunks arrived before they did, but even worse if they were lost on the way.

By the time they reached the outskirts of the city the air seemed cleaner, the smog and coal dust blown away. The taxi crested a hill and a view unrolled before them, water surrounding the hills as if the world had flooded and remained that way—the mountains and moors, the forests and the rocky shores all reflected back at the sky in the rippled mirror of the river Clyde.

Kitty opened her eyes and gazed out at the view in silence.

"So I'm Scottish too?" she asked after a moment.

"Half, if it's just the father."

"And you're not?"

She shook her head no.

In India it often felt as if nearly everyone but her had roots in the old country, as her husband liked to call it. At Christmas the air reeked of mothballs and cloves as Paisley shawls and tartan kilts were brought out of cedar wardrobes or mahogany chests, shaken, pressed, then worn with unself-conscious aplomb. Every Saturday the whole year round, the local bagpipe band played "Scotland the Brave" and "My Bonnie Lies over the Ocean" on the covered terrace of the Darjeeling Planters Club, and increasingly, she had noticed, the newspapers were full of birth announcements for babies named Angus, Hamish, or Fiona. With brighter colors, louder instruments, and stronger accents, Scotland, even from thousands of miles away, seemed to be capable of drowning out the local habitat by sheer volume.

As they drove west, the river widened. A dozen small boats, their sails filled, scudded along the surface. A few miles farther they arrived at a bigger town, the roadside lined with ugly buildings, refineries, warehouses, factories, and a customshouse. The air again turned foul with the smell of charcoal, molasses, and something else—glue, perhaps? Between buildings Cicely caught a glimpse of a harbor, the quays piled high with sacks and wooden crates, the air hazy with smoke from the funnels of ships and the spray of the paddle steamers.

The night before they left home, Cicely had consulted her husband's collection of maps, fragile parchments that he cataloged by continent. Once spread out, the Indian maps were mostly pale pink, dirty yellow, or maroon, all spidered with train lines, but the maps of Argyll, Strathclyde, and the Western Isles were made up of patches of pure color: green, brown, and the most exquisite shades of blue. They were old, however, and had been folded so many times that they had begun to crack and split, the names of some places rendered illegible, as if forgotten halfway through the telling. She had shown the maps to Kitty, pointing out Glenrannoch School near Stirling, and the child had placed her finger on the tiny square set in a rectangle of green to make it disappear.

Cicely had always loved the musical quality of Scottish places. *Skye, Ayr, Troon*, towns named in songs, the sound of each lingering in the mouth like sugar pebbles. It was strange, therefore, to arrive in a land she thought she knew only to find it otherwise. She had pictured mountains and wild seas, pretty villages and harbors, not factories, cranes, and a river full of barges.

"Excuse me," she called to the driver. "Where are we?"

"Tail of the Bank," he enunciated carefully. "Greenock."

This was the town her husband's family wealth had sprung from, where their ships had set sail for the West Indies and where they had opened their warehouses and refineries, first for tobacco and then for sugar. There were some fine villas and a few grand civic buildings, but the streets were narrow and the houses old, many looking on the brink of collapse. Cicely took in the people as they passed: three men in caps and dark jackets sheltering in a doorway to smoke their cigarettes, a woman leaning out of a window to shout at some children below, a group of girls with baskets hanging out sheets on a line. Cicely stared and they stared right back. They looked so thin, so undernourished. It was a strange thing, to her at least, to see such poverty among people with white skin. It was equally novel, so she gathered, to see a woman and child alone in the back of a taxi.

They turned right onto a wide esplanade, elegant mansions on one side and the chop of the river on the other. A light wind blew in from the hills, lifting hats and blowing skirts around the ankles of the ladies who strolled along the waterfront. The driver pointed out a thick seam of land between the water and the sky, the Cowal peninsula, their destination. They would take the steamer, she thought he said, across the water and drive the last few remaining miles. Finally they pulled into a narrow harbor with a small pier and drew to a halt. There was already a small queue of motorcars, horses and carts, and bicycles. Cicely wound down the window just as the sun came out and lit up the view with a golden light. The colors of the hills, the water, the sky, the rocks seemed to deepen and intensify as if a layer had been lifted, a glass washed, and she was sure she had never seen a bluer blue or a blacker black.

She was turning to Kitty to point it out when the sun dipped behind a cloud, and the whole scene—the sky, the water, the rocks on the beach—grew dim and gray, the only color that remained the faded blue paint around the window of the ticket office. A spitting rain began to fall as she wound the window back up again. Although it was supposed to be the height of summer, Cicely's feet felt cold. Her body, though cocooned in her coat, was chilled right through. How could one get used to such weather? How did one stay warm?

A steamer was approaching. It docked and released a stream of vehicles and foot passengers from its decks, their heads covered with newspapers or baskets as they ran for cover. They were close to their destination now, but she was suddenly filled with dread. Would the boat sail in such a downpour? Perhaps they might be delayed? Would their driver turn around and take them back to the station in the city if she paid him double? Before she could ask, the taxi started its engine and followed the other motorcars down the ramp. There would be no delay, no opportunity to change her mind. In eight weeks Kitty would start boarding school, but in the meantime they were heading to an estate called Balmarra with neither prior warning nor an invitation.

At the point where the Clyde widened into an estuary and ran into the Atlantic, several sea lochs, deep and black as molasses, joined the river as it turned from freshwater to brine. It was on the shores of one of these, Loch Long, that Balmarra House was situated, facing east and looking out toward the village of Cove on the other side. Constructed in the 1760s in the Palladian style, the house had a wide shallow staircase flanked by two stone lions, which led to a porch on the main floor. Three stories high with two side wings, it had been built to look bigger than it actually was.

The first sign of the motorcar's approach was the rise of a couple of black crows into the pale summer sky. And then the faintest rumble of wheels on the driveway, the crunch of gears, and the grumble of an engine. The gardener's dog began to bark.

"Are we expecting anyone?" Antonia asked Cook.

Cook shrugged and placed a kettle on the range to boil.

"Just two for dinner as far as I know," she replied. "But then again, no one tells me anything."

Antonia glanced over the accounts once more, then took off her spectacles.

"Now about the tea," she continued.

"It's the best I can get on our budget," Cook replied. "Maybe not the best there is. Depends on what you're used to, I suppose. Your father never complained."

"I find that hard to believe."

Cook, whose name was Edith but who preferred to be addressed thus, sucked in her cheeks, no doubt storing her outrage for later where she would repeat their exchange word for word to anyone who would listen, picking over it for morsels of insult. She was a woman who seemed to lack the muscles for smiling. There was a stiffness about her, not limited to her joints, as if she kept herself boxed in for fear of revealing something unbecoming. But Antonia's father had liked her; he had praised her cooking—plain and wholesome, nothing fancy or foreign—and she had worked for the family for as long as Antonia could remember. It couldn't be much of a life, Antonia reminded herself, serving mediocre food to people who only pretended to appreciate it.

The doorbell rang. Antonia turned her head in an effort to hear. But the mutter of voices was too low to make anything out.

"I wish tradesmen would use the back entrance," she said and returned to the ledger.

After she had finished the accounts, Antonia was hoping to get out into the garden for an hour or two and had left her painting materials packed and ready next to the front door. There was a particularly attractive patch of lily of the valley that she had her eye on up the glen. Housekeeping took up more of her time than she liked, but what was the alternative? They couldn't justify the expense of a housekeeper when she was perfectly capable of doing it herself.

The rhododendrons had been glorious this year, the colors more intense than any pigment or paint. Her father's collection included dwarf specimens from high altitudes in China and Nepal and the much larger plants from lower down, their great shiny leaves almost a foot long and their bark a rich rusty red. Only two other people, the gardeners, saw their annual display, which was a shame. Malcolm, her husband, wasn't interested. The great outdoors, he always said, gave him nothing but chilblains.

Someone was running down the servants' stairs at full tilt. Antonia looked up. Cook lifted the kettle off the range. Dora, the housemaid, tried to catch her breath before she spoke.

"Didn't know where you were—" she said. "A taxicab all the way from the city—"

A large black car had indeed parked in front of Balmarra's main door. The driver seemed to be unloading luggage from the trunk. Three brown leather suitcases had already been placed in the porch. Fastening the button on her cardigan, Antonia stood as tall as she could in her boots and opened the front door.

"Can I help you?" she said.

"It's six shillings all in," the taxi driver replied, slamming shut the boot. He glanced up and saw the look on her face. "At the railway station in Glasgow I gave an estimation of the fare, and the lady agreed."

She was about to ask which lady he was referring to when the door of the taxi swung open to reveal a woman of about thirty. For a moment she was silent, taking Antonia in, so it seemed, from the bottom up. And then, refusing the taxi driver's hand, she climbed down.

"George described you perfectly," she said, adjusting her hat. "You must be his sister, Antonia."

"You know my brother, George?"

"I do indeed. And this"—she turned and held out her arms to a small girl Antonia hadn't noticed, rubbing her eyes in the back seat—"is our daughter, Kitty."

Antonia suddenly needed a chair. But first she needed her purse. Of course she did not have money for the fare and had to ask Dora to ask Cook to raid the housekeeping fund. Before the maid arrived back, however, the woman had paid.

"Here," she said, handing the driver a ten-shilling note as if it were nothing. "And here," she went on, handing over an extra half crown. "Thank you."

"We should have taken care of that," said Antonia, aghast at such a conspicuous display of generosity.

"It's done," she said.

Dressed in a dark-brown velvet coat, trimmed at the collar and wrist with rabbit fur, the woman who had just arrived was both elegant and soft spoken. Her waist was small, and the hem of skirt just skimmed her ankles, making Antonia's floor-length day dress seem woefully dated. Although the play of wind from the water lifted a few strands of hair from underneath her hat, she did not seem to notice. Nor did she acknowledge the taxicab, which, with a toot of the horn, turned and headed back along the driveway. Instead the woman pulled off her gloves, took a step forward, and held out a slim, honey-colored hand.

"I'm Cicely," she said.

"Well, this is most unexpected," Antonia replied as she shook it. "And you've come all the way from—?"

"India, yes. I was going to write. But—"

Antonia waited for an explanation. Was her brother sick? Had something awful happened to him? She braced herself for bad news and realized that this was the moment she had been expecting for years: Was it an accident, an illness, a drowning, an altercation? She imagined limbs lost, temperatures soaring, a body white and lifeless on mountain scree. She hoped George hadn't suffered, she hoped the end was swift and dignified and felt the rise of tears in anticipation.

"But?" she prompted.

"But here we are," her brother's wife replied. There was no bad news. George, she deduced, was still very much alive. A wave of relief was quickly followed by a wave of panic. Judging by the suitcases, they had come to stay. Where would they sleep, was there enough food, what would they think of the house, of the weather, of her, standing on the doorstep in a threadbare cardigan?

The woman inhaled deeply and stretched in a single movement.

"I am stiff as a board of wood," she said. "I thought we'd never arrive! I must say you live so far from anywhere."

"Anywhere?" said Antonia.

"Paris, New York, London—" The woman laughed.

"Dunoon is rather close," Antonia said.

There was a small, slightly awkward pause. Cicely's eyes flicked to the open door behind her.

"Goodness," said Antonia. "What am I doing, letting you stand out here on the doorstep? Please do come in."

Visitors were uncommon. Before Edward Pick's death, the minister had occasionally dropped in for a glass of port and an argument. Other than him, the only people were the grocer, the postman, the roofer, the plumber, and the coal man, and they usually used the back entrance. Although it was not untidy, the house was not prepared for eyes other than the family's own. Antonia was aware too that although she barely noticed it anymore, on damp summer days like this one the house had a particular smell that was not entirely pleasant—of wet wool, dry rot, and burnt toast. A distant toilet flushed, and above their heads a pipe belched and groaned.

"I'm afraid you caught us on the hop. We weren't expecting guests."

"I hope it's not an inconvenience?" replied her brother's wife. "If you'd rather we took accommodation elsewhere—"

"Absolutely not! This is an"—she searched for the appropriate phrase—"unexpected pleasure. And I'm sure my husband, Malcolm, will be thrilled to meet you both. He's heard so much about my younger brother, but of course they've never actually met."

What would Malcolm say? He made no secret of the fact that he disapproved of George. Although he hadn't ever said anything negative, it was obvious in the way he referred to him as "that" brother of hers, as if she had another, better one.

"Why am I not surprised?" she would ask rhetorically when he came home.

"Why indeed?" he would mutter to himself.

All the fires were quickly lit in honor of the guests' arrival. The clouds cleared, and the late afternoon light that fell through the windows—the glass still giving off the faintest whiff of the vinegar used to polish it some time ago—was golden. And even though most of the rooms were still so chilly that you could almost see your breath, Antonia hoped that the flicker of cool yellow flame and the cast of sun across the oak floors would give the impression of warmth if not the physical reality.

While their suitcases were being taken to the guest rooms on the top floor and the beds were being made up, her brother's wife and daughter stood at the drawing-room window and stared out. The girl looked about eight, Antonia guessed, but had the composure of a slightly older child. She wore a blue woolen coat buttoned up to the neck, a straw hat, and a pair of white leather ankle boots. Her face was striking, with sepia skin and pale-green eyes, a face that would probably one day turn heads. And yet for all her poise, there was a restlessness about her: She was a fiddler, a foot tapper, a nail-biter. Strands of her hair fell in corkscrews around her face. The toes of her boots were scuffed, and she had a small hole in one stocking. Did she long to escape, to play? To unbutton that coat and pull it off? She vividly remembered the twin constraints of etiquette and restrictive clothing. As she watched, the girl breathed on the window, lifted her finger, and was about to write on the misted glass when her mother preempted her, taking her hand and holding it still.

"Excellent view," Cicely said.

"When it's not raining, I suppose," Antonia replied.

"What's that down there?" she asked. "Is it an island?"

"That's Karrasay," Antonia said. "It's not really an island. You can reach it by a narrow causeway. I take it George told you all about Balmarra?"

"No," she replied, "not really."

Antonia was momentarily taken aback.

"The gardens look established," Cicely offered.

"As well as the formal one," Antonia explained, "we have about thirty hectares, and I'm sure you saw the glass house on the way here."

"We did," said Cicely. "Impossible to miss, really."

Antonia glanced sidelong at her brother's wife and wondered if she was being facetious. Her words expressed one opinion, her face another.

"I suppose you have plans," Cicely said.

Antonia blinked. Did she mean the gardens? She suddenly felt the weight of responsibility on her shoulders. The upkeep, the expense, the constant battle to keep the weeds from taking over the flower beds. She hadn't got as far as planning.

"Well, of course," she replied. "My father was a collector of exotic species, but he wasn't much of a record keeper. It's all been a little let go in recent years for understandable reasons. But I intend to take it in hand and catalog everything properly."

What was she saying? She no idea how to do such a thing. If she painted a flower, shrub, or tree she didn't recognize, she would collect a specimen and tell herself she would look it up later. But something always came up, and she rarely did.

"Maybe I could take your coats?" she suggested.

A bluster of wind rattled the glazing. The clouds had closed over again, and it began to rain. The outlook from the drawing-room window was now undeniably bleak, or *dreich* as they said in Scots.

"I think we'll keep them on for the moment." Cicely frowned through the glass as the rain grew heavier. Dora came in with a couple of oil lamps even though it was still afternoon. It may have been preferable to sitting in the half dark, but once lit up from the inside, Balmarra sometimes felt like the last house left in the world.

"There were floods in May," Antonia began. "The rain brought down all the blossom. It was almost biblical."

Her brother's wife didn't seem to be listening. She was regarding her daughter with an expression on her face that Antonia couldn't read. Cicely placed her hand on Kitty's shoulder for a fraction of a second before the girl shrugged her off.

"Luckily," Antonia said in a slightly louder voice. It worked. Cicely turned in her direction.

"Luckily we have roses all year round," Antonia continued. "From the glass house. They'll keep us going for decades to come."

There was a moment of what looked like complete incomprehension. Cicely Pick swallowed.

"How splendid," she replied, the corners of her mouth twitching a little before they formed a smile.

Tea was served, along with a Dundee cake and fish paste sandwiches. They took their places at the dining room table. Kitty ate three slices of cake in silence while her mother described their journey:

leaving Bombay at sunset, passing through the Suez Canal, arriving at the island of Malta, the antics of the monkeys in Gibraltar. Almost as suddenly as she had started, however, she stopped.

"I'm afraid I'm not at my best," she admitted, then drained her teacup. "I have the stamina of a mule, George likes to say, but cannot doze when the world is moving beneath me, not even in the ladies' carriage."

Antonia noticed the blue bruise of lack of sleep beneath each eye. But she was determined not to take the hint. She needed to know exactly why this woman and her daughter were there.

"How is my brother?" she asked.

"You know George." Cicely placed her cup back in its saucer.

"Another expedition?"

"Northern Burma," she replied with a wave of her hand. "Or somewhere around there."

"Rong Chu," said the girl.

It was the first thing she had said since they arrived. Antonia suddenly had a horrible premonition that she didn't speak English.

"It's a river," the girl explained, to Antonia's relief. "In the Lohit Valley."

"Wonderful," Antonia said and forced a smile. "What's he hunting now?"

"The usual," his wife replied. "Plants."

"Only the rare ones," said the girl. Then for emphasis, it seemed, she brushed the remainder of her cake from the table to the floor. Ignore, Antonia told herself, and tried to banish the thought of the resident mice feasting on crumbs.

"He was sorry he wasn't able to be here for your father's funeral," Cicely Pick said. "He felt rather bad about it, actually."

"Couldn't be helped, I suppose."

All Antonia had received over the years from George was the odd Christmas card, never in December, to show that he was still alive, postmarked in all manner of places from Mandalay to Calcutta.

Before the funeral, a letter had been dispatched to India, care of the British consul in Bombay, informing him of the news. No acknowledgment had ever been received. And now to find out that not only had George known about their father's death and not sent word, but that he had failed to pass on the news of his marriage and the birth of his progeny, was shocking.

For a moment all three of them stared at the teapot.

"You've come all the way from India?" Antonia offered.

"From Darjeeling, yes," she replied. "It's in the mountains, the Himalayas, that is."

"Place of the Lightning Bolt," said Antonia.

"You know Darjeeling?" asked the girl.

"Only its name. In Tibetan."

"You speak Tibetan?"

"Oh, no," she admitted. "I'd like to learn and travel to Tibet one day, or thereabouts. My geography needs a brushup. Maybe you could . . . ?"

The girl, however, had lost interest and was picking with a fingernail at the gold enamel that edged her side plate.

"Darjeeling is in western Bengal," Cicely explained. "Nepal is in the west, Bhutan in the northeast, and Bengal again in the south."

"And Tibet?"

"The north."

It clearly was a stupid question. Where else could Tibet be but in the north?

"Are your people in tea, Cicely?" she asked.

"Everyone's in tea. But my father initially worked for the railways. One of my grandfathers was in the military."

Antonia nodded. It was not only geography: She knew little about India or railways or tea or the military either, and was reluctant to continue the conversation in case she made even more of a fool of herself. But what were these people doing here without her brother? Why on earth hadn't they written to tell her they were coming? Before she had formulated the right question, the woman yawned theatrically.

"Excuse me," she said. "I hate to be rude, but I'm exhausted."

"Your rooms should be ready," Antonia said brightly as she folded up her napkin and rose to her feet. "You must take a nap. Please come this way."

The guest suite, as it was officially known, consisted of two bedrooms connected by a door opposite the old nursery. They were on the right-hand side of the house, on the top floor, at the back. Once she had shown them the bathroom and the servant's bell beside the fireplace, Antonia excused herself. But when the door closed she hovered around the upstairs hall, straightening the picture frames and polishing the glass with her sleeve. She hoped they wouldn't be too cold; she hoped the beds weren't damp. They hadn't actually been slept in for a decade or more, not since her long-dead great-aunt had once-and-never-again stayed for Christmas.

Now, through the closed door, she heard the girl laugh. Something softened within her. There hadn't been any children at Balmarra for a very long time. This was not something she had herself chosen, but there it was. She would be accommodating, understanding, sympathetic. Her brother's wife and daughter had come from another continent, a place where not that long ago the natives had mutinied and slaughtered dozens of British women and children, a place where tigers roamed and tropical diseases were rampant. Also, it couldn't be easy being married to a man like her brother. The reason for their unexpected visit couldn't be merely social, could it? The journey must have taken weeks. And yet they didn't appear to be staying for long: All they had brought with them were a few suitcases. They must be based elsewhere, with one of Cicely's relatives perhaps? How nice to be remembered, Antonia told herself. Rather than return downstairs, delaying a little longer, she rearranged the glass-house roses in a vase on an occasional table. Finally, from the guest suite, there was a short, devastated sigh.

Antonia knocked, then whispered: "Is anything wrong?"

When there was no answer, she opened the door. Cicely was sitting on the bed, her hat off, an open package on her lap. In her hands was a metal tin filled with what looked like dead seedlings.

"My goodness, you brought them all the way from India?" Antonia asked. "What were they?"

"Orchids," Cicely replied.

"The seeds seem to have germinated," Antonia said as she peered down at the package. "Then died. But really you didn't need to bring us a gift."

"They weren't for you," Kitty replied sharply.

Antonia blushed scarlet. Not that her brother's wife noticed. She put the package on the bed and began to root through her handbag. Finally she pulled out a cigarette, held it to her nose, and sniffed. Only then did she look up and notice Antonia still standing by the door.

"Smoke?" she asked.

"Oh no," said Antonia. "I don't."

A few seconds passed. Cicely's eyebrows raised and her lips opened just a little, a wordless but unmistakable prompt that she should go now.

"Dinner is at seven," Antonia said. "I meant to say."

"I think we'll retire early. We're both so very tired. Could we have ours on a tray?"

"If it's stew I won't eat it," said the girl.

"Kitty!" her mother warned. "Remember your manners."

Antonia stood at the door for another few seconds. What was she waiting for? Gratitude, or at the very least, recognition, but neither was forthcoming. It seemed that manners had been forgotten by both.

"I'll tell Cook," she said. "We breakfast at eight. Just so you know, the nursery is across the hall. You might find something of interest to play with."

Cicely Pick gave a single nod, then lit the cigarette with a match. Kitty didn't respond. She was staring at herself in the mirror, pulling faces. Although Antonia was tempted to point out that the wind might change and the screwed-up face would stick, she turned and quickly let herself out. She paused at the top of the stairs and took a deep, tobacco-smoke-infused breath. To have a sister, even in-law, was a complete surprise. A niece even more so. It was a turnup for the books, a cause for celebration. I am an aunt, she told herself— twice, so it would sink in. And yet they were nothing like any other relative living or imagined. The Picks as a family were fair skinned and blue eyed. Their hands were wide, their feet flat, and they shared a certain pragmatism of both physique and personality. Not only were George's wife and offspring dark skinned and fine boned, their clothes were fashionable but flimsy, cut to be admired rather than to keep a person warm. And Cicely herself? She looked exotic, too exotic, too fragile, too delicate for either a man like George or a place like Balmarra. But what business was it of Antonia's whom her brother married? He had always done exactly what he wanted without a thought to the consequences.

Antonia tucked a strand of hair behind her ear. It was forever escaping its pins, especially in damp summer weather. She had spent a lifetime smoothing and straightening, pinning and arranging, but had given up dressing it unless she went out. Most of the time she wore it in a long plait that hung to her waist. When it was loose, her hair fell in curls and ringlets, a halo of blond frizz quite unlike any-one else's in her family. Unless she was mistaken, Kitty had inherited the same curse. She hoped that, unlike her, she could learn to tame it.

The wind rattled the window that illuminated the stairwell. She felt a sudden impulse to turn around and rush back to the guest rooms, to throw her arms around Cicely and Kitty Pick, to hold them tight and whisper in their ears, "I'm so glad you came." From outside, however, she heard the crunch of wheels on gravel: A mo-torcar was approaching along the driveway. It must be Malcolm. He would know what to do, he always did. It was one thing her father had always commented on. But as she approached the door to greet him, she heard the sound of raised voices.

"No, we are not expecting a delivery," Dora was saying to someone on the porch.

It was not her husband but a small van from the Caledonian Railway. In the back were four large trunks belonging to Cicely Pick and labeled with Balmarra's address. Antonia, it seemed, had been wrong about the fleeting visit.

2

When she opened her eyes, Cicely had no idea if it was day or still night. Only a little light penetrated the gaps in the curtains. A noise had woken her, a disturbance, dragging her from the depths of sleep. She had slept more soundly, however, than she had in weeks. The mattress was soft, the quilts thick, and the air in her room so chilly that it would take a great deal of willpower to actually climb out of bed.

But then she heard it again, faint at first, the sound of raised voices. Antonia and a man—her husband, she presumed—were having a blazing row in a room somewhere on the other side of the house. Undoubtedly their unexpected arrival was the subject of the conflict? Cicely rolled onto her back and tried to ignore the clutch of anxiety in her chest. It was going to be much harder than either she or George had anticipated.

The voices suddenly fell quiet, and then there was the shudder of a door slammed. From outside came the crank of an engine and the crunch of gears as the motorcar sped up the driveway to the main road. Back home, automobiles weren't seen much yet outside Calcutta. In the hill stations European women were still transported in carriages, with their turbaned servants and pairs of ponies, or if they were very unlucky, the *palki*. Since she could ride, Cicely never had to bear the humiliation of being carted around on a boxed-in seat carried on poles. But she knew plenty who had, their voices rising half in hilarity, half in desperation, as the servants tipped the seat back and forth, accidentally on purpose.

In Darjeeling they had let all the servants go except the groom, and paid the rent until Christmas. Her horse would be cared for, ridden twice a day, and fed the occasional sugar lump. Everything else had been packed away, dust sheeted, and locked up. It was something of a relief. Even though she had been the memsahib for eight years, she still found it hugely complicated—only certain castes could sweep a floor or drive a *carriage*—and although they employed fourteen male servants, she could never work out why so many of them seemed to be so idle. But she lacked the energy of her mother's generation, who spent their lives monitoring the minutiae of their domestic situation. Who could be bothered to check the stock in the storeroom once a week, taste a sauce, dust the piano, or track every single rupee? Yes, she was glad to have left it behind—the responsibility, the requisite air of authority, the cost, even for a short time. When they returned she would have to hire all the servants back again—all, that is, except Kitty's beloved ayah. The less said about that the better.

At that moment she missed their *khidtmatgar*, the boy who brought tea on a tray every morning at seven. She missed the noises of home—people working, laughing, cooking—the cries of the wild monkeys in the trees, and the calls of birds who filled the forest with their chatter. She missed the scent of orange flowers in the foothills, the fragrant flush of the tea plantations, and the clear sharp wind that rushed down the valley from the high peaks, rattling the windows and rising through the floorboards, filling the air with the smells of bare rock and fresh snow. Here, apart from the car, the world was so still, so quiet, so reserved.

"Mummy?" Kitty called from the next room. "Are you awake?"

Had Kitty heard the argument, too? If she asked about it, what would Cicely tell her? How could she explain that under normal circumstances she would never dream of arriving the way they had, unexpected and uninvited? But these weren't normal circumstances.

"Almost," she said. "Give me another minute or two."

She looked across at the clock on the mantelpiece; it was already ten.

Two settings had been laid on the table in the breakfast room. Cicely poured herself and Kitty each a cup of tea from the pot only to find it was stone cold. Porridge was brought wordlessly by the housemaid. It had a slightly burnt taste. Was this all they were being offered? No toast, no marmalade, no jam, no eggs?

"It's horrible," whispered Kitty.

Cicely sweetened the porridge with sugar and rang the bell to ask the maid for more tea. As they waited, they heard tires on gravel and the slam of a car door.

"Eat up," she said.

"You try it," Kitty replied.

She raised a spoonful of porridge to her mouth but couldn't bring herself to actually taste it. It had the consistency of glue.

"Peaches!" A man stood in silhouette in the doorway with a newspaper under his arm. He was dressed in a tweed suit, driving gloves, and a flat cap. "Mr. Baillie, our head gardener, picked these this morning from a secret tree. Only he knows where it is, and he's not telling."

He strode into the room, put the newspaper on the table, took off his cap and gloves, and began to empty his pockets, placing three small fruits on the tablecloth.

"Please help yourself."

"You must be Antonia's husband," Cicely offered.

"That's right. The name's Malcolm. Antonia's better half."

No trace of bad humor remained on his face from the argument earlier. He let out a blurt of a laugh at his own joke, and his face concertinaed.

"Anyway, good morning! Or should that be good afternoon?"

She put down her spoon.

"We overslept," she said. "Our long journey seems to have caught up with us."

"Don't apologize. Sleep as late as you like. I, however, have already been out for a spin in the Stuart. It has 15hp, a twin-cylinder engine, and a Cardan shaft drive. Lovely model."

There was something faintly ridiculous about Antonia's husband. Maybe it was the theatrical curl of his mustache or the redness of his cheeks that gave him a vaudevillian air. Kitty tried to catch her mother's eye. Cicely ignored her, took a peach, and picked up a knife.

"Allow me?" Malcolm extended his hand.

"I can cut up a peach," she replied. "And I have been known to peel a mango."

His eyebrows shot up and he sat back. Then he laughed as if she had cracked a great joke. She cut two slices, gave one to Kitty and ate the other herself. It was surprisingly sweet.

"I don't suppose there are many peaches to be had in India?" he asked. He was looking at them as if they had just arrived from the moon. At home, in fact, they had fruit trees in the garden including peach, orange, fig, pomegranate, and mango.

"A few," she lied. "And if we're really lucky, a couple of oranges at Christmas—that is, if the tigers don't get them first. Luckily we're rather fond of mangoes."

Kitty's shoulders shook once, a contained spasm of laughter. Her eyes darted like minnows as she tried to fix on something, anything, before focusing on her porridge spoon and lifting it to her mouth. Antonia's husband, thankfully, was oblivious.

"As I thought," he said. "A mango tree! Now there's an idea. I'll speak to Mr. Baillie."

"It won't grow here," said Kitty.

"And why do you come to that conclusion, young lady?" Malcolm asked.

"Rotten weather." She shrugged.

"Well, we'll see about that! Impossible things do happen. The weather isn't always rotten, you know, and we have the glass house. We can grow just about anything in there we choose. Might take a few years, but we're not going anywhere."

He looked directly at Cicely, and she was forced to glance away. Was it a pointed remark? Did he know more about the situation than his wife? Kitty pushed the porridge to one side of the bowl and then laid down her spoon.

"Aren't you going to eat that?" he said, pointing at the uneaten porridge. "Waste not, want not."

Kitty stared down at the bowl and didn't answer.

"Anyway," Antonia's husband continued, "mustn't linger. Some of us have to work for a living to support the fairer sex. Anything you need?"

"More tea would be nice," Cicely replied.

Malcolm placed his hand around the teapot.

"It's cold. How novel," he said. "You know we drink it hot in Scotland?"

Kitty opened her mouth to speak, but when Cicely widened her eyes in warning, she closed it again. When the maid appeared, Cicely stood up and smoothed her skirt.

"Could we have another pot? And you know, I think I'll try it hot this time!"

Kitty let out a bubble of uncontainable laughter. Cicely knew that she should reprimand her, and yet she too struggled to keep a straight face. Where did he think they came from? The deepest, darkest jungle?

"If you could bring it my room," she continued, "I'd very much appreciate it."

The maid's face fell. Clearly it was not done to take morning tea—at any temperature—in one's room.

"Oh, by the way, your trunks arrived," Malcolm said. "All four of them. Nothing like traveling light!"

He laughed. She smiled politely. Four trunks for two people *was* considered light. Most people wouldn't leave India without at least four each.

"I expect you'll be wanting to see the gardens?" he suggested.

"I would," she said, because it seemed expected.

A blast of wind hit the window, and rain began to lash the glass. A draft whistled through the curtains.

"As the old man used to say, we can't be held hostage by the weather," Malcolm went on. "We'll go, rain or shine. What time would suit?"

In India no one would dream of going out in the rain. But then she reminded herself why they had come and what she must do, and so she mustered a smile.

"In an hour?" she suggested.

"An hour," he confirmed.

The fires were newly lit in the bedrooms but spat sparks and barely heated the still-frigid air. A single white rose stood in a vase on the writing desk. During breakfast their trunks had been brought to the rooms and unpacked. The beds had been made, the blankets and sheets tucked under with such precision that it would take more strength than either of them had to unmake them and climb back in again, no matter how much they wanted to.

"Could you plait my hair?" Kitty asked.

Cicely sat down on the bed and undid her daughter's hair. Unlike her own hair, which was dark and had to be waved using curling irons, Kitty's was fair, like her father's, and curly. Cicely brushed it out, divided it into two sections, and began to plait.

"How long are we staying here?" asked Kitty.

"Not long," she replied. "Why don't you take a look at the nursery when I've finished?"

"Tighter," said Kitty. "You know my ayah does it much tighter."

Cicely started again, pulling each strand of hair as tightly as she could. Kitty let out a small cry.

"That hurts—you're not doing it properly!"

Despite her daughter's protestations, Cicely kept going, pulling and tugging until she had fashioned the hair into two plaits.

"There," she said.

Kitty examined the results silently in the mirror. It was clear to both of them that once again it wasn't up to her usual standard.

"Will you play with me?" asked Kitty.

Did her ayah play games? Whatever she did she was always better, according to Kitty.

"I don't think so," Cicely replied. "I have important business to attend to."

"No you don't."

"Excuse me!" she said. "You have no idea what I must and must not do."

The girl's face started to redden. She stared at the floor.

"I need to bathe and wash my hair," Cicely said. "And then I need to sort something out for Daddy."

"What shall I do, then?" she whispered.

"Use your imagination. You *have* got one? Or did you leave it on the train?"

"Of course I have," said Kitty, her brow furrowing. "I wish Daddy was here."

"Well, he isn't," she replied. "And wishing won't change that."

George had left his family home in Scotland fifteen years earlier and had never returned. Now she began to understand why: There was something stifling about Balmarra, the grandeur of the architecture, the polished wood, the faded chintz, and the parsimonious flower arrangements. There didn't seem to be enough oxygen in the air to breathe. Although deceased, Edward Pick looked out from almost every wall. He must have commissioned at least a dozen portraits, some when he was young, but mostly when he was middle-aged, signaled by a paunching around the jaw and collar. In all of them he appeared austere, judgmental, staring out at the world as if about to give his opinion, sure in the knowledge that he was most definitely correct. As for the gardens, from what she had seen so far, they were nothing special. Though it had been the fashion in the last century to get rid of all the native species and replace them with species from elsewhere in the British Empire, and from China and America, Balmarra seemed to have done a poor job of this. Not that Scotland had many native species. According to George the only one it could claim was the primrose.

Also, George and his sister had never been close. What were the words that he had used to describe her? "Naive," "provincial," "dull"? It was true that although she was in her midthirties, Antonia seemed younger than her years, unripe; she was tentative and, at the same time, overenthusiastic. Her wardrobe, for example, had been chosen with a very conservative hand. Even in India, European women did not wear skirts that reached the floor anymore unless they had given up on appearances or were too old to care. Worst of all, she wore her hair in a long plait like a teenage girl.

But it was more than that. Even though Cicely felt a little sorry for her and wished she had not made such poor choice of husband, she didn't want to get to know her: It would make the whole process harder in the long run.

Cicely locked the bathroom door and turned on the tap in the bath. At least there was hot water. As she took the pins from her hair and unwound her chignon, she tried to decide on a course of action. In her pocketbook she had six guineas in change. The plan had been to sell the orchid seeds to a collector in Glasgow for a hefty sum to give them some disposable income. Maybe they hadn't been properly packed. Maybe their luggage had been left in the sun. Maybe she should have taken better care of them. But hopefully it wouldn't matter. The orchids were a single drop in a sizable ocean.

Ever since they had first met, George had referred to his legacy, to the nest egg that was slowly maturing. Money could be spent, loans taken out, favors asked because sooner rather than later he would inherit his fortune. Over the years George and his father had occasionally corresponded. George had told him about his expeditions, his marriage, and the birth of their daughter. It was strange that his father had not passed on any of this information to Antonia. As for the legacy, it was all in the letter that George's father had written him a year earlier. He instructed that the estate was not to be broken up: It must remain a single entity. Furthermore, he wrote, he was leaving it to his son. Edward Pick was a traditionalist; he believed in primogeniture, that wealth and property be handed down the male line.

In the twelve months since his father's death, they had been expecting a lawyer's letter to arrive any day. When nothing came, Cicely went to the main post office in Darjeeling to make sure it hadn't been mislaid. They checked and checked again, but no letter from Scotland had arrived. First George was puzzled, then angry. What underhand games had his sister and her husband played? Was it possible they had swindled him out of what was rightfully his? How was one to find out?

Cicely had eventually volunteered. Although the idea of traveling halfway around the world to sort out her husband's inheritance was not in the least appealing, it was the obvious solution. She had never been to Scotland and had no particular desire to go, but she had realized that the situation could work in her favor. She made a bargain with her husband: She would sort out his windfall on the condition that, as well as his expedition, it be used to finance their daughter's education in Scotland. Kitty would learn Greek, Latin, mathematics, and science; she would be properly educated. Maybe one day she would go to university. As Cicely expected, George had been totally against the idea of the Scottish boarding school. But beggars can't be choosers, and he eventually had to accept.

Steam had stopped rising from the bath. Cicely held her hand under the tap. The water had gone cold. She undressed, slipped into the lukewarm bath, and washed as quickly as she could. Was it possible ever to feel completely warm in this house? She supposed not; she suspected that one just got used to being permanently chilled. All those high ceilings and huge windows were elegant but came at a high price, and the truth was that few people could afford to run a place like Balmarra the way it was designed to be run, with a dozen servants and a fire burning in every room. They would try to sell the entire estate to a single owner, as George's father had wanted, but there was a good chance it would be sold off in lots or become an institution, a hospital, or a school. Surely that was better, however, than letting the place decay and run to rack and ruin—it was halfway there already.

How long would it take to sort everything out? A week might be enough. She would show Edward Pick's letter to Antonia and her husband at lunch. She hoped they wouldn't hate her: She was only claiming what was rightly her husband's, what his father had wished. In their place, however, she would find it hard to remain civil.

As she dressed her hair in the bedroom mirror, Cicely's hands were trembling, and not just because she was cold. Sweat had collected at the base of her throat and in the creases of her palms. How could she do this? How could she not? The view from her bedroom window at home calmed her, the mountain range, Kanchenjunga, Kabru, and Lashar, rising up on the other side of the valley, snow-capped and wreathed in cloud like the softest down. She closed her eyes and summoned it up in her mind's eye; she listened to the gentle ringing of prayer bells and felt the luminosity through the gauze curtains, so warm that you could feel it seep into your skin until you were as saturated as her grandmother's *gulab jamun* with rosewater syrup.

The letter wasn't in her handbag: She had emptied it twice. She opened the suitcases and trunks, even though they had already been unpacked, and looked in every pocket and pouch. It wasn't with her travel documents, tickets, passports, or letters from the school either. After searching the room four times, she sat down on the bed and tried to remember the last time she had read the letter through. Could it have been on the train from London? Could she have left it in the folds of a newspaper or a napkin, to be screwed up and thrown away? Her face grew hot. Surely she wouldn't have been that careless? But it had gone, vanished. She tried to calm down, to think rationally. It was bound to turn up when she had more time to look for it. Without the backup of the letter, however, explaining the purpose of her visit would not be easy.

"Hello!" George's sister called up the stairs. "We leave in five minutes."

Cicely pinned on her hat and began to button her coat. Her clothes were neither water- nor weatherproof, but they would have to do. A crash came from the nursery.

"Kitty!" she called out. When there was no answer she went to investigate. The nursery was lined with shelves of books, games, and toys. A rocking horse stood beneath the window. Her daughter was sitting in the middle of the floor surrounded by wooden animals and a small wooden boat, the picture of innocence.

"It fell out of the cupboard," she explained. "It's a Noah's Ark, I think."

"It must have been Daddy's," Cicely said. "Or your aunt Antonia's."

"Do you think she would give me this?" Kitty held up a small wooden bear. "I want to give it to my ayah."

Cicely felt the rise of irritation and paused before she spoke.

"You're going to school, remember," she said. "Besides, the animals went in two by two. The other bear will be lonely."

Kitty frowned, and tears welled up in her eyes.

"I don't want to go," she said. "I'll be lonely."

"But you're a big girl now, and big girls go to school and make new friends."

"Not all of them do," she replied. "Some stay at home with their ayah."

"Only babies," she replied, taking the bear and placing it back in the ark. "Don't be scared. You know you can do anything if you set your mind to it."

It wouldn't do to let her daughter know the truth—that just the thought of being apart was almost unbearable to her. But the alternative was even worse. Without an education, Kitty could look forward to nothing other than marriage and motherhood, a life played out in the doll's house of domesticity, with a husband who, like George, might follow his own whims and desires while she was left to pick up the pieces. Was she a terrible mother? All she wanted was something different for her daughter than her own experience.

"I don't suppose you want to come for a walk?" she asked Kitty.

Kitty glanced up at the window as a bluster of fresh rain hit the glass; she shook her head. Silently she lined up the other wooden animals side by side. The rain outside cascaded down from the guttering and they could hear it splashing on the ground below.

"I think we may need a boat," Cicely said lightly. "Can I borrow that one? 'I Once Loved a Sailor.'"

It was a popular song they'd learned on the steamer. A tiny smile formed on Kitty's face.

"Once a sailor loved me," sang Cicely softly.

"But he was not a sailor," sang Kitty in return. "That sailed on the wide blue sea."

Cicely reached out and stroked Kitty's hair.

"You don't know how lucky you are," she said. "When you grow up, you'll never have to use a curling iron."

"My ayah says only silly ladies with nothing better to do use a curling iron," Kitty replied.

"Does she now," said Cicely.

Antonia strode up the path beneath an avenue of lime trees to the top of a small col. Here there was a stone bench with a view across the island and water to the rise of mountains beyond. It was too damp to sit, so she ran her fingertips along the stone, over the soft green moss and crumbling surface of the backrest. The pounding in her chest was lessening, yet the bruise from her argument that morning with Malcolm, while invisible, still seeped through her in shades of dark blue and brooding purple. She would not think of it now; she would resist the urge to work out all the things she should have said. Let it go, she told herself. Instead she focused on how much she liked this view, this spot, this bench. Today the garden was awash with rain, the grass soggy underfoot and the bright green lime leaves above cascading showers of droplets.

Her fingertips almost itched, and she wished she had her materials to hand. The bag packed with her sketchbook, watercolors, and brushes was still lying where she had left it, abandoned after Cicely and Kitty's arrival. She had always found solace in painting, in botanical illustration. As a girl she had been encouraged by her father to paint flowers and shrubs, and found she had a talent for it. She had grown to love the rhythm of the seasons, the long fallow winters and the short intense summers, and the annual miracle of snowdrops or the haze of bluebells. She would pull on her waxed coat and galoshes, go out in any weather, ignoring the damp or the rain that fell from the brim of her hat, and paint. Her sketchbook was a diary of sorts, a visual journal, the plants and flowers acting as a record of her shifting moods.

There had been a time when she had thought she might take it further and attend art school. The Haldane Academy was opposite the Glasgow Green in the East End, and sometimes, on trips to the city, she persuaded her family to take a stroll on the Green so she could pass the school, with its white facade and sculpture of a young scholar above the west wing, and imagine herself inside.

And yet she had gotten ahead of herself and was brought down, she remembered, with a crash. Without asking her, her father had shown some of her work to a professional, and the verdict was that although her work was "pretty," she lacked natural talent. Art school, her father said bluntly, would be a waste of time and money. Even after all those years she still felt a stab of hurt when she recalled that dinner.

"Don't take offense," George had said. "Your work is lovely. But isn't art school for serious artists, not illustrators?"

"That's why I want to go," she retaliated. "I want to learn."

"My dear sister, I just can't see it, you with plaster on your hands and paint in your hair—"

"Leave the challenging vocations to those who are built for it," her father interjected. "To men."

Antonia had kept her temper, she had swallowed the rise inside.

"Surely a person's sex has nothing to do with it?" she replied.

"Can you imagine a woman painting the Sistine Chapel?" George laughed. "She'd be standing at the bottom of the scaffolding drinking tea and talking about the price of bread."

Her father had snorted with amusement while she sat there puce faced, pushing her food around her plate before eventually being excused. She hoped they both jumped in their seats when she slammed her bedroom door so hard the house seemed to shake. Not that it did any good in the long run. She hadn't argued; what was the point? The disappointment was so acute that she barely left her room for weeks. But eventually, once she got over the shock, she decided to continue but keep her work to herself. No one knew about her painting anymore, not even Malcolm.

To compensate for his daughter's perceived failings, perhaps, her father had taken a keen interest in art. As well as self-portraits, he had commissioned a painting of Balmarra from a local artist. The picture captured the house and gardens as seen from Karrasay, the mountain rising behind and a golden evening sky all reflected in the loch. At her father's insistence, the artist, Henry Morris, had added a stag grazing at the shore and an eagle wheeling above. Although it was undeniably accomplished, Antonia hated it. Not only was its tone cloying and sentimental, it suggested a wholly fictional reality rather than a dour, real, wet Scottish one. It had hung in the hallway for years, placed so it was the first thing visitors saw. Every time Antonia passed it, which was often, she turned her head the other way so she wouldn't have to look at it.

There were no stags in evidence from the stone bench that day, no wheeling eagles or heroic beasts beneath the lime trees. There were a couple of blackbirds, and she'd seen a siskin and a couple of blue tits—nothing special—and the rain had finally stopped. A steamer sailed from Hunter's Point toward Gourock, its wake a stroke of chalk on a blue canvas. The sun came out and lit up the moorland on the other side of the loch, and the world beyond was suddenly illuminated with vibrant color: dark orange, mustard, and the palest lilac. And at the center of it all, partly hidden by trees, was Balmarra, the house she had been born in and had lived in all her life. The wind in the sycamore tree above lulled, and her husband's voice was suddenly audible.

"According to the forecast it will be overcast until Tuesday," Malcolm was telling Cicely. "After that a band of high pressure will sweep in from the west."

"Really," she replied, barely disguising the blade of disinterest.

They were walking slowly up the hill. Her husband had taken the morning off work to be here, to be hospitable, but their unexpected guest appeared completely oblivious. Though she was still angry with him, Antonia felt a surge of indignation on his behalf. Finally they reached the col.

"This is one of my favorite spots," said Antonia, rising.

Cicely took in the view, what there was of it, with a glance, then stamped her feet and rubbed her arms.

"Surely summer can be cool in the mountains in India, too?" Antonia asked.

"You can't compare it," she replied.

Antonia suddenly felt the urge to apologize for the climate, for the precipitation, but swallowed it. The phrase "Like it or lump it," one of her father's, suddenly came into her head. Cicely Pick yawned. Would nothing please her? Not the light, the ruffled water, the colors of velvet-covered hills?

"Tell me," said Malcolm. "What occupation is your husband currently pursuing in India?"

Cicely pulled her shoulders back.

"He's a horticultural explorer and collector, as I mentioned yesterday."

"But surely that is simply a hobby," Malcolm replied, "not an occupation."

"A hobby?" she repeated. "No, botany is his life and his occupation."

"But is botanizing"—Malcolm struggled for words—"lucrative?"

When Cicely finally spoke it was with much deliberation.

"For plant hunters, the collection of rare and undiscovered botanical species is more than a vocation," she said. "It's a calling, a métier. Look around you, there's barely a garden in Europe that doesn't display discoveries made by my husband's profession."

"Perfectly true," said Antonia. "That's a *Hamamelis virginiana* from North America. And over there, that's a *Euodia hupehensis* from China."

These were two trees that she had recently painted, and for once looked up and memorized their Latin names.

"But hasn't everything already been found?" he asked.

"Well, obviously not," Cicely said. "Or why would he be looking?"

There was a small, ringing silence.

"One flower, to me, looks very like another," he admitted.

"Indeed," said Antonia. "You don't even know the difference between a daffodil and a dandelion."

She immediately felt a twinge of guilt. She shouldn't side with George's wife, not against her husband. As usual, however, he tried to make it into a huge joke.

"Must be rather fun tramping through the back of beyond, eating yak. Where is he, anyway?"

Cicely sighed, then replaced her hat.

"Have you heard of the Mekong?"

"No," said Malcolm. "I haven't."

"There is a valley, and the river that runs through it empties into another called the Mekong. In this valley are alpine meadows that are filled with a profusion of flowers, anemones and primulas and gentians as well as many other as-yet-undiscovered species. So yes, I suppose it is the back of beyond to some people, but to George it is the center of everything."

Cicely took a deep breath and gazed into the middle distance.

"And yak meat can be rather good, actually," she added, then smiling such a smile that Antonia could actually see her husband lose his train of thought. Even in the rain, in the pale green light that filtered through the leaves above, Cicely was striking, her chin raised, her back straight, her eyes half closed as if looking down at the world. She had the look of a dancer and skin the color of caramel. No wonder, Antonia thought, her brother had married her. She couldn't have been an easy catch, not like the girls from Dunoon or Gourock George had gone with as a younger man, some of whom he hadn't even bothered to tell he was leaving the country.

Malcolm looked at his pocket watch, his hand, Antonia noticed, trembling ever so slightly.

"Goodness, it's later than I thought," he said, thrusting both his hand and his watch back into his pocket. "I am in court tomorrow. Working for the Crown one can't afford to be ill prepared. Please excuse me, ladies."

He started back down the path.

"Take her up the glen," he called over his shoulder. "Show her the American redwoods. There, see, I know a plant or two!"

They both watched until the path turned and he was gone.

"What does your husband do?" Cicely asked.

"He's an advocate depute," she replied. "That's what we call a barrister in Scotland."

Cicely turned and glanced at her strangely, a look of incomprehension that was there and then gone again. Antonia felt momentarily winded.

"He was your father's lawyer?" she asked.

"Oh no," she replied. "He's not that sort. He works for the Crown Office, prosecuting criminals."

"Oh, I see."

Maybe, Antonia considered, she had imagined it. She searched Cicely's face once more but found nothing changed.

"People are usually fascinated by Malcolm's occupation and ask all sorts of grisly questions," said Antonia.

"Do they?" said Cicely.

"Let's see those trees, then," Antonia suggested. "Before the rain comes on again."

As they walked up the glen, she could see a splatter of mud on the hem of Cicely's coat. Her heels left tiny indentations in the path, and her shoes would no doubt be wet through by now. She wore such beautiful clothes but seemed unconcerned by their ruin. She must have plenty more in her multiple trunks and suitcases. Even so, maybe Antonia should have offered galoshes and an overcoat. And yet there was something gloriously nonchalant, something fanciful, about Cicely's appearance. To say she looked out of place would be an understatement. She looked positively alien. But it was not just her sense of fashion.

"Her skin's a little dark," Malcolm had said that morning. "And so is the girl's. They seem, well, foreign."

"The Indian sun would color anyone's skin," she replied. "Don't be ridiculous."

"Hmm," said Malcolm doubtfully. "What reason did they give for coming?"

"They didn't say!" she said, her exasperation building. "Look, I was doing the accounts, a taxicab arrived, and there they were with a pile of suitcases."

"I hope you didn't pay the fare."

"I tried," she replied. "Seemed rude not to. But she wouldn't let me. She's clearly wealthy. You should have seen the way she tipped the driver. It was positively excessive."

"Maybe she hasn't come to grips with the currency?"

"Or maybe she's just generous. Must be nice not to have to count every farthing."

"Oh, Antonia," he said in that voice that made her bristle despite herself. "Why must you grasp the wrong end of the stick every time?"

Arguments were like trains. They ran away with themselves, belching smoke and hot steam and going so fast that nothing could stop them. They usually ran out of momentum eventually, or rather *she* would, backing down, her admission of fault water on his fire. This time was different: This time she would not back down.

"The thing is, and don't take this the wrong way, my dear"—he said, his tone eventually conciliatory—"how do we even know that they are who they say they are? They could be anybody!"

"Don't be silly, Malcolm," she had replied. "I mean, to what end? What have we got that a woman like that could possibly want?"

"You mean apart from the house? And the gardens?"

Antonia laughed.

"George has always hated Balmarra. Besides, people just don't just turn up on your doorstep and expect to move in."

"I suppose I'll have to find out why they're here and how long they intend to stay," he said. "I mean, one of us has to!"

"No," she had replied. "Don't you dare. George is my brother, after all."

As usual, he had challenged her, had questioned the wisdom of her approach. She had stood her ground; for once she had kept her voice level and her emotions in check.

"Whatever she wants, she'll play us like fools," he said under his breath. "A woman like that? I can see it coming."

Antonia pinched herself on the arm. Don't rise, she told herself; don't take the bait.

"I wouldn't be so sure," she said. "And I, for one, am happy they came. Apart from you they're the only family I have left."

After briefly admiring the redwood trees and making a small detour to see the glass house, Antonia and Cicely walked back to the house past the servants' cottages. Half of them were empty now. They didn't have the staff they used to, not for the two of them. The rain came on again, more heavily this time, and so she suggested they make a dash for home. Antonia stopped for a moment to tuck in the lace of her boot. Her sister-in-law ran on ahead without waiting. Antonia picked up a small silk rosebud that lay in a puddle in the gravel. It had fallen off Cicely Pick's hat. She put it in her pocket.

3

Lunch was lukewarm, which meant that it could have been eaten quickly. Instead the meal was long and awkward. Cicely ate out of politeness rather than hunger. Her appetite was gone, replaced by a gnawing, low-level panic. Antonia, however, intent on her role as hostess, filled any pauses in the conversation with monologues and gave a hugely detailed account of recent roof repairs. This meant that she took far longer than anyone else to clean her plate. They waited as she chewed every single mouthful, Kitty squirming in her seat with boredom.

Then, once the plates had been cleared, she turned to more personal matters.

"So how did you and my brother meet?" she asked.

Cicely took a deep breath. She had been expecting this, and decided to give as few details as possible.

"It was my father who met him first," she replied. "In the Planters Club."

Antonia cocked her head: Surely there was more?

"He invited George for dinner. And that was that."

"Love at first sight, how wonderful. Lucky old George."

Antonia folded up her napkin and stood up; lunch was over. Kitty pounded up the stairs to the nursery. Cicely declined coffee and said she might take a short nap. Not only did she need to get away from any more prying questions, she needed space to think. The letter was gone. As an alternative, she would try to find out Edward Pick's solicitor's address and pay him a visit. Then, once she had a copy of Pick's will, she would politely inform Antonia and Malcolm that the ownership of Balmarra had been passed down to George. Once the process was rolling, it shouldn't take long. While the paperwork was being drawn up, she would start to instigate the sale of the estate, contacting agents in Glasgow and Edinburgh. But how would she find out who oversaw Edward Pick's legal affairs? She could hardly just ask. If only George had given her the details before he set off, she wouldn't be in this predicament.

At the top of the stairs, distracted, she turned right instead of left and found herself in a corridor on the other side of the house from the guest rooms. Here were two bedrooms, Antonia and Malcolm's, she deduced, one with a dressing table and the scent of Parma violets and the other with a suit stand and the lingering aroma of pomade. Each room contained a single bed. No wonder the couple were childless. The maid was coming up the servant's stairs, singing softly to herself. Not wanting to be caught in her host's sleeping quarters, Cicely headed back to the main stairs as quietly as she could. Antonia was in the hallway below, and so Cicely turned to the nearest door, opened it, and slipped inside.

It was a library, the walls lined with shelves and the room lit by a long window at the far end. There were books on botany, geology, ornithology, natural history, zoology, and horticulture. One shelf held copies of periodicals—the *Journal of the Linnaean Society* and the *Botanical Magazine*. Another was devoted to the *Journal of the Royal Geographical Society*. The library, the books, the magazines looked well-read, a personal space that reflected a singular passion. She hadn't been expecting this: George had never referred to his father as anything other than an ignorant enthusiast. But it was the same with the glass house, the last stop on her garden tour that morning. If the library was the late Edward Pick's head, the glass house was evidently his heart. Although the house had been built by his ancestors, Pick had constructed the circular palace for his plants, and no expense had been spared. It was quite unlike any structure she had ever seen before, the central dome at least twenty feet high and filled with palms. Hot pipes heated by a coal-fired boiler ran around the outer and inner edges of the beds, and thousands of panes of glass kept the heat in and glazed the elegant ribs of the dome. The ironwork was lavish. Leaves wound their way up the pillars and fronds curled around the pediments. While the central area, the warmest, housed the tropical plants, the palms and yuccas, the outer areas were split into sections for fruit trees, orchids, and roses.

Cicely had lingered, taking in the smells and relishing the heat while Antonia listed some of the plants in what seemed like a single exhalation. Most of them, however, she didn't seem able to identify, which was a little surprising, as there were some rare orchids that even Cicely knew were highly prized. With the boiler burning day and night, she guessed it must cost a small fortune to run. Once a buyer was found, she hoped they would have the money to keep this place going. Or if not, there was surely some money to be made by selling off the plants. But it would be a shame to do that.

After leafing through a periodical that had been left lying on the desk, Cicely noticed a large wooden filing cabinet. The handles were made of polished brass, cool beneath her fingertips. For a moment Cicely faltered. This felt wrong, intrusive. But she had to finish what she had set out to do, for Kitty, for George, for herself. She had no other option.

The first drawer was full of receipts for building work, from plumbers, roofers, blacksmiths, and joiners going back at least fifty years. The middle drawer held auction house catalog from London, Paris, and New York. A door slammed. Someone was coming along the corridor. She closed the drawer and picked up a book. Whoever it was passed by, and the hall fell silent again.

As quietly as possible, Cicely pulled out the bottom drawer of the filing cabinet. As well as folders for correspondence and old Christmas cards, there was one labeled "Family Documents." Inside were birth, marriage, and death certificates, doctors' and funeral bills. Almost without trying she found some correspondence from Edward Pick's solicitor, a Charles Drummond Esq., with an address in Dunoon.

Another door slammed in the hallway, followed by footfalls on the stairs. Cicely slipped the letter back into its envelope and put it in her pocket. Before she closed the drawer, her eye fell on a postcard. It was a photograph of snow on the Himalayas taken a from vantage point she knew: the Mall in Darjeeling. The hall was silent again. She picked up the card and turned it over.

"Just passing through," George had written. "Home by Christmas."

The postmark was 1903. He had not been home by Christmas; in fact, he had not returned at all. They had married in 1904, and Kitty had been born six months later. Was it love at first sight, as Antonia had said? Or was it all a matter of chance and happenstance, the sum of their collective capacity for self-delusion?

George Pick wasn't the first man to go to India and not come back. Her own father had relocated temporarily to Darjeeling as a young man to work on the new railway from Siliguri. He liked the climate, found her mother at a dance, married her, and when he could afford it, bought a small tea plantation in the Kanchenjunga foothills. Although he planned many times to return to England to see his long-neglected family—a sister and a couple of elderly aunts—he never did. There was always too much to do, a tea planting or a polo match or a whist drive. Also, in Darjeeling he was a man who might be invited to events, asked his opinion, proposed for committees and teams and boards, a man who one day might have had his name spelled out in gold leaf on members' lists. In England, she suspected, people would always see him for what he was, an errant son from a lower-middle-class family who had run off to foreign climes to work on the railways.

For a few years, shortly after he bought the tea plantation, her father had become interested in botany, in propagation and soil acidity. When he had struck up a conversation with the young Scot in the cocktail bar of the Planters Club, a man "just passing through," a man who not only knew what *Camellia sinensis* was but suggested ways to increase yield, he believed he had found a kindred spirit.

Darjeeling was full of Scottish plant hunters that summer, men with broad accents, crude jokes, and dirt under their fingernails. In Britain, orchids were all the rage, and the rarest specimens could be auctioned for hundreds of guineas. In habit, dress, and attitude, George Pick set himself apart from the others. Although he too was in search of rare plants, he claimed he was an expert rather than an opportunist, out to discover new species, not pander to the market. After a few drinks her father invited him for dinner to show off various botanical successes such as his *Persea odoratissima*, or fragrant bay tree, that he had had grown from seed.

Cicely remembered that evening vividly. The young plant hunter had stared across the table at Cicely, and she had stared right back. She was eighteen, had never been courted, and—he said later—her skin was perfect as a winter rose. It seemed that while her father's eye had been fixed on his beloved bay tree, she had blossomed without him noticing. He was therefore oblivious to what was going on and fell for all of George's subtle manipulation and gentle flattery, for all his feigned interest in tea plant propagation. It had the desired result. Cicely's father eventually suggested that he could partly sponsor George's next expedition in return for a place on the trip. Maybe his daughter, George proposed over the cheese course, could join them? It would be an educational, enlightening experience. Put on the spot, Cicely's father had to acquiesce. Though he was a man of his time, even to him the reason that immediately sprang to mind—the obvious one, that she was a girl—was too crass to utter.

"Well, I suppose," he had said. "If Cicely wants to."

Cicely did want to. Cicely was bored out of her mind. She was convinced that nothing interesting would ever happen to her if she remained in Darjeeling, and she longed for places well out of her reach: Paris, London, New York. A plant-hunting trip hadn't been on her list, but it was better than nothing. Especially if it involved George Pick.

The expedition was duly organized and scheduled to depart in a week. With her father's investment, George bought more supplies and hired grooms and porters. And then came the question of transportation. Cicely balked at being carried in a *palki* and said she would ride instead.

"You'll get tired," her father had told her. "You'll slow us down."

"A *palki* will slow us down," she had replied.

George had admitted that she was right.

"But it won't be a hack along the Mall," he added. "It's a two-day trek—some of it on horseback but often on foot—followed by three days in a rudimentary camp. It will be hot and uncomfortable, with no warm bath and cocktail at the end of a long day."

"I think I can live without them," she had replied. "For a short while, at least."

George had laughed out loud—even though her response was not particularly witty—and then he had looked at her for longer than was polite as if wanting more, as if she had stimulated an appetite in him, a thirst. For the first time in her adult life, in her female skin, in the body that had changed so much in the previous year, she had the sense that somehow, without any effort whatsoever, she had the undivided attention of a member of the opposite sex. It was absolutely, undeniably the most exciting thing that had ever happened to her.

The local tailor made her a brand-new riding dress in gabardine and a couple of tweed skirts, recommended for keeping out the heat.

She packed an umbrella, stockings, undergarments, and a pith helmet, none of which she ever opened or wore, but which some poor soul carried all the way to camp and all the way back again. What did she remember of the expedition now? The lessening humidity as they headed out of the plantations into the forests above, the small Bhutia ponies they rode in single file, and the grooms who walked alongside flicking away the flies with a stick. The porters carried the supplies on their backs, their long hair plaited; and beyond, she remembered, the five peaks of Mount Kanchenjunga, the home of the goddess Yuma Sammang, appeared in fleeting snatches through the clouds.

"Thank you," she silently told the goddess, "for bringing George to me."

"Orchids are either saprophytic"—George explained as they walked through a forest of birch trees near the place he had chosen to set up camp—"which means they grow on dead or decaying trees, or terrestrial, they grow on the ground, or epiphytic, they grow on trees or shrubs. They are each highly adapted to attract very specific insect pollinators."

He stopped, glanced up, and hit a branch above with his stick. His face was shadowed by the leaf canopy.

"I'm sorry, once I start I become a frightful bore."

Her heart beat faster beneath the gabardine.

"No, please do go on," said Cicely. "I'm not bored at all."

A breeze parted the leaves above, and he was suddenly lit by a shaft of light. She saw his left eye, his cheekbone, the film of sweat on his upper lip, a small scar that cut through his eyebrow. He pushed his hair away from his forehead in one fluid move, then frowned in her general direction, where she stood concealed in the gathering gloom.

"You see, orchids are masters of attraction," he continued. "Some of the male insects—"

He stopped, cleared his throat, perhaps remembering that he was walking through the foothills of the Himalayas and not on the po-dium of the Royal Horticultural Society. The wind suddenly blew apart the leaves again until they were both standing in bright sun-shine like actors on a stage.

"The male insects—" he repeated, looking straight at her. "I'm sorry, but I've completely lost my train of thought."

A shout sounded from one of the porters at the front of the march.

"And with perfect timing," George said, "a discovery is made."

The porter was poking a plant at the base of an oak tree with a stick. It had tiny pink-and-white flowers with a yellow center. Cice-ly's father approached at a run, out of breath and red faced.

"You've found something?" he asked.

"A *Dendrobium amoenum*," said George. He looked around and pointed out another and another.

"What's that one?" she asked, pointing to a profusion of pale-yellow flowers attached to a single stem.

"Hello! That's a *Dendrobium pubescens*. I'm so glad your daughter came, Mr. Anderson. As well as having sharp eyes, she seems to have brought us good fortune."

"Nothing new, though?" her father asked. "Nothing like the Snow Tree?"

"I'm afraid not," George replied.

"But it's early days, surely," her father said.

"Absolutely." His eyes met hers again for the briefest of seconds.

She had been warned at her convent school of the peril of toying with the male sex. Flirting was a sin, she was taught by the nuns, dangerous and pernicious, while coyness was indicative of an unsta-ble mind. At the time of the expedition, she had never met a man she liked enough to do anything potentially damaging with. The young men she had been introduced to at dances, balls, and polo matches could barely string two words together, let alone make conversa-tion. Flirting was impossible even if she had been tempted to try it.

George Pick, however, was a man of the nuns' worst nightmares. Not only was he eloquent, but his hair was fair, his eyes the palest gray, his cheekbones high, and he had a habit of leaning in a little too close when conversing, due to a slight deafness he attributed to his childhood bout of measles. She also could not ignore the fact that he was nicely built—tall, slim, descended, he joked, from a Viking chieftain. And when he stood at the base of a tree while a porter shimmied up the trunk to fetch rare blooms or seedpods, or he climbed up the side of a waterfall to get his bearings, it was not too hard to believe that what he claimed was true.

That night they camped next to bend in a river. While her father rested and the cook prepared dinner, Cicely and George sat on an outcrop of rock on the bank, smoked his packet of Rothmans, and talked. And as the mountain water rushed by and the campfire filled the air with the smell of roasting spices, as he described traversing ravines and meeting natives who were not particularly friendly, her eye fixed on the curve of his ear and the turn of his lip. She took in the sound of his voice when he spoke her name, which he did frequently. And even though at that point she had known him for only a matter of weeks, she was already in the grip of an infatuation that she believed was the first stirring of love. Until, that is, over dinner her father uttered those hateful words:

"I suppose, George, you'll want to get back for Christmas to see your intended."

Cicely had put down her plate of half-eaten stew and walked down to the riverbank alone. The shock, she remembered, was visceral, painful, sudden, like a slap across the cheek. How could he have talked so much about his life and failed to mention that he had a fiancée? She felt idiotic. It wasn't entirely his fault: What claim did she have on him? she asked herself. What right did she have to feel so wronged?

Away from the campfire's bright blaze the river reflected the yellow disk of a full moon. In the darkness no one could see her face crumple and her heart contract. And then he was there, at her elbow, standing close, much closer than he would have dared had it been light.

"Cicely?" George said softly.

"You don't need to explain anything," she replied. "It's quite all right."

"There is no intended," he whispered. "I invented one so your father would let you come on the trip. I so wanted to be with you. . . ."

And so her cards were played; his too. He turned her face around and kissed it, hot tears and all, in the dark, beside the boil and roll of the river, his body pressing into hers as if he were a force of nature that could not be stopped.

"Cicely?" her father called.

They pulled apart, a sheet of paper torn; then she sauntered back to camp alone. George appeared a little later from the forest, carrying an armful of tinder for the fire. How clever they thought they were, how discreet. Thankfully Cicely's mother, who could sense a white lie from a bitten lip or the turn of a gaze, wasn't there.

The rest of the trip was taken up with carefully packing and drying precious specimens to ship back to England. It was quite a haul. Cicely gravitated to George's side whenever she could. To be near him was to be filled with an energy she had never felt before; her pulse quickened, her mouth parched, her stomach turned over; it was unbearably wonderful.

"I have never found such a perfect spot for orchids," George said more than once.

"I'm glad," she said. "So glad I came."

"Here you are," a voice cut through the memory.

Cicely came back with a jolt to the present, to Scotland, to the library in Balmarra. Antonia was standing in the doorway.

"Looking for anything in particular?" she asked.

From the corner of her eye, Cicely noticed that the bottom drawer of the filing cabinet was still open. How careless she had been.

"I was just admiring your fine collection of books," Cicely replied. "But I couldn't manage to open the window. Could you try?"

Antonia strode across the library and with both hands lifted the window easily. Cicely closed the drawer gently with her calf but was unable to return the postcard without Antonia noticing.

"What have you got there?" Antonia asked.

"This? An old card," Cicely said. "From George."

"Wherever did you find it?" Antonia asked.

"On a shelf," she lied. "At the back."

"Can I have a look?"

Antonia smoothed the image with the flat of her hand, then turned it over.

"'Home by Christmas,'" she read. "Famous last words."

She smiled, but there was something of a rebuke in her manner, Cicely noted. Surely it was not her fault that in ten years George had never once returned to see his family? She had hardly entrapped him. Nothing and no one had that power over George except, perhaps, his vocation.

"It was so thoughtful of my brother to suggest you pay us a visit," Antonia said. "I only wish he were here with you."

Here was her chance to tell Antonia the truth. The words were on the tip of her tongue, all she had to do was to open her mouth and let them out. I have come to claim George's inheritance. All this will soon be gone, sold, auctioned. You are about to lose Balmarra. Antonia was looking at her, waiting for a response.

"We're glad to be here," she found herself saying, a platitude that was absolutely false. "George would have come himself if the political situation had not arisen."

"The political situation?" echoed Antonia.

"In China," she replied

Antonia looked completely lost. Did she never pick up a newspaper? The Qing Dynasty was crumbling, and the army had staged an uprising. Chinese troops were withdrawing from Tibet. All the former restrictions on travel would be lifted.

"Ah," Antonia said, straightening the spines of the books on the nearest shelf. "*That* political situation."

They were silent.

"Did he send any message?" Antonia continued. "A letter perhaps? It's been so long since we've seen him."

"I think he meant to," she replied. "But he has been rather occupied of late."

She remembered the wastepaper bin in his study that she found filled to the brim with sheets of writing paper, each screwed into a ball. "Dear Antonia," George had written in one. "It has been longer than I intended." "I regret I wasn't around more," he had written in another. "I hope we can remain on the best terms." She also remembered their argument on the day before he left.

"Maybe you should write and tell them we are coming?" she had suggested.

"And tell them what?" he had replied.

Too much time had passed. Too little contact had been sustained. Even without the difficult issue of the inheritance, the ties appeared irreparably broken.

"Tell me," Cicely said. "Was George always more interested in plants than anything else?"

Antonia ran a hand along the length of a shelf and then examined her finger for dust.

"First it was insects," she said. "He kept them in a jar. Then he had another phase—tadpoles. Then it was birds."

"Then plants?"

"Yes. My father was absolutely against him becoming a botanizer," said Antonia, looking at her directly. "I think that was why George pursued it."

"Really?" She smiled. "But your father himself collected plants."

"He was a man of contradiction." Antonia shrugged. "I think he had some kind of bad experience. Anyway, take this." Antonia held out a volume that had been lying faceup on a shelf. "It might come in useful when you and your daughter explore the estate. You know you're welcome to stay here for as long as you wish. We have a lot of catching up to do."

Cicely took the book, a much-thumbed copy of *Familiar Garden Flowers,* thanked Antonia, and excused herself, the book snug in her pocket beside the solicitor's letter. She wished Antonia would stop being so accommodating. Did she really have no idea? As for the "bad experience," it was probably something clerical, such as being overcharged or sent the wrong species. He seemed like a man who could hold a grudge against an entire profession. Now that she had the lawyer's details, however, it was perfectly possible that she could be home before the monsoon season was over. The idea calmed her a little. She was back on track.

Antonia closed the door of the library behind her. The first emotion she had felt on seeing Cicely in the library was alarm. She kept her sketchbooks on the top shelf—dozens of them, all filled with notes, drawings, and paintings from the last twenty years or so. They were safe up there, she had thought. Malcolm wasn't interested in books, and her father hadn't spent any time in the library since his eyesight began to fail. It didn't look as if Cicely had discovered them. But where on earth had she found that old postcard? What was the woman doing in there? If one was being cynical, it looked a little like snooping. Maybe Malcolm's suspicions were correct. There was no letter, no message. How could they be sure that the woman was George's wife? And the child? Was she really her niece? And if they were, what would it mean? Had her father known about Cicely and Kitty before he died? Did this change anything? And if so, what?

Antonia walked along the corridor to her bedroom, closed the door, and placed the silk rose from Cicely's hat in her top drawer. It was here she kept her secret collection of "borrowed" objects: a single gold cuff link from the painter Henry Morris; a copper thimble from sewing class at school; a silver bangle and an enameled hair clip from a former school friend. She had vowed to herself that she would stop. At best it could be seen as a compliment, at worst as theft. It was after the death of her mother when she was twelve years old that she had become attached to small mementos: a tram ticket, a tortoiseshell comb, an embroidered handkerchief. And now she found the compulsion to pocket things that belonged to other people and wouldn't immediately be missed nearly overwhelming. She had become addicted to the race of her heart and heady rush of adrenaline, the sense of power and the thrill of duplicity, especially when enlisted to search for the lost object. Would she ever return them? One day, perhaps, planting them in obscure places to turn up unexpectedly—in the lining of an old jacket, for example, or in the toe of a Wellington boot.

Maybe it was the house, the estate, the weight of all the responsibility on her shoulders that made her do it? Sometimes she dreamed of walking away from it all and into an alternate life where she was an artist more concerned with the slant of light than the cost of coal. An image of Henry flickered through her mind. His hair was long, his face clean shaven, and he smelled not of French cologne like Malcolm, but of turpentine and fresh air. How many years ago was it now? How many decades? Two? Long before she was married, anyway.

At first it had been awkward, difficult. She would wander down to the causeway where he sat with his easel, his canvas, and a case of paint, and take a quick look at how the painting was progressing. She loved to watch him work, the way he held himself, tense, like a cat about to spring, his brush in his hand and his eyes narrowed as he took in the angle of a roof or the shiver of the trees. And then he had spoiled everything, painting in that stag and eagle at her father's request, and she saw that like her, he was not free after all.

She sat down in front of her dressing table and tried to look at herself objectively in the mirror. She knew how she appeared to the world. She read it on Cicely's face the moment they first met. She was cosseted, sheltered, as fragile and ridiculous as a fig tree wrapped up in muslin in winter to guard it from frost. Portraiture had never interested her, but she wondered now if she should have painted herself at eighteen just to compare. She smoothed her face around her eyes to see if the skin was already wrinkling. To her dismay she noticed a slight droop under the jawline. It was not surprising given the events of the last five years. They had taken their toll. Strands of hair had escaped from their pins and formed a pale halo around her face. Her father used to call her "the Bitter Angel," an insult and compliment rolled into one. She was neither an angel nor was she bitter. Or only slightly. She had once wanted so much for herself; she had dreamed of days infused with the smell of linseed oil and pigment, of light on scrubbed wooden floors, and of the soft strokes of black charcoal on white paper. She would have liked to have spread her wings, bitter or not, and be taught, be challenged, and meet new people. She would have liked just a little for herself, not recognition exactly, but the possibility of praise. But it was not to be. She had stayed at home with her father while George had gone away.

A door slammed somewhere in the house, and she jumped despite herself. Cicely's daughter certainly made her presence known. Ever since they had arrived, doors were always banging, taps running, floors creaking, toilets flushing. At least they had come in summer; winter was not a comfortable season at Balmarra. Seen from their angle, however, maybe Kitty wasn't too noisy but the house itself too quiet.

Earlier that morning, just after breakfast, she had heard a noise coming from the room above. Not squirrels again? But this didn't sound like rodents, no manic racing and sudden silences. Maybe it was a pigeon? The room directly above her own was the nursery. Another noise, this time a muffled crash. Maybe it was the roof? It seemed that not a month went by without another dozen slates becoming dislodged by the wind and needing to be replaced.

She glided up the stairs; in her father's last few months she had become adept at moving silently around the house, avoiding loose floorboards and walking on tiptoe. The nursery door was slightly ajar, and from inside came a rhythmic squeaking. She peered through the gap—the rug was covered with toys she recognized, wooden soldiers and wooden animals from a Noah's Ark. A mechanical tumbling bear stood on its head, and a game of bagatelle lay open, its pieces scattered everywhere. Underneath the window, sitting on the rocking horse, was the girl.

"Here we go round the mulberry bush," she sang softly as she rocked. "Come on, horsey, giddyap."

In the soft winter light, the resemblance between the girl and her brother was striking. Would her own daughter have looked a little like Kitty?

Antonia shivered and felt a sense of loss as keen as if a door had opened to let in the chill. Malcolm had done his best. He had taken time off work to accompany her to doctor's appointments, he had uttered all the right words. But she hated the way he patted her on the arm while they waited; she couldn't bear the way he way he nodded gently when the doctor had explained her predicament as if he understood what it felt like to be her. And as they sat in the chemist's waiting for her prescription, a tonic to help her sleep, and Malcolm leafed through the local newspaper, she had wanted to rip it out of his hands and burn it. The fault wasn't his, however, but hers. She had thought that she might be a better mother than she was an artist, but apparently this was not the case.

"We could continue trying," Malcolm had suggested more than once. But they had tried, and she had failed several times already. When she saw how easily other women fell pregnant, her blood turned to vinegar. How could she let herself be touched when she was so sour inside? Several months after the last mishap, as he called it, Malcolm had given up. They had slept apart for years now, and—she told herself—had probably both forgotten all they once knew. How quickly they had moved from being bedfellows to being friends, and sometimes she wasn't even sure if they were that.

Kitty had started to hum and began to sing another song with words Antonia struggled to make out.

"*Roti, makhan, chini,*" she sang. "*Chota, baba nini.*"

The girl was not like George or any of her unborn children. She was foreign, different, strange.

At lunch Cicely had told Antonia they were sending Kitty to boarding school, somewhere she had never heard of called Glenrannoch, near Stirling. Antonia felt a pang for the girl. How would she fit in?

At her dressing table, Antonia unfastened her plait. They had never discussed what would happen to the estate when he died, but her father had always assured her that it would eventually belong to its caretakers, and that, surely, meant her and Malcolm. George had done his best to disinherit himself. Anyway, her husband wasn't worried. Malcolm was her father's son-in-law, and more important, he kept an eye on his legal affairs. If there was any chance that anything was about to be snatched from under their noses, so to speak, he would have told her. Besides, there was nothing much of value at Balmarra. And she doubted George had the money or the will to finance its ruinously expensive upkeep, especially not from five thousand miles away.

She tried to flatten her hair with the palm of her hand, but still it bounded back again, coiling into thick spirals. It was impossible. Sometimes it felt as if her life was a series of challenges that defeated her every time. She picked up the pompadour frame she had bought in Glasgow several years earlier and placed it on her head. The process was painful, difficult, and the style never turned out the way it was supposed to. First she began to roll the front of her hair over the frame, and when it was lifted away from her face, to anchor it in place with pins. Next she rolled up the rest of her hair into a "foundation tail" and wrapped it in a figure eight the way the hairdresser had shown her. Then she threaded in hairpins until her hair was piled into a loose chignon. The results were better than usual: Finally she looked presentable. But before she even rose from her stool, one hairpin and then another began to loosen. The frame wasn't straight, the roll of hair was sliding forward, and strands sprang out on both sides.

This time, she decided, she would not give up. If Cicely made the effort, then so would she. After all, she was the lady of the house. She pulled out all the pins, removed the frame, brushed out her hair, and started again.

4

Cicely followed the footpath that led down to the boathouse on the shores of the loch. The rain was soft, fine, and came down in blusters and wisps like pale smoke. It was too late to go to Dunoon and see the solicitor. She would go first thing in the morning. In the meantime she craved fresh air and open spaces, a place to escape. She had rushed out of the house, ignoring the skies that threatened rain, taking no account of the rough terrain. By the time she reached the bottom of the hill, her shoes were sodden.

All of a sudden, the birds stopped singing and it started to rain so heavily that she was forced to take shelter under a holly tree. There was a taste in the air she recognized. This was more like the rain she knew, this was a deluge, this was almost a *manasuni*. As she stood beneath the dripping leaves, she wondered what George was doing at that particular moment. Was it raining too? Had he reached the valley high up in the mountains that he had told her about or was he still in the foothills? How many specimens had he collected? She remembered the one he had given her after the first expedition: a *Cymbidium mastersii*, a winter-blooming orchid with white petals, a pale yellow lip, and an almond scent. Its flowers, George had explained, never fully opened. And then he had kissed her again, the taste of him like nothing she had ever tasted before: flash floods and waterfalls and lightning.

"Should I stop?" he whispered. "Should I?"

Even now the imprint of George's mouth, the pressure of his lips on hers, the small of his back and softness of his skin beneath her fingertips were locked in her body's memory. Afterward there were buttons fumbled, laces unknotted, voices swallowed, each of them growing increasingly bolder in a series of meeting places. Despite the hours before and after when she agonized over every detail, it was over before she knew it. Kitty was conceived in the space between a heartbeat and the tick of a minute hand. When she missed her monthly bleed she knew enough about biology to realize that they had done something that could not be easily undone. George was silent when she told him. His eye followed a bird as it glided into the distance, and his jaw hardened.

"Well, that's that, then," he said.

What about the fiancée in Scotland? her father had demanded the night George came around unannounced and uninvited. Fictional, George admitted. You are not only a fantasist but a liar and a seducer, her father had yelled. And what was more, he continued, how did he think he could support his daughter with such a precarious profession? All the aspects of George Pick's personality and background that had initially impressed him, that he had lauded with praise only a matter of weeks before, were now proof of his blatant unsuitability. Her father, sweating in the morning jacket that he had hastily thrown on over his nightshirt, must have read George's face and realized it was already too late. No wonder he was furious: He too had been seduced.

The marriage was without fuss, a brief ceremony in St. Andrew's Anglican Church on the Darjeeling Mall Road. Did she regret it now? Of course. Although she could never imagine her life without Kitty, she regretted her haste, her impulsiveness, which rather than opening up her world had narrowed it.

Her mother had died suddenly that summer, the newly conceived and the newly deceased passing each other so closely that Kitty seemed to have picked up some of her mother's mannerisms and facial expressions on the way. Her father had married again six months later to a much younger woman and set up a new home, throwing away most of the detritus of the last. His new wife was gay, sociable, jealous, and crammed every spare moment with dinner parties and bridge evenings, leaving no time for anything or anyone else. Apart from Cicely to prove it otherwise, sometimes it was as if his first marriage had never happened.

Kitty was born a month prematurely while George was away on another expedition. On that trip he found a valley where there were so many orchids, so many thousands of different species, that he made a huge collection. On hearing the news of Kitty's birth, however, he rushed back, leaving hundreds of plants behind, their roots cruelly exposed, their flowers already wilting in the heat. Later he tried to return, but the valley seemed to have disappeared, like the location of a fairy tale, never to be found again.

George's green thumb, his exhaustive knowledge of plants, and talent for specimen collection made him famous throughout Bengal. But for all his singular passion, or because of it, there was a side to George that was sometimes hard to like. His gentleness, she knew, was tempered by brutality. He had wide hands scored with scars, and his touch was exacting, perceptive, merciless. At one consultation with a potential client it was alleged that he had uprooted an entire tray of magnolia seedlings that the client's gardener had just planted at vast expense, leaving just one, which then failed to thrive and died. He didn't receive many bookings after that.

After Kitty's birth they had lived in a series of rented villas, each a little farther out of town, each a little less expensive than the last. They had been in the current villa, which sat in an abandoned tea plantation, for a year. It was cheap and a little run down but, according to George, purely temporary. She could put up with it for a short while, couldn't she? Soon they could move anywhere she wanted, a house on the Mall, or to one of the other hill towns, or maybe, if she wanted, to Europe. The brightest of futures was always just ahead of them, so close that they could almost touch it. It was always, however, also just out of reach.

The setting of the tea plantation was beautiful but isolated. Sometimes it felt like a prison, her only escape long rides through the forests on her horse. When she came back breathless, exhilarated, her skirts, her hands, her face spotted with mud and her hair filled with the scent of mountain snow, George would barely glance at her, his silence filled with accusations he didn't voice. And then, more often than not, he would take his bicycle and pedal off to town, and be gone for two days, possibly three. George, she discovered, had something missing—an emotional hole. Food, wine, expensive hotels did not impress him. The only currency he valued was the new, the unexplored.

On the March morning when George had started to plan his current expedition, the air was filled with his itch of impatience. He would travel to Siliguri and then change trains three—or was it four?—times until he reached Saikhowaghat, the end of the line, in Assam. There he would hire mules and muleteers and load his equipment on their sturdy wooden frames; he would employ a cook, buy food from the bazaar—rice, eggs, flour, tinned meat—and then head off on a pony along paths that had been there for thousands of years to transport cotton, walnuts, and opium. Eventually the mule caravan would turn off the beaten track and head into the mountains guarded by tribesmen, the majority of it unexplored, uninhabited, and filled, George hoped, with a profusion of rare and unidentified flowers, trees, and shrubs.

"You know I support your decision," she'd said. "But in all honesty I have to say that I would rather you didn't go. Not right away. Not until we have everything sorted out."

It was not only the length of time—a year or more at his own estimation—or the fact that an expedition on this scale was dangerous, difficult, speculative; it was the expense, which was ruinous.

There was a stack of unpaid bills on the hall table, and each day's post brought another final demand for payment.

"Why don't we at least generate some income first? We could plant some tea."

"That would take years. I have to leave before the mountains are teeming with plant hunters," he had insisted. "I want to go to the Mekong River, to the Lohit, set up a base at Rima, and explore that whole area. There are valleys up there that haven't been charted, where few Westerners have ever set foot. It's everything I've been waiting for, Cicely. It's why I came to this part of the world in the first place."

She remembered how distracted he had been in the weeks before he left, as if he were halfway there in his head already. His eyes were full of light, he could not sleep, he did not eat, he spent hours looking at maps, running his fingers over the brown ridges of mountain ranges and tracing river valleys, the thin black lines like wrinkles on a piece of cloth. It was, she thought at the time, as if he had been overcome by a kind of madness.

"This trip will make me," he had told her. "The timing could not have been better. With the inheritance and my experience I can't fail. Just imagine, my dearest Cicely, your name immortalized in a rare bloom!"

He gave her that look, a look that said: I'm in love with everything, you, the world, the ground we walk on. It was hard to resist. She made herself turn away.

His desire was a shifting, corrosive appetite that ate at him from the inside. She had not seen it in him at first. When she closed her eyes, even here in Scotland, she could still smell the jungle; she could see the colors of the orchids, the blues, the creams, the purples; she could feel the heat rising. After almost a decade she could remember every single aspect of that first expedition with George. Imagine a flower, a shrub, nothing like anyone had seen before, she remembered he had told her: a striking shade, a fragrant scent, an azalea or a clematis of a new color or shape or size.

"Cymbidium elegans," his voice whispered in her head. *"Crepidium purpureum. Calanthe whiteana."*

She wondered if he would ever find what he was looking for, if he would ever satisfy the craving that consumed him or if it would destroy them all first.

Cicely took a deep breath and let it go. She must calm down. Take one step at a time. Think of the task at hand. Tomorrow morning the solicitor would confirm their claim, and she could start to make plans. At the base of a holly tree, she spotted a tiny flower with small pink starry petals and a slender stem. She took off her gloves, knelt down, and carefully uprooted it with her fingertips. Maybe this was one of the rare species that Antonia had mentioned?

The gardener's wheelbarrow, empty now, had been left beside the glass-house door. A dog, a brown Labrador, lay sprawled out at the entrance and raised its head, its tail beating the ground in greeting. Inside the air smelled of steaming loam and tar wash, of horse manure and seaweed. The windows were clouded with condensation, a steady drip came from the roof. How ironic, she thought, that the Picks keep their glass house warmer than their bedrooms. At the far end, steps led down to a doorway, and she could hear the low rumble of the subterranean boiler.

"Hello!" she called out. "Mr. Baillie?"

The man who emerged from the boiler room was not Mr. Baillie. He was young, at least younger than the head gardener, his sleeves were rolled up, his hands were blackened, and his face was flushed—it seemed she had caught him in the middle of things.

"I was looking for the gardener," she explained.

He inspected his palms and then rubbed them with a clean white handkerchief.

"My uncle's gone for tea," he said. "Maybe I can help?"

"I don't think so," she said. "This is about a horticultural matter."

"Try me," he replied.

Her face began to color. Was this how the staff addressed the

Pick family? He'd be calling her "duckie" next, she thought, or "pet," as the cabdriver had in London.

"I was wondering if you knew what this flower is?"

She held out her right palm to show him.

"If not, then I'm sure I can find it in here," she said, bringing *Familiar Garden Flowers* from her pocket, slightly damp from the rain.

There was a flash of white as the solicitor's letter fell to the ground. The gardener hadn't noticed. Cicely thought it best to ignore it. It wouldn't do for the staff to find out she had been stealing the Picks' private correspondence.

"Let's have a look," he said, indicating that she should place the flower in his palm. "Where did you find it?"

"On the island, near the shore."

The envelope was wedged halfway beneath a terra-cotta pot six inches from his foot.

"Were there many of them?"

"I only saw one. Is it rare?"

Although he tried to hide it, a small smile appeared on his face.

"It's thrift," he said. "Common thrift. It grows all over."

He knelt down and picked up the envelope—he must have noticed it after all—and peered inside.

"Another one?" he said.

She frowned at him, uncomprehending.

"Excuse me?"

"Can't say I know this," he said. "Maybe I could look it up later. When I'm not so busy?"

And before she could stop him he had placed the envelope in his pocket.

"Wait!" she said.

He stopped, he turned. How could she demand the envelope back without raising suspicion? Would he go straight to Antonia with it? How could she explain what she was doing with the solicitor's letter?

"I was almost away with this," the gardener said and carefully placed the thrift back in Cicely's palm. "It's Mrs. Pick, isn't it?" He gestured at the book in her other hand, and she looked down.

The solicitor's letter was still wedged inside. There must have been another envelope between the pages of *Familiar Garden Flowers.*

"Everything all right?" he asked.

Her heart was still pounding. She forced her face into a smile.

"Everything is fine. Thank you."

Antonia glanced up as Cicely left the glass house. What could she possibly have been talking about with the gardener? Young Baillie watched her go, his face expressionless, then headed back down to the boiler room. Antonia picked up the secateurs and began to select some roses for the dining room table. They had to be just right, the heads still tight, the blooms not in imminent danger of blowing.

Young Mr. Baillie was old Mr. Baillie's great-nephew. He had arrived a few years earlier from Glasgow, where he had worked for a spell in the Botanic Gardens. In all the time he had worked for them, she had conversed with him only twice. He was, however, good at his job, and kept the boiler topped up and the glass house warm. And now that his uncle was getting on a bit, they needed him. Old Mr. Baillie had worked for her father for as long as she could remember— much longer, in fact—and he had helped establish the gardens and her father's collection. Her mother had wanted a fernery, which was at the time the height of fashion. But her father had won out, since he was paying for it. He had hired a horticultural engineer, sketched out a few designs, and then, as if to make a point, had built a huge glass house quite out of proportion with Balmarra House.

As well as his tropical plants, his orchids, and his fruit trees, Edward Pick had been especially proud of his roses, his Bourbons and his Albas, and positioned them in beds around the entrance. But you had to be disciplined, he had told Antonia, with Rosaceae, and cut them back after they had flowered; otherwise they would grow leggy and unproductive. This year, for the first time, on her instructions, the roses had not been cut down to the ground; they had not been hard-pruned in the autumn. New shoots were already appearing, their tiny leaves curled in on themselves like fists.

The rest of the estate was harder to control. There was always something that needed urgent attention. The house and gardens were in a constant state of decay from woodworm or rot or rust, or from siege by mice, squirrels, and ants. Twenty years earlier, however, Balmarra's garden and glass house had been much admired. A journalist had visited and written a short feature for the *Dunoon Courier*. Several botanists from the Royal Botanic Gardens in Edinburgh had planned to come and take a look, but their ferry had been canceled due to bad weather and the trip had never been rescheduled.

Although the glass house was kept a constant temperature of seventy degrees, the rest of the garden was now not well maintained; there had once been a team of gardeners, not just a couple. The old paths were blocked by fallen trees that hadn't been removed, and the decorative ponds were clogged with blanket weed and algae. Just keeping the area around the house free of encroaching vegetation and stoking the boilers for the hothouses took up most of the Baillies' time. Maybe Antonia did need a plan. She would have to do something about it, but what? There wasn't any money to employ extra staff.

Suddenly Kitty yanked open the glass-house door. The girl stood, slightly breathless, and looked around at the damasks and tea roses, climbing on trellises or staked in pots.

"Why is this place so hot?" she asked.

"The plants need heat to thrive," Antonia replied. "Most of them come from other countries, hotter countries."

"Like me," said Kitty.

She placed her fingertips around a dark red rose, an Alba, and for a moment Antonia was sure she was going to pluck off the head. Instead she lowered her head and sniffed.

"They smell more fragrant in the early morning," Antonia explained.

"Really?" Kitty said. "May I have some? For Mummy?"

Without waiting for an answer she took the secateurs from Antonia's hands and started to snip. In a matter of moments ten, twelve, fourteen, twenty heads, white and yellow and pink, red and cream and orange, were severed.

"You don't mind, do you?" she said as the bunch of flowers grew larger.

There was a moment when the pipes rattled and the rain began to patter on the glass above.

"No," said Antonia. "Be my guest."

They walked back to the house in silence, Kitty's arms full of roses, Antonia with her half dozen. She was filled with a kind of furious panic. The rose bed was now practically barren; only a few small buds were left. How would she decorate the house in the coming weeks? What would her father have said? Antonia had never seen such extravagant, wasteful behavior.

They met Cicely on the front steps. If she was embarrassed by her daughter's haul, her face didn't show it.

"These are for you, Mummy," said Kitty. "From the hothouse."

Kitty went to ask Dora for some vases, and they walked into the house in silence.

"Come to my room," said Cicely when they reached the bottom of the stairs. "I have something for you."

"That's really not necessary," Antonia replied without looking up.

"Let me put these in water first. But come. Soon."

Cicely's room smelled glorious. The flowers had been arranged, and the vases placed on every possible surface from the mantelpiece to the bedside table.

"It was very generous of you to let Kitty pick so many," Cicely said. "I would never have allowed it."

Antonia gave a small smile. She realized that she had a lot to learn about children and how to deal with them.

The cashmere scarf was the deepest, sweetest red. Around the fringe was a border of embroidery; tiny flowers and minuscule bees picked out in silver, yellow, and black thread. It was a beautiful scarf, the fabric soft, the decoration intricate. Cicely wrapped it around Antonia's shoulders and let it fall to the ground.

"There we are," she said. "It suits you."

"Oh no, I couldn't possibly . . . ," Antonia began. "It's far too special."

"It's yours," she said. "In India we have a saying. It is not the value of the gift but the sincerity with which it is given which is important."

For a second Antonia wondered if Cicely was making fun of her. Was she sincere? If the scarf had really been intended for her, then why hadn't she given it to her the day she arrived? Or was it not sincerity but guilt that motivated the action? Antonia ran the tips of her fingers down the beautiful scarf. She desired it so much she practically ached. Should she accept it? How could she not without making a scene? On balance, she made a decision. She would take Cicely at face value; she would give her the benefit of the doubt.

"Well, I suppose," Antonia began. "If you insist, then thank you."

"Going anywhere special?" Cicely asked, gesturing at Antonia's hair.

Antonia's hand immediately rose to her head, to smooth down any stray hairs, and her cheeks flushed.

"What?" she said. "No, oh no."

"I thought we might go to Dunoon."

"Really? When?"

"Tomorrow morning," Cicely said. "We could do with a walk."

"I'm rather busy," said Antonia. "I'm sorry."

Cicely gave her a smile, that smile, as Antonia took in that she hadn't actually been invited.

5

They had just reached the village of Sandbank when Kitty heard it, a rumbling, a spluttering, high above. Cicely looked up, shading her eyes with her hand. It was a biplane, making a great circle through the sky, its shadow looping across the hills, the river, the sugar refineries, before it headed out to sea.

"Where is it going?" asked Kitty.

"Probably just out for a spin," she replied. "Like we are."

It was a relief to get away from Balmarra. They had breakfasted at eight and left the house an hour later. George would have been impressed; he was always complaining about how long it took Cicely to get ready. Would he really have preferred the alternative? Her hair in a plait and her clothes thrown on? Did he want her to look like Antonia? She doubted it.

Kitty skipped as they crossed a bridge and then followed the road for at least a mile. Several carriages and motorcars passed by, the occupants staring down at them curiously. Otherwise the only people they saw were on foot: a couple of young girls who giggled behind their hands, a farmer with a sheepdog that barked at them, and finally Mr. Baillie's nephew. He was wearing a dark overcoat and carrying a heavy leather satchel.

"Morning," she said as she passed him.

"Same to you," he replied.

"Was that—?" Kitty whispered.

"Yes," she replied. "The younger gardener."

"Where has he been?" Kitty asked.

She was at the age where she believed that her mother knew everything. Cicely stole a glance over her shoulder. Mr. Baillie's nephew was walking backward, looking after them. She turned, but not quickly enough for Kitty. She stopped and then gave a small wave. Cicely spun her around by the shoulders, took her hand, and walked faster.

"Don't want to miss the post office," she said. "It might close."

"When does it close?"

"Half past hurry up," she said.

Kitty laughed.

"Two minutes to slow coach," she suggested. "Quarter to quickly."

"Enough," she said after Kitty had reeled off several more.

George had arranged he would write to her care of the local post office. It wouldn't do for his sister or her husband to open and read any of their correspondence accidentally. And there was the other reason she needed to visit Dunoon, the more pressing one—to pay a visit to Edward Pick's solicitor. She hoped he would see her without an appointment.

An ocean liner sailing down the Clyde Estuary to the Irish Sea passed by so close that they could almost see the faces of the men, women, and children on the decks, all heading, she supposed, to America or Canada to start new lives. Kitty was silent, maybe thinking, as she was, of the continent they had left behind, of India. Did one ever sever the link with one's homeland? It pulled like a current, and she compared every taste, every color, every smell. She dreamed of the mountains, of Darjeeling, and woke up disoriented, surprised to find herself in another land and another climate.

A seagull glided in the sky above. The wind boomed in her ears.

Once they reached the headland, the town was visible in the distance. Kitty liked the sound of it in her mouth and sang a little song, "Dunoon, Dunoon, Dunoon." Across a small inlet was a huge red sandstone castle. Unlike Balmarra, it looked as if it had been built in the last fifty years and was bigger, grander, with a sweep of lawn and an exquisitely planted garden.

Maybe Antonia and Malcolm had never expected that George would come back and claim what was his; maybe they had thought he would let them live there for as long as they wanted. After all, his life was elsewhere; it was doubtful that he had thought of Balmarra more than a couple of times in years. But now he needed the money, desperately, immediately, and that drive was stronger than any sense of filial loyalty.

Hopefully the solicitor would be able to suggest a palatable solution. A buyout, perhaps? Would Antonia and Malcolm have enough money for that? Would their marriage survive? And if not, what would happen? She pictured Antonia alone on a deck with a suitcase at her ankle, sailing off to another, more turbulent life. The worst thing was that she seemed to have absolutely no idea, no inkling, of what was coming.

By the time they reached Dunoon, the sky had clouded over again, a raw wind was coming off the water, and large waves buffeted the pier. The cafés on the seafront were open for the season and faded bunting, strung from the lampposts, snapped in the wind. A few holidaymakers strolled about eating ice cream, and several families were camped out on the shingle beach shivering in their swimming costumes, only the very brave or very young venturing into the water.

In the post office a man with leather flying goggles on his head was chatting with the clerk. The queue stretched out the door, and the other customers were becoming impatient.

"Do we have all day?" one elderly man said under his breath. "Oh no, we don't!"

"I'll wait for it," the man at the front said, and finally stepped aside. When he saw the queue he apologized profusely and then he stood, his elbow on the counter, and began to whistle. As they stood in line, Cicely scrutinized him: mid- to late-thirties, she guessed. As well as the goggles, he wore a leather flying jacket and a bright yellow silk scarf knotted around his neck. It was a slash of color in swaths of gray and black wool. His hair was dark, and he had a small scar on his right temple. Was it his plane they had seen in the sky? The whistling, the goggles, the scarf, the way he leaned on the counter as if he owned it, were in sharp contrast to the people queuing up to buy a stamp. He was clearly someone in this small town.

After twenty minutes Kitty and Cicely finally reached the front of the queue.

"I wondered if you had any post for me?" she asked, writing her name on a piece of paper and slipping it across the counter to the clerk.

"A letter came for you from India, Mrs. Pick," he said.

As he went to fetch it, she sensed a presence. The whistling man was standing at her elbow gazing down at her.

"I couldn't help overhearing, but you don't happen to be related to the late Edward Pick?"

"I am, yes," she replied. "I'm his son George's wife. And this is our daughter, Kitty."

He took a sharp intake of breath, as if surprised, and then his face widened into a smile. It was an expression quite without diffidence, of a man at complete ease with himself, more than a little disarming.

"Keir Lorimer," he said by way of introduction. "I had great respect for your father-in-law and was sorry to hear of his death. My condolences."

"Thank you," she replied. "I'm afraid I never met him, but I'll pass them on to his family."

He cocked his head.

"We are visiting from abroad," she explained. "From Darjeeling. It's in India."

"I know where it is," he replied.

The office door opened, and the man appeared, handing Cicely a letter and Lorimer a parcel.

"Just arrived, Mr. Lorimer," he said.

"Come to dinner," Lorimer told Cicely as they turned to leave the post office. "I'll send word to Balmarra, and we can work out a date."

"Oh no," she replied. "We won't be staying for long."

"All the more reason to make it sooner rather than later," he said before he headed out of the door, whistling once more.

Dunoon was much smaller than Darjeeling. After walking the length of the main street, Cicely and Kitty took refuge in the restaurant of a hotel on Argyll Street. The dining room was paneled with dark wood, and four electric lights flickered dismally behind their orange shades. Three elderly men sat at a table overlooking the gardens, and several groups of middle-aged ladies perched in booths at the back. Their entrance caused a small stir, a turning of heads, as if they had let in a bluster of air of another temperature. First they were shown to a table in the middle of the room—the very worst, second only to one next to the kitchens. Cicely asked for another table, and they were grudgingly shown a slightly better one at the window and given menus.

With some swallowed-down amusement—what *were* black pudding, haggis, neeps, or stovies?—they both ordered the roast lamb. When it came, the meat overcooked and the gravy congealed, Kitty moved the food around the plate with her fork but didn't eat much of it. Cicely admonished but couldn't really blame her. Once the plates had been cleared without comment, she brought out George's letter.

"Now. I thought we could read it together," she said as she slipped open the envelope with her finger.

Her daughter was staring out the window.

"Kitty?" she asked.

"I wish he was here too," Kitty said.

"I know," she said unfolding the thin blue paper. "Now, are you listening?"

Dear Cicely and Kitty, if you are reading this, then you must have arrived safely in Scotland. Since I last saw you I have walked too many miles to count, over mountain passes, across rope bridges and through lush valleys. I have paid my respects to a maharajah, and stayed in a village on the Holy mountain where nothing can be killed. In some of the places I have been, they have never seen white people before and the crowds gather.

As I predicted, much of the land hasn't been explored. One day I slipped from a path and fell down a cliff. Please don't concern yourself; obviously all was well. I grabbed on to some greenery to save myself from falling further only to find it was a species of buddleia that I didn't recognise. If it is indeed a new species, I will instruct the Regius Keeper in Edinburgh to call it Buddleia kittii. *I am sending this letter with a muleteer who is heading back to civilization and has promised he will post it. He is waiting outside now, so I must stop. Much affection, George.*

Cicely folded up the letter and put it back in the envelope.

"Seems he's having quite an adventure," she said.

"I think he's making a terrible mistake," said Kitty, still staring out the window. "You both are."

How much did she know?

"Everyone goes to school," she told her. "And you'll be happy at the one we've chosen."

"That's not what I mean," she replied.

Kitty's face was set, her jaw clenched. Maybe she shouldn't have brought her to Balmarra after all.

"You don't want to live in that draughty old place, do you?" Cicely said brightly.

"You never even asked me."

"Well, do you? Do you want to live there and not go to school, to molder away like . . . like . . . your aunt Antonia?"

Kitty didn't answer. Cicely signaled for the bill

"Why is everything always about money?" Kitty said eventually.

"Why, indeed?" said Cicely.

The solicitor, Mr. Drummond, was an elderly man with scant hair the color of house dust. His office was on the first floor above a dentist. While Kitty waited in reception he ushered Cicely in, then whacked the seat several times with his handkerchief before he invited her to sit. It was clearly quite an inconvenience for her to simply turn up rather than make an appointment.

"I am sorry to disappoint," he said once she had explained the reason for her visit. "But I still need more time to go through the paperwork."

"Is there a problem?" she asked. "It has been over twelve months."

He smiled and bowed his head.

"It shouldn't take long," he replied. "However, there have been a few unforeseen complications."

"What kinds of complications?" she asked.

His threaded his fingers together and placed his hands on the desk in front of him.

"For reasons of confidentiality," he replied, "I am unable to give you any further information, Mrs. Pick. I'm sorry."

This was not the news she had been expecting at all.

"Mr. Drummond," she said. "I have come all the way from India."

"I realize that," he replied. "But all I can do is assure you that I'm doing everything I can. You're staying at the estate, I take it?"

"We are. For the time being."

How could she have come all this way to find the situation so unresolved? Maybe Edward Pick had changed his mind before he died? Maybe he had changed his will?

"I'll write as soon as I have news," he said.

As she closed the door of the solicitor's office behind her, she clung to the brass door handle for support.

"What's the matter?" Kitty asked her. "Mummy?"

She turned and forced a smile. Best not to think about the school fees, the unpaid debts, the soaring cost of the expedition. Edward Pick clearly stated he was leaving Balmarra to his son. She had read the letter herself.

On the walk home, the sun shone. The weather had turned fair. She looked up at the sky half expecting to see the same plane scoring the blue. They would have to stay and find a way to make the situation work to their advantage. What else could she do?

After Cicely and Kitty had gone, the house was so quiet that the air seemed to pause, like a body of water settling after a storm. It was midmorning. A weekday. Cook was out, Dora too. Antonia walked from room to room, running her fingers over the cool porcelain of the door handles, the pale green linen weave of the wallpaper, and the smooth curve of the banister's polished mahogany. There was a certain security, she knew, in the feel of familiar objects, in the texture of the permanent. Most likely the house would still be standing when she was long gone. A sudden vision struck her, of Balmarra as a huge stone tomb, for both the living and the dead. She shuddered. It was her lot in life, she thought grimly, to be perpetually cold.

George's room had lain untouched since he had left it—a single bed with a blue woolen counterpane, a washstand, an empty mahogany suit stand, and a bookshelf stacked with *Boy's Own* annuals. Antonia stepped inside and crossed to the window. Mist was drifting in from the north, obliterating the water with a thickening breath of white. She ran her hand over the bedcover. It was cold and slightly damp. But it didn't seem that long ago that George was sitting on this bed, his rucksack packed, tying his bootlaces.

"I'm walking to Italy to see the orange blossom," he had told them the night before he left.

"Well, you better hurry," her father had replied facetiously. "Or you'll miss it."

It had taken him five months, and he had almost died, he told her later, in a snowstorm in the Alps. But he had made it: He had walked thousands of miles with nothing more than a change of clothes and a compass, to lie in an Italian orange grove, *Citrus sinensis*, to be exact, the air heavy with the drift of fragrant blossom, just as he had dreamed it would be.

And was it worth it? she had asked him once he had returned. George had looked at her with unmistakable pity in his eyes.

"Seeing the world is the greatest thing a man can do," he had replied.

Antonia was not so lucky. She was not a man, and the female sex rarely walked anywhere unaccompanied, especially not across continents. George had always had the odds stacked in his favor. While George was sent away to school, Antonia was educated at home by a series of governesses whose subject matter was limited to needlework, piano, and conversational French. Whatever the difference in their education, the siblings had grown up with a sense of mutual distrust and the knowledge that nothing either of them ever did would be quite good enough for their father. He could be cruel, unkind, and divisive, encouraging sibling to compete against sibling at every opportunity. He offered prizes for the fastest runner, the highest climber—the best, the biggest, the longest, the rarest, whatever took his fancy. Once he even had them racing snails. Not only did he expect the winner to make fun of the loser, he often forgot about the prize. Even though he was younger by two years, George nearly always won. On one of the rare occasions she won,

Antonia had reminded her father that he owed her a shilling, and he had been so angry that she had been banished, sent to bed without any supper for a week. While George had absented himself, running away from Balmarra as soon as he could, she had remained, turned inward, and folded into herself until the face she showed the world was as blank as crockery.

But it could have been worse. A few years later a friend of her father had introduced her to the solicitor Malcolm McCulloch, who was unmarried and available. They began to court, and he had soon proposed. The wedding was a private affair attended only by close family and her father's friend, followed by a short honeymoon in North Berwick, where she had caught cold and had to spend most of it in bed. On their return it was decided that the newlyweds would base themselves at Balmarra with her elderly father, until his inevitable demise.

Would her life have been different if George had not abandoned her? It was impossible to know. One day she hoped they could heal their relationship. He was her brother, after all, and until Cicely and Kitty arrived, her own only living relative. She opened his bedside drawers one by one, to see if he had left anything behind, but apart from a scattering of dried lavender flowers, they were empty. She looked around her brother's room for a final time and then opened the door to let herself out.

At the end of the corridor, a staircase circled up to the attics. The huge space above hung in her chest like a weight; for months she had been intending to sort through her father's collections of china, paintings, and Roman artifacts. He had been an avid collector of the rare and the ancient and the obscure. He had accounts at all the major auction houses in Edinburgh and London and was often approached by dealers looking to make a private sale. His taste was eclectic, and he spent hours poring over auction catalogs looking for bargains. Some of his collection was valuable; some of it was junk. The problem was that she wasn't sure which was which. Today was the day, she decided, to start the process. No more procrastination, no more delays.

Daylight revealed the narrow gaps and holes in the eaves made by squirrels and roosting birds over the years. Lit up by the cracks of light were suitcases and winter galoshes, Christmas decorations and boxes of her old things—toys, threadbare animals, and books, their covers faded or spotted with mildew. She lifted a rag doll that had once been beloved, held it to her face and sniffed. But nothing of her childhood self remained; it smelled of damp with a hint of mouse. In fact there was a hole in the doll's arm and kapok stuffing was falling out like snow. What was the use of keeping these things now, she asked herself, when there would be no children to hand them down to, no new toys to replace them?

Her father's collection of books, antiques, and paintings had been bought, he was fond of boasting, for a song. Antonia doubted that was true. Once the thrill of the purchase had faded, he stored most of it out of sight as if the memory of how much it had cost had become vulgar to him. Beneath a blanket was a stack of oil paintings, their gilded frames scuffed and peeling. In the dim light she looked through them; landscapes and still lifes that depicted fruit, dead birds, tarnished copper plates, and drooping flowers. Others were figurative: portraits of her father he clearly hadn't liked; a young African woman in a pale blue gown; some nudes, where pairs of young women with puckered buttocks and plump breasts gazed out of the canvas as if inviting the viewer to touch them. Antonia quickly pulled the blanket back over the paintings again. No wonder her father had kept these hidden. What would her mother have thought? Did she know what he had bought, or had he started to collect them only after her death? Antonia began to suspect that she hadn't known her father as well as she thought. What other secrets had he kept from her?

After an hour Antonia had managed to unpack only one tea chest containing a few pieces of china and a set of silver teaspoons. There were at least forty more tea chests as well as stacks of paintings. It was a mammoth task. She vowed not to leave such a mess behind when she died. What was the point of accumulating so much? The only things she valued and would be sad to lose were her sketchbooks in the library.

On her way back downstairs, she noticed Cicely had left the door to her room ajar. After a moment's hesitation, she pushed it open and stepped inside. What was she looking for? A clue, evidence? She opened the wardrobe and ran her hand over Cicely's gowns. As she expected, they were beautiful, made in fine fabrics and bold shades that would never suit her own insipid coloring. She picked up a scent from the dressing table, sprayed it on her wrist, and sniffed. It smelled different on her skin, sharper, almost sour.

The drawers contained nothing but undergarments and stockings. She looked in the bedside cabinet, the back of the wardrobe, the single drawer of the writing table, but there was nothing personal or private. She was about to look under the mattress when she heard the sound of someone knocking at the back door downstairs. She felt herself blush deep red, as if she had been caught in the act. Quickly she checked that everything was as she had had found it, then she let herself out and ran down the servants' stairs.

The knocking had stopped by the time she reached the back door. Mr. Baillie's nephew was standing on the doormat, deep in thought, his hat in one hand and a notebook in the other.

"Oh, hello," she said as she opened the door. "Are you looking for Cook? It's her day off. Would you like a cup of tea?"

"Only if it's no trouble," he said.

She filled the kettle and placed it on the range to boil. It was no trouble, but it was certainly novel. Cook would have a fit if she found out. But what nonsense it all was, Antonia told herself. She might be the lady of the house and he might be the gardener's nephew, but fundamentally they were just two people who needed a cup of tea. And so they stood, he at the door and she at the stove, and waited for the kettle to boil.

"So how is it?" she said when she could not bear the silence anymore. "The garden, I mean?"

Mr. Baillie's nephew seemed to be holding his breath.

"Well," he blurted out, "a few trees came down in the spring gales, but otherwise—"

At last, after a small eternity, the kettle boiled, steam whistling through its spout. She filled the teapot and took out two cups and saucers.

"Milk?"

He shook his head no. She handed him the cup and saucer. They looked too small in his hands, like toy crockery. He raised the cup to his lips and blew on the tea to cool it. Was she going to have to stand there while he sipped the whole cup? She had rather hoped he was a swig-it-down-in-one-go kind of man.

"Remember when we used to play in the forest?" he asked suddenly. "I think you were about nine. I was eight. Your brother was younger."

She frowned. For a moment she had no idea what he was talking about. And then a memory came back as faint and jumbled as a dream. A boy on a tree stump with a stick in his hand.

"I used to come for summer. With my mother. Maybe you don't remember?"

Antonia stared at the gardener.

"Oh, my goodness, yes!"

"You fell into the stream once. I tried to pull you out and fell in too."

She did remember. The wet rocks, the green moss, the smell of leaf mold and rain.

"And then my governess wouldn't let me play with you anymore."

Antonia remembered whispered discussions, doors closed, the sense that there was something wrong with him, something shameful. What was it? And then it came back to her. He didn't have a father. Now she felt sorry for him, sorry for what had transpired all those years ago.

He cleared his throat and then put the teacup and saucer on the table. For a moment they were silent. Then they seemed to fall back into themselves, into their roles.

"Well, anyway," she said. "Can I pass on a message to Cook?"

"It was you I was coming to see, actually," he said. "I was wondering if I could borrow a few books from your library."

Antonia frowned.

"Whatever for?" she asked before she could stop herself.

His face turned red. But any embarrassment he felt did not dissuade him.

"I thought there might be some works of reference I could use," he said. "I tried the library in Dunoon, but they had nothing. My great-uncle said you had quite an extensive collection of books relating to botany and horticulture and the like."

"Did he now?"

She turned and put the kettle back on the stove. Ever since her father had taken ill, the library had become her own personal space. When she had found her brother's wife there, she had felt somewhat invaded. And now before she could stop herself she pictured mud on the Persian carpet, dirty handprints on the walls, a lingering smell of manure and loam.

"I wouldn't ask," he said softly. "But it's either this or I take some time off and go to the library at the Royal Botanic Gardens in Edinburgh. And I wouldn't want to leave the stoking of the boiler to my great-uncle, not when he's been so poorly."

"Absolutely," she replied. She had no idea that old Mr. Baillie had been poorly. She would tell Cook to make him up a basket of fruit. "You're most welcome to use the library—"

"Jacob," he said.

"Of course," she replied. "Jacob."

"Thank you, Mrs. McCulloch."

She remembered him quite clearly now, his knees all muddy and his blue eyes clear as marbles in the sunlight. He hadn't come back the next summer, and she had missed him. George had been never been one for playing imaginary games. But after a few years of playing alone she had forgotten all about him.

"You can use the back stairs," she said. "The library is directly across the hallway at the top."

As she listened to the soft pace of his boots up the servants' stairs, she felt the peace of the house dissipate. The library door opened and closed again. Now, whatever she was doing, her ears would strain for the smallest disturbance, a cough, a sigh, the slap of a closing book.

She poured the rest of the tea down the drain—a terrible waste, and just as well Cook wasn't there to witness it—and then made the rounds of the servants' quarters to make sure, she told herself, that all was in order, all was well. The larder was tidy, as was the boot room. The laundry smelled of starch and soap. Washing day was tomorrow and all the household's whites had been left to steep in a sink in a mixture of soap and soda, just the way her mother had always insisted. Over the years she had been tempted by advertisements for rotary washing machines that were meant to save time and labor. But Malcolm had balked at the price and said that he didn't want to put Dora out of a job. He had a point, in a way.

A door closed upstairs. The gardener, Jacob, was finished in the library. How strange it was to realize who he was after all those years. And how strange that she had completely blocked him out of her memory—that without a prompt, whole sections of her childhood were inaccessible to her. She wondered what else she had lost. She listened to him coming down the stairs, walking along the hallway and through the kitchen, then letting himself out the back door. The house was quiet again. Still.

Her eye was drawn to a small pile of tickets and receipts on the draining board, the contents of her husband's pockets. She was about to throw the lot into the dustbin when she noticed that one of the receipts was from a hotel in Dunoon. It was for two drinks, a whisky and a port and lemon. She put it in her pocket and stepped into the hallway. Light was streaming through the trees outside and through the glass pane above the front door to create a shifting, moving carpet. She put one foot forward, half expecting the wooden floor to bend and buckle beneath her weight. Her heel struck the parquet; the ground was still solid. And yet she felt something slide within her, a sense of vertigo, a loss of balance, as if the world were spinning beneath her feet and she had only just noticed. A small nap, she told herself, would sort her out. As she lay down on the coverlet of her bed, however, the feeling did not diminish. She had closed the curtains to shut out the light, but she could not make herself unsee what she had seen. She pulled out the receipt from her pocket and smoothed it with her fingers. Port and lemon. A woman's drink.

6

Kitty slammed the front door hard when they returned, the glass shivering in its frame, the wood creaking in its joints.

"Hellooo!" she yelled. "We're back!"

There was no response. Cicely suspected that everyone in the house was pursing their lips or rolling their eyes, or both. The house was colder inside than it was out. The fire in the drawing room, although laid, was unlit.

"Let's make a cup of tea," Cicely suggested.

"And a piece of toast?" Kitty suggested. "With butter and honey?"

Although there was no one there, the kitchen was cozy, the range lit. They both stood for a moment and warmed their hands.

"Now, where's that tea?" She had just reached for a tin on the shelf above the sink when they heard the bustle of someone approaching.

"Madam!" Cook's voice rang out. "What on *earth* are you doing?"

As Cicely turned, the tin flew out of her hand and into the air. Landing with a crash, it sprang open and sent tea leaves scattering all over the tiled floor. For a second they all just stared.

"I'm so sorry . . . ," Cicely began.

Cook could barely contain her fury. She looked at the wasted tea and the mess on the floor and the houseguests who had come, uninvited, and Cicely knew that everything that had been bothering her—the inconvenience of two extra people to her menu plan, the pain in her feet, the son who had taken up with a girl she didn't like or some such quandary—was suddenly all their fault.

"If Madam wanted tea," Cook said through gritted teeth, "then Madam should have rung the bell and requested it."

"I thought it was your day off," Cicely said.

Cook's mouth quivered. She was wearing a coat over her apron. It looked as if she had just returned from somewhere.

"We still provide a basic service," she replied. "If we are able to accommodate, we will. The point is to ring. And if there is no answer, then . . ."

Then, the suggestion was, they do without.

"Very well," Cicely said. "Next time I'll ring."

"Do you not have domestic staff in India? Or do your kind get their own tea?"

Cicely blinked.

"Our kind?" she repeated.

Cook grabbed the kettle, strode to the sink, and began to fill it.

"Please go to the drawing room," she said. "Tea will be sent forthwith."

Cicely hesitated. Was it worth a confrontation? Cook's gaze was fixed on the kettle, her great bosom rising up and down.

"We'll have toast and honey, too," Cicely added. "Thank you so much."

They left the warmth of the kitchen and headed up the stairs toward the drawing room.

"Mummy!" said Kitty, looking at her in amazement once they were out of earshot. "You made her practically explode. I thought her eyes were going to pop! What did she mean by 'your kind'?"

"From India, I expect," she said.

Cicely knew what the cook was really referring to, though she was surprised to hear it vocalized. In Scotland she had seen very few people of color. Apart from an illustration of a Negro on the marmalade jar, the culture was predominantly white. On the voyage Cicely had been taken for Italian or Greek. Her hair was brown and her skin a few shades darker than Kitty's, but she had not expected a servant to comment on it.

Her grandmother, Nani, had married her grandfather, a British soldier, in secret. Her family had been aghast, heartbroken. She had already been promised to a suitor, and his family demanded half of her dowry as compensation. Instead Nani became part of the community that was called *kutcha butcha*, or half-baked bread. Although she gave up her sari and adopted Western dress, a corset and crinoline, she still wore traditional glass bangles on her wrist that jangled as she moved. Rejected by both her own family and the resident British population, hers had not been an easy life by all accounts. Shortly before she died, she started to wear the *bindi* again, a red spot made of turmeric and lemon juice that she applied between her eyes.

Cicely's mother had been raised by an ayah. At eighteen she knew how to sew and enough math to keep the household accounts but that was all. Cicely had been sent to a day school in Darjeeling run by Catholic nuns. She had grown up playing with poor Europeans and children of mixed blood like herself, Anglo-Indians or *chi-chis*—which meant dirt. Although she had been schooled in algebra and Latin, she had been badly informed about many things, including human biology and social engineering. She had thought race did not matter, that in Britain no one would care about her ancestry. It was a shock to find it otherwise.

They heard the rattle of the tea tray long before it arrived. Cook had calmed down and now proudly placed a pot of tea along with a plate of hot toast spread with butter and honey on the dresser.

"Will there be anything else?" she asked from the doorway.

Cicely was of half a mind to request something just to see the look on her face.

"No thank you," she said.

Cook gave a tight smile. She ran her finger down the polished brass fingerplate on the door with a proprietorial air. She had no doubt lived and worked at Balmarra for years, maybe decades. A change would be good for her. She hadn't just become stale: She was practically fossilized.

Cicely cradled her cup and watched as Kitty ate her toast.

"Do you think we can swim in the water here?" Kitty asked when she had finished the toast.

"I don't think so," she said. "Too cold."

"I knew you'd say that."

For a moment they were silent. Cicely had, she realized, spent longer with her daughter on this trip than at any other time in her eight years. Even when they had been together, they were never really alone, there were always other people—Kitty's ayah, the groom, the houseboy to carry their things. Cicely had been blocking it out, but now the truth of their situation rushed forth in an unwelcome torrent. Once her daughter was gone, how long would it be before she would see her again? What if they couldn't afford for her to come home in the holidays? They could be parted for years. She would come back a stranger, all grown up and silent, raised in quite a different soil from her own. How could Cicely bear it? She was certain it was the right thing to do, but she would miss her so.

"Remember the day we went on that picnic next to Senchal Lake," Cicely said, "when Daddy taught you to swim?"

"The day I almost drowned?"

Cicely remembered it vividly. George had thrown Kitty in where the water was deep and murky and then simply watched as she went under. Cicely had been on the brink of jumping in to save her, but George had held her back until her girl, her precious little girl, had surfaced, coughing and spluttering, and had splashed and kicked her way to shore.

"But you did it," she reminded Kitty. "You swam."

"And then he carried me all the way home."

She pictured George with Kitty on his shoulders, both wet through, their clothes sticking to their skin and their hair dark with lake water. She recalled how Kitty had clung to George's chin for balance, and the grip George had on Kitty's slender ankles. This was her family, her husband and child, laughing and ducking as they walked through the forest, and her heart chimed in her chest with the memory of that afternoon, the beautiful autumn day, when the birds sang and the wind soothed.

"I want to swim," Kitty said, her voice edged with a whine.

"Well, you can't," she replied. "Not here. You'd freeze."

"No I wouldn't."

"I'm not going to argue about it," Cicely replied, her voice level.

Kitty's mouth clamped shut, and her eyes narrowed.

"You never let me do anything!" she said before storming upstairs.

After that day at the Senchal Lake, there were no more picnics. The situation in China took precedence. George spent his days writing letters and planning, while the mountain wind rushed through the house and banged the shutters. It made no difference: George wasn't completely there anymore, she knew, but already halfway up a mountain in his imagination. He was distracted, distant, silent.

One evening, however, he noticed her staring at him instead of reading her novel.

"What?" he asked.

"Perhaps when you come back," she said, "we could move back into town, take a place near the Mall?"

"Or we could travel," he suggested. "Go to London and Paris."

She didn't answer; she had heard this before.

"I know how hard this is for you," he said. "You worry that I'm wasting my time, that I won't find anything, but I always find something."

This was true. He never came back empty handed from his plant-hunting trips. Recently, however, the amount had decreased. The days of finding whole valleys of orchids were over.

"Maybe you could find a patron," she suggested, "who could sponsor the trip?"

"And give them all my seeds, my discoveries? Not likely."

Everything she suggested was immediately rebuked. Sometimes he was impossible. She turned the page of her book and continued reading.

"Just for the sake of argument," he said, "imagine that this time I don't find anything."

"All right," she said. "What then?"

"Then this will be the last expedition," he said. "I promise."

Finally she looked up.

"You don't mean that?"

"I'll learn how to cultivate tea as you suggested," he replied. "Start a family business."

He came over and knelt down in front of her.

"With all the children we haven't made yet," he whispered and kissed her hand.

His lips were cold against her skin. He knew none of the details of Kitty's birth; he hadn't been there. He had no memories of the throb of blood on the white sheets and the taste of death overlapping the smell of new life. Her hips were narrow, her placenta flimsily attached; after so narrowly surviving the first birth, she was certain then that another would kill her.

"We already have Kitty," she replied. "Why would you want more children?"

George dropped her hand, picked up his pen, and turned his back to her.

"I can't win," he said. "Whatever I suggest is somehow unpalatable to you. But yes, one day I want a son. Or two. Perhaps three. Is that really so surprising?"

She imagined a motherless brood, for if not the first, then the second or third birth would do it, out there in the foothills of the mountains.

"Everything hinges on this trip," he continued. "And if it doesn't work out, I'll need sons to help run the business."

"Couldn't Kitty do it?" Cicely asked.

"She's a girl," he replied as if stating the obvious. "Besides, I'm rather good at making babies."

In hindsight the audacity of his words was quite striking. She hadn't read all of George's letter to Kitty because there was a separate sheet with "Confidential" written in his tiny hand along the top. Once Kitty had clattered up the stairs and slammed the nursery door, Cicely unfolded and reread it.

> *Dearest Cicely, I know I should have told you this before*
> *and I apologize. I am afraid I have an admission to make*
> *that may be relevant with respect to my father's last will*
> *and testament. I would not put it past him to change the*
> *terms, hence the prolonged delay. Several years ago I had*
> *an affair and there were consequences. I kept it from you*
> *to spare your feelings.*

Here it was—the unforeseen complication. A small bay gelding was tied up outside the stables. Cicely asked Bill, the groom, to saddle him up. He frowned at her.

"This one isn't for riding," he said.

"Well, which ones are?"

He shook his head. Balmarra's horses pulled the trap and nothing else. Well, she would have to make do with what there was. Cicely took the reins, stood on a box, hitched up her skirt, and mounted the bay. There was no saddle that fit, so she'd ride him bareback. It wouldn't be the first time. She'd been riding for almost as long as she could walk. She gave the pony a sharp clip with her heels and he bolted, as ponies do, clattering out of the stables, the gardens, the valley, then up, up, following paths at random, first through trees, then over grass, then across moorland, climbing higher and higher until the paths petered out. Still the pony flew forward, following ancient trails that only he could sense, his ears peaked, half in irritation with the load on his back and half with the sheer exhilaration of being able to run beyond the limit of the paddock. Soon his coat was slick with sweat, his tail a flag in the wind. Riding without a saddle, all Cicely had was the rhythm, the rush of the animal's pace, to hold on to. She was ten years old again; she was free. Up and up they went until they were so high they broached the cloud line. Soft white pillowed around gray crags. The air had a sharp mineral taste. Her hair was loose, her cheeks pinched with cold, her heartbeat rose up in her chest.

The grouse rose without warning, a burst of squawk and fluster. The bay swerved, and before she could help herself, she was falling, head over the pony's ears, tumbling onto the soft, damp ground. For a moment she lay there, motionless. She was not hurt, nothing was sprained or broken or bruised except her pride, but as she watched the pony trot home without her, she found herself weeping. For what? Not for herself or Kitty or George, but for the whole sorry mess they had made. Not that it mattered—there was no one to see, there was nothing for miles, no one to hear her or see her curl up into a ball like a child and sob. They had never been honest with each other. Both had hidden the truth from the other: She didn't want any more pregnancies or children, any more milk-filled breasts or sleepless nights, and was flushed with relief at every monthly bleed. And he had been keeping secrets from her for years. How many other women had he loved? Were there "consequences" from any other relationships? Was their marriage a sham? How could she not have known? It was then that she considered the possibility of leaving George Pick. In whatever circumstances, rich or poor, maybe she would be better off alone?

It was dark by the time she reached Balmarra. The heels of her hands were grazed, her tortoiseshell combs were lost, the hem of her skirts damp and streaked with mud, but she was calmer than she had been for weeks. On the mountain she had watched the light change, purple shadows ascending like the slow indelible spread of a wine stain. The wind lifted her hair. A skylark sang. And she had been filled with calm, with serenity, with a new certainty. All the lights were on inside the house. Antonia opened the door as soon as she approached it.

"At last!" she said. "When the pony came back without you we all thought you'd been thrown. We were about to send out a search party! What happened? Are you all right?"

"I've never been better," Cicely said. And for once, it was true. "Is Kitty—?"

"Right as rain," she replied. "We gave her a nursery tea, and Dora has been reading her bedtime stories."

"She'll like that."

Antonia barely glanced at Cicely's disheveled clothes. There were clearly more important happenings afoot.

"Now. An invitation has arrived by hand from Keir Lorimer," her sister-in-law announced. "He says you met in Dunoon?"

"He introduced himself in the post office."

"Well, you must have charmed him, because he's invited us all for dinner."

Antonia's eyes were liquid in the lamplight. Her hands almost fluttered as she showed off the invitation, a thick card with an embossed crest.

"He told me he was a friend of your father," Cicely explained.

"News to me," she said. "As far as I knew they were sworn enemies, especially when it came to plant collections. Anyway, I'll need to find something to wear. Heavens!"

This was clearly not just a dinner.

"I was wondering," Antonia continued. "Would you be able to come with me to the dressmaker? I need help to choose an outfit for the dinner."

Cicely's mind was immediately drawn back to the contents of

George's letter. Her stomach turned just at the thought of it. But it had to be done, the sooner the better.

"Certainly," she replied. "You have one in Glasgow, I presume. I don't expect you'd be able to find anyone decent around here?"

Antonia swallowed. Clearly she was still going to the same dressmaker her mother went to, with the same drab fabrics and out-of-date fashions.

"I'd have to try for a last-minute appointment," she replied, "but if I can, would tomorrow suit?"

"Tomorrow would be perfect."

"We can take the train together. Thank you, Cicely."

It was the first time Antonia had used her first name, and she half whispered it, like a secret.

"My pleasure. Is Mr. Lorimer—?"

"Rich? Why, yes."

"I was going to say 'good company,'" Cicely finished.

"He's in threads," said Antonia as if that explained anything. "He's a self-made man by all accounts. It's just as well he dabbles in philanthropy or one might be tempted to despise him. He owns that big castle on the coast, but he's always dashing to London or wherever to meet eligible young ladies."

"The one you can see on the road to Dunoon?"

"That's right," she said. "The huge place on the coast. He has hothouses, a fernery, a whole avenue of Sequoioideae and a dozen gardeners to look after them. Makes Balmarra look like a summer pavilion."

To Antonia the city of Glasgow tasted of oiled steel, of puddles and cold tea. That day it was smudged with smoke and steam and condensation. The rigid grid of the streets, the hunch of men inside the public houses, the crosshatching of railway bridges and cantilever cranes straining on their rivets were all blurred, rendering the whole place as nebulous as a painting by Whistler. Typically there was little flora on display, just a few decorative plantings outside the public parks. At first glance the only green was the livery of the corporation buses that wheezed down Jamaica Street. But it was there if one looked for it; cascades of foliage sprouting from gutters and brick-work or reaching up through tiny gaps in the cobblestones in the narrow back lanes. While the city gave the impression of being bar-ren and monochrome, it was in fact teeming with plant life of the kind that clung to every drop of moisture or inch of soil and reached for a sun that was more a memory than a physical presence. And occasionally, if the spring was particularly clement or the summer drier than usual, there were fronds of vivid purple lilac waving from building sites, and the brief yellow joy of dandelions on waste ground before the heads turned fine and white and blew away.

Antonia's appointment with the dressmaker was at half past two. She had written the day before and received notice of a cancellation by return. She didn't come up to the city often, unwilling to pay those inflated prices, but for dinner at Lorimer's she needed to look the part.

With an hour or so to spend before the appointment, Antonia and her sister-in-law strolled the length of the Argyll Arcade and back again, past the jewelers, drapers, glovers, and hosiers, the booksell-ers and toymakers. The arcade was the city's most expensive covered street and was filled with light from the glass panes in its ceiling. The two entrances were lined with mahogany paneling, the names of the shopkeepers picked out in gold paint. Outside a westerly wind kept most of the smog at bay, and the air in the arcade was heady with the smell of roasting coffee from the grinders on the corner and the scent of soaps and colognes that wafted from the counter of Penhaligon's.

It was a Saturday afternoon, and the place was packed with peo-ple, strolling, laughing, clustering around shopwindows, most dis-playing their wealth in the cut of their clothes or the width of the hats. Some of the ladies wore huge bows or enormous bunches of fabric flowers on the brim. Others bared their ankles in skirts that were daringly short. Antonia had to steel herself, take many deep breaths—crowds unnerved her and she didn't care for being jostled by strangers. Nevertheless, once one became accustomed to it, she discovered, one could enjoy the atmosphere. If you wanted to save money on women's periodicals, Malcolm used to joke, take a walk down the arcade to see the styles on Bond Street or the Champs-Élysées. It wasn't strictly true, or so she had heard. Glasgow was a long way from London and Paris and tended to lag behind by at least a year or so, but it was graphic confirmation, should she need it, that her own clothes were woefully out of fashion.

"And what will you wear?" she had asked Cicely.

"I think I have something suitable," she had replied with a dismissive wave of her hand.

Why had Keir Lorimer invited them? Antonia wondered. Had Cicely caught his eye? She would stand out in the small town of Dunoon. George's wife carried herself as if she was somehow beyond the quotidian, as if she had seen places and sights, as if she had experienced emotions and sensations that other people hadn't. Even here in the Argyll Arcade, men stared openly; women glanced around at them from beneath their ridiculous hats. They were a strange couple, she supposed, both noticeable for quite different reasons.

The glovemaker's window displayed gloves for all occasions made of satin or leather or lace. Inside, Cicely picked out a pair of sage-green kid gloves and tried them on.

"They're pretty but I'm not sure I need them," she said.

"Let me buy them," said Antonia. "As a gift."

Cicely tried to dissuade her, but she was insistent.

"Well, thank you," she said. "How kind."

"Do you want them wrapped?" the girl asked.

"No, I'll wear them," Cicely replied.

Antonia tried on several pairs in the palest pink, lilac, and burnt copper.

"What do you think?" she asked. "You hate them, don't you?"

Cicely's face was expressionless.

"I like the pink," she replied.

Antonia wasn't sure. She thought they made her skin look jaundiced, and the light color of the leather would show every mark.

"I think you found the best pair," she told her sister-in-law as she paid the bill, which was larger than she had estimated.

"Have them," Cicely said and started to remove the left glove.

"Oh, no," said Antonia. "No."

It was the same in the milliner's. As soon as they crossed the threshold Antonia was overwhelmed by feathers, ribbons, veils, and fringes.

"It's so hard to choose," she said.

Cicely took one glance around and pointed to a small but perfect blue velvet hat at the back.

"I'll try that one," she said.

"I didn't see that one," said Antonia.

Cicely placed the hat on her head, tying the ribbon under her chin and adjusting the hat to sit at an angle.

"Suits you," said the milliner.

"I don't think so," said Cicely, taking it off again. "I have one a little too similar already."

"Can I try it?" asked Antonia.

And yet although Antonia tied and tilted the hat several times over, it didn't look the same as it had on Cicely.

"Maybe you need a softer line," the milliner suggested and brought out a straw hat in a plainer style.

"No, I'll take the blue," Antonia instructed.

She knew she would return it before they had even stepped out of the shop but she bought it anyway.

The dressmaker was on the third floor of a block in Buchanan Street. As they waited in the salon, Antonia flicked through the periodicals and paused at fashion plates. Cicely, however, had grown increasingly fidgety.

"What do you think of this gown?" Antonia had asked, passing over a copy of *The Queen*.

"Fabulous," Cicely said, with a glance.

Ever since she had taken one of the horses and disappeared for a few hours the day before, Cicely had seemed preoccupied.

The noise from the street rose up to the dressmaker's open window: a train letting off its low whistle before it departed, the clatter of a tram, the shout of a newspaper seller. From the closed door of the fitting room, however, came a resolute silence.

"She must be running late," Antonia suggested.

"It certainly looks that way," Cicely agreed.

"Bright colors suit you," said Antonia, glancing down at Cicely's new gloves. "You have such a lovely skin tone."

"My grandmother was from Calcutta."

Antonia turned to face her sister-in-law.

"So she was—Indian?"

"It was not unusual in those days for British soldiers to take an Indian wife, which is what my grandfather did."

Malcolm had been right after all. Cicely and Kitty had mixed blood.

"So she wasn't Christian?" Antonia asked carefully.

"No," she replied. "She was Hindustani."

Antonia picked up an illustrated journal and started to flick through the pages as she processed this new information.

Cicely stood up and stretched. "I need a breath of fresh air," she announced. "I'll be back soon."

Moments later the dressmaker opened the door, ushered out the previous client, and invited Antonia into the fitting room. She would mull over the implications of Cicely and Kitty's ancestry later. First there was more urgent business to attend to. Rolls of silk, satin, taffeta, faille, wool, and chenille in every shade were stacked on shelves that reached the ceiling. How could one begin to pick a fabric, a color, a length?

"What style are you looking for?" asked the dressmaker after Antonia had mentioned that she was looking for an evening gown.

Cicely would know. But Cicely wasn't there. Had she offended her? She didn't seem put out when she left. The dressmaker sighed, and so Antonia turned and glanced around the room. A ball gown in purple taffeta with several layers of flounce, in a style similar to one that she had admired in *The Queen*, was displayed on a mannequin.

"Now that," said Antonia, "might be just the ticket."

The dressmaker wiped her palms on her skirts and began to remove the dress from its stand.

Antonia tried not to look at herself in the glass as the dressmaker fussed around the neckline, her mouth full of pins; she didn't want to spoil the impact. She knew that she was nothing special, that she was no longer young, that she had the kind of face that people forgot. Eventually the dressmaker stood back.

"There we are," she said.

As the afternoon light streamed through the window, Antonia finally looked at herself, turning one way and then the other. The color of the fabric made her skin look pale, milk white, almost the opposite of tan. Her cheeks, however, were pinched ruddy. And yet she didn't look as terrible as she thought she might. The dress reminded her of a rhododendron bloom, the petals pleated and the flowers blowsy. The high bodice flattered her, and the small train made her look taller. What would Malcolm say? Would he think it too revealing? Too fussy? Too expensive? Did she have the nerve to wear a dress like this? Maybe she should choose something in a plainer color, one more suited to a woman of her age?

"What do you think, Cicely?" she called out through the open door.

But the salon was still empty; her sister-in-law had not returned.

"She probably got confused," the dressmaker suggested. "One city street looks very much like another if you're not familiar with it. Now, when do you need it by?"

First Antonia strode the length of the Argyll Arcade, walking twice the pace of everyone else and peering into the shops. There was no sign of her. Then, on Buchanan Street, she hailed a horse-drawn cab and rode all the way along to the Trongate, scanning both sides of the street, but to no avail. Glasgow suddenly seemed huge and unfriendly. How would Cicely find her way home to Balmarra? For that matter, how would she find her way to the station? She was a foreigner, unused to British cities. She might be preyed upon by thieves, abducted by criminals. Antonia would have to inform the police. A search party would be sent out. The newspapers would carry a description and a plea for information. Once more Malcolm would blame her.

When she had driven back and forth half a dozen times along every major street, she asked the driver to head along the Saltmarket toward the river—not the river, please, not a drowning!—in case Cicely had lost her bearings and taken a wrong turn. It was an area that Antonia wasn't familiar with. Unlike the streets farther west, the air was thick with the stink of the boiling glue and effluent from the factories and tanneries. The tenements were overcrowded and crumbling—slums, basically, that housed too many people in too little space. And yet it was here that she at last found Cicely Pick, coming out of a narrow alleyway, or wynd, as they were known, strung with washing above gutters filled with sewage. She was easy to spot—a well-dressed woman walking alone on the Saltmarket—and had already drawn a small crowd of people who stopped and stared.

"There she is. Cicely!" Antonia called out.

She walked on, unhearing. The street noise, the trams, the factories, and the tanneries were too loud.

"I'll fetch her," said the cabdriver, pulling in, then climbing down from his bench. "It's not a place for a lady."

"What were you thinking?!" said Antonia when Cicely finally climbed into the cab beside her. "You could have caught something! You could have been robbed, murdered, or worse!"

"Well, I obviously wasn't, was I?" Cicely replied.

After that, George's wife was silent. She didn't ask about the dressmaker's or say a word all the way through high tea at the Grosvenor on Gordon Street. She refused both cake and scone, which prompted Antonia to explain that she hadn't had any lunch before she piled her plate. It was a such a waste, otherwise. And so finally, in Central Station, while the porter was looking for some seats in the first-class carriage on the train to Gourock, Antonia confronted her.

"Well?" she asked. "Are you going to explain? What were you doing down there?"

Cicely climbed aboard the train and took her seat.

"I was looking for you for ages!" Antonia continued as she followed her into the carriage. "I thought you were lost!"

As the train doors slammed and the engine let off a long, low whistle, Cicely sighed.

"I took a wrong turn," she said. "I knocked on a door to ask for directions. It really isn't that complicated."

"Then where are your new gloves?"

Cicely's mouth pursed. She looked out of the window as the train began to move out of the station.

"I must have mislaid them," she replied flatly.

"But I only just bought them!"

"Does it really matter? You chose a gown, I presume. Mission accomplished. Heavens above, what a proverbial storm in a teacup!"

Cicely started to laugh as if the whole thing was a joke. Her behavior, Antonia thought, was not only mysterious, it was down-right peculiar.

"You *are* all right?" Antonia asked and laid a hand on her arm.

"Everything is fine," she replied. "Nothing to worry about. Nothing at all."

The city began to flash past in a blur of gray and green. Cicely sat back and closed her eyes. But Antonia could not doze. Something was going on, something she wasn't party to. Maybe Malcolm had been right: Maybe Cicely was playing her for a fool.

7

Kitty had been bathed and put to bed, then put to bed again after she appeared at the top of the stairs in her nightdress.

"See you in the morning," Cicely had said.

"Where are you going again?" Kitty had asked.

"To dinner. With a friend of your grandfather's."

And Kitty had looked at her reproachfully.

"You're sure I can't come?"

"Too late for you. Besides, it will be very dull, I wish I didn't have to go."

"Then why are you going?"

She didn't answer as she tucked Kitty up and stroked her head. Her eyelids were already heavy; she would be fast asleep within ten minutes. Kitty had been out all day playing in the gardens. Unlike home, there were no poisonous snakes or scorpions, but still she had collected a small armory of sticks to defend herself with just in case. As Cicely was about to close the door she sat up in bed.

"Mummy," she said, "I want it."

"Want what? What are you talking about?"

"Balmarra," she said.

If only Kitty knew the lengths she had gone to secure her inheritance. Life twists and turns, George had written, and washes you up in places you never expect. The place she had never expected was the open doorway on the Saltmarket and the filthy stone stairs that led to the first floor. Despite claiming the opposite, George had had a fiancée back in Glasgow after all, whom he dropped most unkindly by letter. George should have returned to Scotland; he should have married the fiancée as he had promised. That was the right thing, the honorable thing to do. Instead he stayed in India and married Cicely. Three years later his former fiancée had come to Darjeeling to look for him. He wasn't hard to find. Everyone knew George Pick. It seemed that she had forgiven him, accepted all his excuses—he had been forced into marriage against his will or some such fiction—and they had resumed their relationship where it had been broken off. George was, as usual, careless. A child was conceived. The former fiancée had returned home to give birth, and George had once again broken off all contact.

While Antonia was discussing hemlines and silhouettes with the dressmaker, Cicely had the task of finding George's former fiancée. If his illegitimate child was male, George feared, he was legally entitled to make a claim on the family estate if George should die. At first Cicely had decided she would not do it, she would not go and look for George's mistress and her progeny. It was humiliating, demeaning. But how could she not? She owed it to Kitty to find out what she could.

The address that George had given her was in a run-down part of town. As she had walked up the steps, Cicely felt physically sick. The door was painted black and was scuffed along the bottom, as if kicked by dozens of tiny feet. Cicely raised her hand but could not knock; her courage failed her. She was about to turn and head back down the stairs when the door swung open to reveal the silhouette of a woman standing in the doorway.

"I thought I could hear someone coming up the stairs," she said. Her accent was more genteel than her surroundings. "Can I help you?"

"I'm sorry to disturb you," Cicely had said. "I'm looking for a Miss Fintry?"

"I'm Miss Fintry," the woman replied. A flash of panic crossed her face. "Is anything the matter?"

Cicely paused and frowned at her in the half-light. It was hardly a social call. But what was it? And so she came right to the point.

"I think you were once acquainted with George Pick," she said. "My husband."

Jane Fintry had been surprisingly civil under the circumstances; she invited her in, brewed a pot of tea, and unwrapped a cake. Jane's face, although the skin clung a little too tightly to the bones, had clearly once been beautiful, the eyes blue and the teeth even. Cicely had felt a sudden rush of solidarity; she too had fallen for George. Cicely sat on the chair she was offered and took off her gloves. While Jane Fintry cut the cake, Cicely glanced around. The room was full of piles of material spiked with pins, and a chair was positioned at the window to make the most of the daylight. From the way she frowned as she sliced, Cicely assumed Jane Fintry's sight was bad.

"You must excuse the mess," Jane said, her eyes lifting. "I'm not usually in such a muddle."

There was a small pause, a shifting of hands on lap and feet on the floor.

"Did George ask you to come?" Jane asked.

"He did," she replied.

How could he have asked her to do this? It wasn't fair to either of them.

"You have a child, don't you?" Jane asked.

"I do. A girl. She's eight."

Somewhere nearby, a bell tolled the hour. One, two, three, four. She must get it over with.

"Is this about my son, Georgie?" Jane prompted. "A solicitor also wrote to me."

Cicely nodded. Jane's mouth tightened. She picked up a teaspoon and gave her tea a stir. It was then that Cicely noticed that there were no toys, no children's shoes, nothing to suggest that a child lived there too.

"He passed," she said simply. "He was only two. It's been a little difficult, as you can imagine."

Estranged from her family as a consequence of the affair, Jane took in sewing to make a living. Occasionally over the years she had received a small amount of money from George.

"He never forgot me," she said. "I'll give him that."

Cicely felt a lump swell in her throat. In her situation, she would never have forgiven George.

"Weren't you angry with him?" Cicely asked.

"What would be the point?"

There was a knock on the door, and without waiting to be invited, an old woman with a bundle of what looked like rags in a pram let herself in. While Jane Fintry discussed what was to be done, Cicely excused herself, leaving her pair of new gloves and a ten-shilling note, her last, beneath the sugar bowl.

So this was not the unforeseen complication. What else could it be? Who was the other one Jane Fintry mentioned? What else had George done?

"Mummy," Kitty said, "are you all right?"

Cicely pulled her face into a smile for her daughter.

"Be good," she told Kitty as she closed her door. "And sleep tight."

Malcolm and Antonia were waiting for her in the pony-and-trap—the motorcar was a two-seater. Malcolm wore a dinner suit that smelled of mothballs, and Antonia a fur stole, white gloves, and the new purple evening gown that had been delivered the day before. She glanced at Cicely's much plainer dress, a silk sheath in dark blue, but didn't comment.

"We might be late," Antonia said as the carriage headed out through the gateposts. "Shouldn't we go a little faster?"

"No, it's better to be fashionably late than unfashionably early," her husband replied.

"Who else do you think will be there?" Antonia continued.

"The gin set, I expect," Malcolm replied. "None of your hoi polloi."

"I hear people socialize a lot in India?" Antonia asked Cicely.

Cicely thought of the balls, the parties and theatricals, the Polo Club picnic. At one point in her life they had carried great weight. It would take her a week to choose a hat; a choice of color would keep her up at night—eau de nile or emerald, salmon pink or cerise? How could she have been so wrapped up, she asked herself now, in such insignificant concerns? Antonia seemed to be expecting an answer, and so she said the first thing that came into her head.

"The hill stations are rather gay, especially in the summer season before the monsoon."

"That's what I heard," said Antonia.

They rode on in silence, the scent of Malcolm's cologne mixing with the smell of starch and new fabric.

"Should we have brought something?" asked Antonia suddenly. "A bottle of wine?"

"He has a whole cellar full of wine," Malcolm replied with a wave of his hand. "If he had a wife, then that would be a different matter. We could have brought flowers."

"He had a fiancée once, so I hear," Malcolm continued. "But it all went pear-shaped. Her parents didn't think he was the right sort."

"Do you have to go into this now?" said Antonia. "It's all gossip and hearsay."

"Well, I've started now. So I might as well finish—"

"Too late. We're here," said Antonia.

The carriage had turned onto a long, curved driveway that led to the house. The gardens were well tended and the lawns neatly man-icured, scattered with newly planted monkey puzzle trees.

"My father was convinced Lorimer sent someone round to

Balmarra to snoop or steal cuttings," said Antonia. "But my father thought everyone was out to cheat him."

All the lights were on inside the house, and as they climbed down from the carriage at the main entrance, the sound of distant chatter and the light clink of crockery drifted through the open windows toward them. It was an enormous place with turrets and battlements and a view across the Firth of Clyde.

"Very nouveau riche," Antonia whispered.

A butler met them at the door, and after they had handed their wraps to a maid, he accompanied them to the drawing room.

"Mr. and Mrs. Malcolm McCulloch and Mrs. George Pick," the butler announced.

Keir Lorimer was standing at the fireplace. There were a half dozen other guests, all of whom seemed to break off their conversations in midsentence and turn.

"Here you are!" Lorimer said to all three, but directing the comment straight at Cicely. "I was beginning to think you'd changed your mind."

Dressed in tweeds with Argyll socks beneath his plus fours, Lorimer looked like a country laird. The other male guests were dressed in dinner suits, thankfully for Malcolm.

"We're not late, are we?" said Antonia, her face blanching.

"Not at all." He laughed to make sure they knew he was joking. "You're all looking smart as a button, I must say."

Once they had each been handed a glass of champagne, they were whisked off, at Lorimer's insistence, on "the tour." The house was even larger than it looked on the outside, and their host opened door after door to sitting rooms, guest wings, libraries—one for pleasure and one for reference—bedrooms and studies.

"It's much larger than I wanted," he seemed to apologize. "To be honest, it's far too big for one person. I'm rattling around."

Had he built it for himself, Cicely wondered, or the fiancée whose family spurned him? They ended up climbing a narrow stair to the highest turret, where a telescope had been set up.

"Can we see Balmarra from here?" Malcolm asked.

"I prefer to look at the stars," Lorimer said. "Botany and astronomy. My two favorite pastimes."

Dinner was six courses, according to the menu laid at each place, starting with soup and sherry and finishing with ice cream and a glass of Madeira. While Cicely had been seated to Lorimer's right, Antonia and Malcolm were at the far end of the table, next to a very ancient lady with a huge ear trumpet.

Lorimer asked about India, about Darjeeling, and Cicely gave him a tourist's itinerary of things to do and sights not to miss: walking to the top of Tiger Hill, picnics at the lake, and taking a trip to Ghum, the highest hill station in India, on the Himalayan Railway.

"And the social life," he asked. "That's well established, I suppose?"

Once again she gave a glowing account.

"You make it sound almost magical, Mrs. Pick," said Lorimer. "And when are you planning on returning?"

It was a benign question, but even so it caught her unawares. She drained her glass of champagne, and it was immediately refilled.

"Soon," said Cicely. "There are a few things that I have to sort out here."

"But you are enjoying your time in Scotland? Even out here in the sticks?"

"Very much," she replied.

"I always liked Balmarra. Haven't set foot in the place for years," Lorimer said. He looked along the table, catching Antonia's eye. "I was just telling Mrs. Pick here that I'd love to take a look at that glass house of yours again."

"Well, you must come," Antonia said. "You must all come!"

Everyone turned to Antonia.

"Perhaps I could throw a party," she continued. "In the Oriental style. In honour of my sister-in-law, Cicely Pick."

Malcolm stared at his glass of wine and then drank it down in one gulp.

"Isn't it just the most perfect idea?" Antonia said to Malcolm.

Malcolm cleared his throat and forced his face into a smile.

"Fine by me," he added. "Absolutely!"

The conversation turned to the coronation and George V's love of hunting.

"I hear he got quite a haul," said Lorimer. "Twenty-one tigers and eight rhinoceroses in Nepal. Personally I had no idea there *were* any rhinoceroses in Nepal."

"Well there won't be for much longer," Cicely replied. "Not if the king keeps shooting them."

Lorimer threw back his head and laughed out loud. Her glass was empty again, and she couldn't remember finishing it.

"You're witty," he said. "Can't say the same of many people round here."

"I'm not usually," she said. "It's just the champagne talking."

"Well then, have some more," he said. "The champagne is clearly enjoying herself."

The problems that had seemed insurmountable earlier that evening had melted away. Her glass refilled, she began to feel light-headed, even a little drunk. As she swallowed another mouthful, an idea occurred to her, an idea so seemingly obvious that she wondered why she hadn't thought of it before.

"Mr. Lorimer," she said.

"Mrs. Pick?" He bowed his head and leaned toward her. "Has the champagne got a message for me?"

"No," Cicely said softly. "This time it's me. I have a proposition for you."

He turned and looked at her briefly. He moistened his lips.

"Really?" he said.

"A business proposition," she clarified. "Can we have a word in private?"

"Of course," he replied. "But not tonight. We can meet during the week if you're not busy."

"Thank you, yes."

"I'll be in touch," he said, then turned and began to speak to the doctor. On Cicely's other side the hotel owner was deep in conversation with the doctor's wife. Cicely picked up her glass of champagne, then felt the pull of someone's gaze. While Antonia was shouting into the old woman's ear trumpet, Malcolm was staring at her. As soon as she looked back, he glanced away. Then he pulled out a crumpled handkerchief and blew his nose loudly. What *did* Antonia see in him? In the right clothes, with her hair dressed, Antonia could be striking. She had a natural grace that she didn't seem aware of. But Malcolm? He had all the grace of a turnip. Why hadn't she chosen someone more charismatic, someone like Lorimer? Lorimer and Antonia. But even the imagined image of the two of them together filled her with an emotion she would not admit. As soon as the thought passed through her mind, Lorimer turned to her and for a second she was sure he had read her mind.

"Everything all right?" He laid a hand briefly on her forearm.

She nodded yes. Her voice was gone, swallowed up.

"It's time for the men to depart to the smoking room and for the ladies to drink coffee and eat sweet things," he said. "What would happen if I wanted to drink coffee and you wanted to smoke? A truly stupid custom, but there you are. I wouldn't continue it personally, but people expect it. In truth I would far rather stay and talk to you."

Slowly she raised her eyes to his. A jolt ran through her, from her eyes to the base of her spine, in the opposite direction as a bubble in a glass of champagne but with the same velocity, the same small pop as it reached its spot.

Three other female guests and two dogs were arranged on sofas and easy chairs around a roaring fire. The dogs were huge and slightly smelly—hunting dogs, Antonia suspected—and she was reluctant to shoo them from the cushioned hollows in which they so comfortably curled and sit in the slobber and hair left in their place. And so she pretended to be particularly interested in the ceramic vases that were displayed on plinths, and tried not to draw attention to herself.

As soon as they had stepped into the reception room of Lorimer's mansion, she realized that she had dressed for a ball and not a formal dinner. What had she been thinking? Her eyes burned. Cicely should have said something, she could have pointed out her folly.

"No one cares about your shoes," her father had once said when she dithered at the door before going out. "No one's looking."

Maybe this time, too, no one cared; no one was looking. But that was merely wishful thinking. The other women her own age, the wives of the doctor and the owner of the hotel, wore long tunics with high waistlines in shades of gray and cream. They *were* looking; she saw the way they glanced at her. Much too old to wear that shade, the arch of their eyebrows seemed to say. Too many ruffles for someone so plain. She wished she could change, take the dress off, and pull on something more comfortable, more fitting, more suited to her looks. Now she saw that her dress was wrong in every way. It had been designed to be worn in a different season, a different occasion, by a different woman, for a party with enough guests to thoroughly warm a room.

The fire cracked and she shivered. Like Balmarra, Lorimer's mansion, once you left the fireside, was freezing even in summer. Who could survive Scotland without cardigans and slippers? How long must they remain here before it would be polite to leave? Dinner had been lengthy, and the food served in very small portions. She was still hungry despite eating six courses. She also had the distinct feeling that there was a pecking order in place and that she and Malcolm were near the bottom. Even Lorimer's elderly aunt, who was both deaf and seemingly demented, had been given a place nearer the center of the table than they had. Her brother's wife, however, had been seated at Lorimer's right, a queen to Antonia's castle, and now she felt sure that this was how she appeared to the world—all sharp angles and crenellation. And then there was the matter of Lorimer's announcement about visiting Balmarra. What had possessed her to suggest they throw a party? Her heart stampeded at the thought of it. She no more knew how to throw a party than to sing a madrigal. And the cost? However would they pay for it? Cicely had gone to the lavatory and not returned. She was always absenting herself, disappearing. It was infuriating.

A silence had descended in the drawing room. She glanced over her shoulder to find the three women and two dogs staring at her expectantly. What had been asked? She had no clue. Did she take milk and sugar in her coffee? Did she want coffee at all? Not really, was the answer; what she desired more than anything was a stiff drink, a malt whisky, like the men were knocking back in the smoking room. But it wasn't done. Women didn't drink the hard stuff. Not in public anyway. They sipped weak coffee from china cups, ate Turkish delight, and made meaningless small talk.

"Sorry," Antonia said. "Did you ask me something?"

"Are you going on," the doctor's wife asked, "to another occasion?"

"How lovely to have two events on the same night," said the other wife and took a small gulp of her coffee.

"Same night?" echoed the elderly aunt.

"Oh, no," Antonia said with a laugh. "Just this. I so rarely . . ."

They waited for more. No more words came. Antonia swallowed and cleared her throat.

Grace, that's what she needed, grace and self-assurance. Who cared what they thought? Had they nothing else to think about? Were their lives so dull that the dress of another guest was worthy of extensive pondering? It was pathetic. In an act of modest defiance, Antonia took a handful of skirt, of the bright purple, sumptuous, expensive silk, and spun around. Only she forgot the train, the beautiful train that made her look so elegant, the dressmaker had said, and the force of her sudden movement propelled the train into the plinth in a tidal wave of fabric. The vase wobbled on its stand and then fell forward, bouncing once before exploding into a million pieces on the polished parquet floor.

The women's hands flew to their mouths, the dogs' ears dropped, and the pressure in the room suddenly changed. To Antonia the walls curved, the windows seemed about to crack, and her eyes began to ache inside her head.

"Was it—?" she began.

"Sèvres?" one woman exclaimed.

"Probably," said another.

"Oh dear," said Antonia. Could the evening get any worse? At least Malcolm wasn't in the room to witness it; that was some consolation.

The butler was summoned, and he removed the dogs, placed Antonia in an armchair, swept up the broken china, and refilled every coffee cup, all with a minimum of fuss.

"I once broke a side plate in the Dorchester Hotel," said the doctor's wife. "But they had plenty more."

There was another short silence, this one even worse than the first.

"It was so nice of Mr. Lorimer to invite us," Antonia began in a desperate effort to change the subject.

"Yes," said the wife of the hotel owner. "It was."

Everyone sipped at once.

"We were both wondering where your friend hails from?" said the doctor's wife.

"India. She's George's wife, actually. My brother."

They looked at her blankly.

"George is a botanist, a hunter of rare plants. Just an excuse to go tramping into the middle of nowhere for months on end, if you ask me."

She laughed. Alone.

"How long will she be with you, Antonia?" asked the doctor's wife.

"Oh, not long, I expect. She'll be wanting to see Edinburgh. And her daughter starts school here in September."

"Where is she going?"

"Glenrannoch, I think?"

There was a small bewildered silence. It seemed that no one had heard of the school either. One by one the women glanced at the door, as if expecting Cicely to walk in at any moment. Where on earth was she? Surely no one could spend that long in the lavatory?

"How nice of you to throw a party in her honor," said the hotel owner's wife.

"Yes," said Antonia before draining her coffee cup.

"Lovely-looking woman," she went on.

"She has an interesting appearance," the doctor's wife added. "Exotic. In fact, if one didn't know she was white, one might assume—in a dark room, that is—that she, you know—"

"Touch of the tar brush," agreed the hotel owner's wife.

Antonia stared at her. The woman met her eye and then looked away. They suspect, Antonia realized. And she was suddenly both amused and relieved. The dress, the broken vase, the seating arrangement at dinner, the proposed party, all paled into insignificance. They didn't care about any of it. This was what they would talk about in the days ahead: the color of George Pick's wife's skin.

"My sister-in-law's grandmother," said Antonia, "was Hindustani."

No coffee cup was left unslurped. A log cracked in the grate, making every woman jump a little in her seat.

Cicely locked the door of the lavatory behind her. Like everywhere else in Lorimer's house it was lavish: a huge room with a wooden stall and a large wash-hand basin with French lavender soap. On the walls were prints of racehorses. Had he chosen them himself or had he hired someone to do it for him? There was nothing personal, no hint as to the type of man he was or where he had come from.

She washed her hands, then her face. Her hair was still in place, rolled up and away from her forehead. She could hear the guffaws of laughter from the men in the smoking room. The women, in the drawing room, were much quieter, their voices barely audible. From downstairs came the clatter of crockery as the scullery maid washed the dishes. She was singing as she worked. She had a sweet voice, high and light, almost unaware of itself. How lovely, Cicely thought. The singing stopped suddenly. A door shuddered shut. Someone had come in. What a shame.

In the hallway, footsteps approached the lavatory. The door handle turned. The person, a man by the sound of his tread, sighed, then walked away. She should hurry. She picked up a hand towel, dried her hands, then raised it to her face and sniffed, searching for any trace of Lorimer in its soft folds. What was she doing? She was married.

She had a child. This was not the thrill she had felt when she first met George, the crazy churn of infatuation. It was something else, something altogether more complicated. She placed the towel back on the rail. He had probably never used it. He was bound to have his own personal lavatory and his own personal hand towels. She must get back. She unlocked the door and stepped into the hall.

Lorimer was waiting at the foot of the stairs. Was it he who had tried the door? He looked as surprised as she felt.

"It's you!" he said.

"I'm so sorry," she said, "to make you wait."

"Oh, don't worry," he said. "Listen, I was thinking. When we meet next week, would you like to come with me for a ride in my plane?"

She blinked.

"It's quite safe," he said. "I've had my license for four years now."

"Is it a good idea," she asked softly, "to mix business with pleasure?"

"In my experience," he said with a smile, "it's the only idea."

When Cicely finally appeared in the drawing room, her face was flushed and her eyes were glassy. Had she heard the women's conversation? Had she been lurking outside listening? Thankfully it didn't appear so.

"Is that coffee?" she asked with a smile. The pot, however, was empty.

Space was made on the sofa for her to sit down. But only a few moments later the butler summoned them to the smoking room to join the men for a spot of musical entertainment. The room was a fug of blue smoke. Antonia found it hard to stop herself from coughing. Even Malcolm had succumbed to the lure of a Cuban cigar, and it did not suit him. She glanced sidelong at her sister-in-law and could see in her dark hair and brown eyes what the other women meant.

"Are you all right?" Antonia whispered to Cicely.

"Why do you ask?" Cicely replied. "I'm fine."

The doctor had discovered the pianola and was excitedly thumbing through the scrolls.

"We know this one," he said to his wife. "And this!"

The doctor started to pedal, and even though the player piano was out of tune, his wife began to sing.

"Well, this is rather jolly," Lorimer said to everyone. "I don't think anyone's played that thing for years!"

The song had many verses. Once it finished they raced straight into a second.

"It's rather late," whispered Cicely. "Shall we head home soon?"

Antonia had wanted to leave for the last hour. But first she needed to apologize for the vase. Her heart pounded in its cage of whalebone, her palms were clammy, her head felt light. She would offer to pay for it, to replace it. Now she knew the name, Sèvres, and had an inkling that it was French. Surely it couldn't have been *that* valuable: It was an ugly thing, shaped like an urn with two handles like thin arms propped on hips. It certainly wasn't a receptacle for flowers. What was it for? she wondered. And how much was it worth? Judging by the other women's reactions, it was an antique. Maybe there was something similar in the attic at Balmarra? In fact she had the distinct impression that she had seen a vase just like it in the tea chest she had sorted.

Malcolm accepted a top-up of malt. He already looked intoxicated, his face rosy and his red hair brassy in the gaslight. He turned, caught her eye, and raised an eyebrow. She swallowed and wiped her palms on her skirts. This is why, she told herself, they never went anywhere. Later she would have to admit to Malcolm what she had done, that she had broken the vase. She braced herself internally. And once he knew, she was sure, they would never go anywhere again.

"Antonia?" Cicely was standing at her elbow, her hand on her arm as if she was just about to pinch it.

"What is it?" Antonia replied in a tone a little harsher than she had intended.

Although she tried to hide it, her sister-in-law's impatience was palpable.

"We don't want to overstay our welcome," she said. "Do we?"

"Neither do we want to be the first to leave. And I, for one, am having a wonderful time."

For a moment Cicely was silent. She stared at the doctor's wife with a small frown as she began a third song. They seemed to be enjoying themselves immensely, though it was doubtful that anyone else was. The fire had burned down, the whisky decanter was empty, and the butler hovered at the back with his eyes closed. On and on the doctor's wife sang as the guests' attention span was stretched to its limit. At the end of the song they clapped, more in relief than as an expression of enjoyment.

"I think they liked us, David," the doctor's wife said. "One more for the road?"

To Antonia's horror, before they could begin Cicely stepped forward and announced that she was leaving.

"Many thanks, Mr. Lorimer," she said, "for a splendid evening."

"It's been a pleasure," he replied. "And I look forward to the party at Balmarra."

"Wait a minute !" Antonia blurted out. "We're not ready to leave quite yet."

"You stay, Antonia," she replied. "I'm going to walk."

"In the dark?" the doctor's wife exclaimed. "Surely that isn't safe!"

"I'm sure it's quite safe," replied Cicely. "Besides, I could do with some fresh air."

And with a nod to the assembly, Cicely Pick walked out of the drawing room and was gone.

For a moment everyone was silent. Would someone suggest they go after her? Or instruct a coachman to pick her up? As one, they all looked to Lorimer for instruction. He was sucking on a cigarette.

"Are you going to play another, or what?" he said.

9

The moon was almost full and the light that fell between the black tangle of trees was bright as zinc. Cicely walked fast, but she was wearing silk slippers with heels that had been made for dancing, not for outdoors. The driveway was paved up to the gatepost; then the road was unsurfaced, two thin ruts made by carriage wheels and a strip of mud churned up by carthorses' hooves in the middle. She had to escape, to get out of Lorimer's house, but maybe she shouldn't have insisted on going on foot. Too strong-willed, George would have said. But that wasn't true at all on this occasion. Her will was weak; that was the problem.

The wind blew in gusts around the headland, plastering her dress to her body and riffling through the trees as if looking for something lost. A few drops of rain fell. Her feet lost their feeling first, her fingers, even in gloves, followed soon after. She tied her evening wrap as tightly around her shoulders as she could, but she still shivered.

It had occurred to her during dinner—the idea that Lorimer could sponsor her husband's expedition, that he could be George's patron, that this would solve everything. Now, however, the champagne was wearing off and with it the sense that she had made some horrendous mistake, some terrible error of judgment.

In the sky above she heard the flap of a bird—an owl, she guessed, hunting for prey. It called out, a single cry, before it headed away up the valley. In India the jungle was denser, noisier, thick with cries of fear and alarm. At dusk and during the night, the big cats came out to hunt: leopards, who might drop on you from a branch, or tigers, who were almost impossible to see in the undergrowth. But she knew what to listen for, the barking of the deer and the cry of monkeys warning one another of a tiger's prowl. Here she had no clue; she couldn't read this country as she could her own, she couldn't decipher the cries of the birds and the direction of the wind. The landscape spoke a language she didn't understand.

At home she had seen a tiger once, sitting on the opposite side of a river, its jaws red with the blood of a sambar.

"It's all right," their guide had whispered. "She already has her supper. Shall I?"

He raised his gun. And as they watched, the tigress went back to rip herself another hunk of fresh deer meat. Out of the shadows came two cubs.

"Leave them be," George had told him.

She had loved him then, for the way he had spared the family. And yet she saw a different parallel now: He had let it be because the tiger was female, the sex that killed and cared for and sacrificed their own lives for their offspring, while the male went off to follow his own path, thinking only of himself.

A noise came from somewhere nearby, the snap and rustle of broken branches and a flurry of leaves. She narrowed her eyes but could make out nothing. Was it animal or human? Should she call out? No, she must be quiet, invisible, and so she made herself imagine that she was a drop of black ink on a blacker page; she was part of the night, swallowed whole, dissolved. She tried to follow the road but twice she found herself stepping into the ditch at the edge and stumbling. She had to walk more slowly, cautiously, her arms stretched in front like a blind person's. Surely she should be almost back at Balmarra by now?

It was impossible to tell exactly where the streams and rivers were; they seemed to be everywhere, the roar and tumble of water both ahead and behind, making her lose her sense of direction, unable to judge distance or speed.

It wasn't just out here. She seemed to have completely lost her bearings. It would be different if Lorimer were old and ugly and fat. But he was not. She pictured his face, the curve of his mouth, the line of his wrist.

Cicely heard the approach of a horse and cart long before she saw it. It came around a corner with a clatter of hooves and the snap of leather, a storm lantern held by the driver and lighting up the road.

"Goodness me!" he said when he saw her. "I've been out looking for you for the last half hour. If you're wanting to get back to Balmarra, then you're on the wrong road. This one's the back road to Dunoon."

He held out his hand. For a moment she hesitated.

"I'm Jim," he explained. "Mr. Lorimer's coachman."

"Really, there was no need—" she began.

The wind blew the rest of her words away. She took his hand and he pulled her up to the seat beside him.

Antonia and Malcolm weren't home yet. Young Mr. Baillie came out of his cottage to greet them. He held the horses while she climbed down.

"I'll let Mr. Lorimer know," said the coachman before he drove off.

There wasn't a single light on inside the main house. The fires would have been swept and set for the morning. Kitty would be fast asleep, her breath steady and sweet. But Cicely was cold, the coldest, perhaps, she'd ever been. The gardener seemed to notice her hesitation; perhaps he saw the stiffness in her limbs and the clench of her jaw.

"My uncle has a fire going, Mrs. Pick," he said. "Maybe you could come in and warm up for a minute or two?"

She knew she should go straight to bed, slowly thaw, and try to forget the dinner and the long walk home in the wrong direction. And yet she knew too that she would lie awake for hours, trying to warm up, unable to stop her mind going round and round and over and over the same small snippets of conversations, the same face.

In the front room of the gardener's cottage was a range with a blazing coal fire, a bed recess, a small table, and a couple of armchairs. Old Mr. Baillie greeted her with a nod, then climbed the ladder to another bed, she guessed, in the attic. Baillie cleared stacks of books from the kitchen table and took the kettle off the range above the fire.

"Tea?"

"Please," she replied, looking around.

"Smaller than you're used to, I suppose?" he said.

"Not really."

The scale of the room was closer to the scale of the house she had grown up in, and unlike the cavernous rooms of Balmarra, it held the heat. In India, however, she would never have entered a servant's quarters. The caste system did not allow it. She was regarded as "unclean" and anything that she touched would have to be thrown away. She was pretty sure that in Scotland women of a certain class didn't drink tea with their gardeners. But what did she care? And who else would know unless someone told them? She doubted either young or old Mr. Baillie would gossip.

She picked up a book at random from the kitchen table. It was a volume of botanical drawings. She flicked through its glossy color plates while the gardener swirled the tea around in the pot, then poured it into two cups.

"How long has your uncle worked here?" she asked.

"Over fifty years," he replied. "The only job he has ever had."

"And what brought you here?"

"My mother liked the place. We used to spend the summer holidays with the old man."

"And your father?" she said.

"He was out of the country."

"Really? Where?"

He didn't appear to hear the question.

"Please," he said. "Sit down."

She took a seat at the table, and he handed her a cup of tea. Then he placed a jug of milk and a bowl of sugar beside a jam jar full of wildflowers. Maybe "out of the country" was a euphemism. She thought about Jane Fintry, about bringing up a child alone. It couldn't have been easy.

The gardener sat down at the table.

"Remember that envelope you gave me?" he asked. "The one with the flower and the seeds inside? I've searched all three volumes of Hooker's *Genera Plantarum* and couldn't find it. I'm going to keep on looking."

Did he have her mixed up with Antonia? She had no idea what he was talking about. "Wonderful," she replied vaguely.

All the bravado she had felt before had gone. George's admission of his infidelity was devastating, but did she have the courage to leave him? And if she so, what kind of life would she and Kitty have?

The fire crackled in the grate. Jacob Baillie seemed to relax. He sat back and sipped his tea. He didn't seem to expect conversation. After Antonia, the silence was a relief. Eventually the clock struck midnight. Cicely drained the cup.

"I'd better be going," she said, rising to her feet. "Thank you so much for the tea."

"Glad to be of service," he said.

"Good night, Mr. Baillie."

Cicely hoped the new owners would keep the Baillies on. She doubted anyone else would employ old Mr. Baillie, not at his age, but she would do what she could for both of them, offer references, recommendations. There was no action without a reaction, her mother used to say.

Antonia slept badly. At her insistence they had been the last to leave Lorimer's dinner, engaging him in conversation long after everyone else had left.

"Do you think he really wanted to discuss politics at midnight?" Malcolm had asked her on the way home. "I mean, *really*, Antonia!"

She sat and stared out at the dark, her mouth a straight line. There were two reasons. First, she was making sure that they didn't overtake Cicely walking back along the road; they were giving her a head start. That was what her sister-in-law wanted, surely? To make her point. To make them look bad. But the night was colder, windier, more inhospitable than she had realized, and the journey home in the carriage made her feel guilty and then angry that she had been made to feel guilty and then guilty that she felt angry. It was all Cicely's fault. Second, she wanted to apologize about the vase. She had been on the brink, but then someone had brought up the prime minister and the problems of Irish home rule, and the moment had passed.

"And as for your brother's wife," Malcolm went on, "I have to admire her. Got out when the going was good."

"I thought it was quite rude. But then etiquette doesn't seem to matter to her. I mean, as you said, they just turned up on the doorstep expecting to stay indefinitely?"

Antonia sounded harsher than she intended.

"But then again, they are family. Maybe it's a marital issue?"

"Marital?" repeated Malcolm as if the thought had never occurred to him. "Do you think that's a possibility?"

"My brother can't be the easiest man to be married to," said Antonia.

When they had arrived back at Balmarra she was relieved to hear that Cicely had made it home safely. All was well that ended well, as Malcolm said more than once. During the night, however, Antonia lay awake, the sound of her own voice chafing in her head, the events of the previous evening churning like indigestion. If she didn't throw the party, no one would ever invite them anywhere again. Their social pariah status would be confirmed now and forever more. And what about Lorimer's vase? Could she ever live down the embarrassment? And finally she thought about Cicely. Maybe she had come to

Balmarra for help and was too proud to ask. Her face burned at the thought of it. How could she have been so insensitive?

The next morning she listened to Malcolm getting up and going to work. When he was gone, she rose and ate breakfast alone, then climbed up the stairs to the attic. It didn't take long to find what she was looking for. It was in the tea chest nearest the door, wrapped up in newspaper from the late 1880s. The vase was not exactly the same as Lorimer's but similar. It had two gold handles, a lid with a gold pineapple-shaped knob, and a painted image of cherubs on one side. She lifted it up and found a mark on the base, two lines crossing twice to make a double cross, with the letter *C* in the middle. Was this a Sèvres? She would wrap it up and send the groom over with it later that day with an apology.

Antonia wiped her palms on her skirts and took a final look around the attic. It would take some time to sort through it all, but it must be done. A door slammed on the floor below, and she jumped. The visitors were louder than a crowd of laborers. Later that day, however, she would ask Cicely what was going on and if she could be of assistance. In return Cicely could help her throw the party. The more she thought about it, the more she convinced herself that it was not only desirable, it was essential. Such an event would put them on the social map; it would announce their intention to be recognized as members of the landed class. But it would not be the kind of party that people might expect, there would be no chamber orchestra, weak bowls of fruit punch, and postage-stamp-size sandwiches. Instead they would throw a party like nothing anyone had ever experienced in those parts before. It would be a big hurrah, a celebration with an Indian theme. Yes, Antonia told herself, a lavish party was just the ticket.

10

The morning was crisp and cold, the blue sky above streaked with white mackerel clouds. Although it was only August, the taste of autumn was already in the air. Across the water, the mountains looked as soft as felt, while the tangled garden that had seemed so sinister to Cicely the night before now rustled benignly in the breeze. Everything always looks better in the morning, her ayah used to tell her when nightmares had woken her, but this time, although the world looked transformed, her mood was still unchanged: She was an awful person, accepting her sister-in-law's hospitality under false pretenses and exchanging looks with a man who was not her husband. She had to stop.

Dora brought tea, toast, and boiled eggs to the breakfast table. It was only eight thirty, but, she said, Antonia had already breakfasted. Cicely poured the tea. She would take Kitty a cup. In India, Kitty's school uniform would have been pressed and mended, the brown paper that wrapped her exercise books replaced, her writing pencils sharpened, and the slate she used for homework wiped clean. During the trip they had grown closer—at least there was one positive outcome. Soon she would be packed up and dispatched to her Scottish school. Kitty would need a brand-new uniform, shoes, textbooks, and sports clothes plus a small trunk for personal belongings. The list the school had sent covered both sides of three pieces of paper. How could she possibly pay for it all?

The breakfast room door opened and Antonia came in, dressed as usual in so many layers of cardigan that she looked like an Eskimo.

"Good morning," Antonia said. "Sleep well?"

Cicely said she had, even though she had not slept well at all.

"Is the tea hot?" she asked.

"Yes, but I'm afraid there is only a little left," Cicely replied.

"I'll ring for more."

For a moment they were both silent. Cicely took a sip of tea and placed the cup carefully back in its saucer. Antonia sat forward in her chair and lowered her voice.

"I don't know how to say this tactfully, but is everything all right between you and my brother?"

Antonia was staring at her with real concern.

"George and I are. . . ." Cicely began. A lump had risen to her throat, and she couldn't continue. Were they really fine?

"It's just . . . ," she tried again, her gaze fixed on the teapot. "We miss him. It isn't easy being apart for so long but—the truth is—"

"Go on," said Antonia.

"The truth is that his current trip is expensive—more, much more, than we can possibly afford."

There, she had told her.

"Why didn't you say so before?" asked Antonia. She inhaled deeply then pushed her spectacles up her nose. "I can help you with that."

It's only money, Cicely told herself. It doesn't matter. And yet a yawning chasm had opened up inside her. How would Antonia feel once she discovered that Cicely borrowed money from her only to go on and claim the whole estate?

"We'll pay it back," Cicely said. "With interest. And if you don't mind, would you be able to keep it just between ourselves?"

"Malcolm will never know," Antonia replied. "Leave it with me. And don't be silly about the interest. I'm not a bank, you know."

At that moment Dora bustled in with a fresh pot, and the subject was dropped. More tea was poured, and Antonia started to talk about the awful brew they had been made to drink at school as well as the dreadful food that was served up for dinnertime. Cicely let the rest of her sister-in-law's words wash over her. She was so like George sometimes. She looked nothing like her brother, but when she had an idea, a plan, her eyes widened, just a little, and caught the light—polished stone in sunshine, slate to his flint. Her offer of financial help was completely unexpected. Maybe she and Malcolm could afford to buy them out after all? Maybe they lived frugally but had a large amount stashed away? There was one thing, however, that worried her. Antonia hadn't asked how much they required. But surely she would have some idea. She began to calculate—at least three hundred guineas for Kitty's school, and George could keep going on seven hundred for a month or two. A thousand guineas was not a fortune, was it?

"Let's talk about lighter topics," Antonia said. "I'm very excited about the party!"

Antonia elaborated on the idea she had proposed the night before, an event that no one, she enthused, would ever forget. Invitations would go out to all the gentry on the Peninsula as far west as Kilfinan, plus clients from Malcolm's firm, and ex-employees from the sugar refinery as well as the so-called Dunoon gin set.

"I never did have a coming-out ball," she continued. "Father didn't believe in them. He called them cattle markets."

Although she had never met Edward Pick, Cicely had heard so many of his opinions and sayings that at this point that she felt she had. She had to agree with him on the cattle market idea. Cicely's own coming-out had been for more than one hundred guests and featured a small orchestra, a banquet, and elephant rides. The young women had been instructed to line up on one side of the ballroom and the young men on the other. One by one the women were chosen, until only the plain ones or the older ones were left. It was nothing more than an exercise in humiliation, in herding. Since she had married George she rarely attended any social events unless she absolutely had to. It didn't seem, however, to be the right time to mention this.

"But the space," Antonia said. "We don't have the space."

"Why not hold it in the glass house?" Cicely suggested. "It's certainly big enough."

Antonia turned and looked at her, her eyes wide.

"Why didn't I think of that?" she said. "We could have dancing in the orangery and drinks next to the roses. We could string colored-paper lanterns from pillar to pillar and have a band playing beneath the palms. It's perfect!"

Kitty ran past the window with a wooden sword in her hand. When it was dry outside she kept herself occupied for hours, playing long imaginary games and sometimes building dens out of sticks and fallen branches.

"How about a masked ball?" Antonia went on. "With an Indian theme? We could eat kedgeree, and there would be cushions to sit on of instead of chairs. It would all be rather fun, I think. Unless—"

"Unless?"

"When are you thinking of leaving Balmarra?"

Antonia had caught her off guard.

"I received a letter from George," she began, "asking me to take his specimens to the Regius Keeper in Edinburgh in person. When they arrive, that is. Also, Kitty doesn't start school until the end of September."

"Well, then we have plenty of time. I'll look at dates and come up with a few possibilities."

There was no letter from the solicitor that afternoon or the next, nothing but a card from Keir Lorimer suggesting a time he might pick her up the following day. Cicely pictured his face, the way he had looked at her at the foot of the stairs, and felt herself flush. She had had too much champagne at dinner. She couldn't see him again. Before she could change her mind, she threw the card away without answering.

If only she could find that letter from Edward Pick, then it could all be sorted out. In her bedroom she checked through her suitcase, her handbag, her bedside drawers once more. She was down on her knees looking under the bed when Kitty walked in.

"Lost something?" she asked.

"A letter," she replied. "I've looked everywhere."

"You and Daddy are always losing things."

Cicely straightened and stared at Kitty.

"What's that supposed to mean?"

"It's just that you don't look after things very well," she said.

"We try," she said. "It's not always easy."

Kitty shrugged and tried to smile, but her mouth was turned down at the corners.

"It's not easy for me either," she whispered.

"I know," Cicely replied.

She held her hand out to Kitty, but Kitty did not take it. Instead she let herself out of the room and ran down the stairs, out of the house, and, as Cicely watched from her bedroom window, across the lawn to the woods.

Malcolm dealt with their finances; he didn't even trust her with a checkbook. But Antonia had promised that he wouldn't be involved. No, this was something she would sort out on her own. She had noticed as soon as she had come into the breakfast room that the honey of her sister-in-law's skin had faded and she had a blue smudge beneath each eye. She looked pale, exhausted, crumpled. When she had brought up the subject of her marriage, Cicely's eyes had filled with tears. It was not only the strain of being married to her brother that was causing her grief but the cost of the expedition. Well, she could help with that.

The pony-and-trap went at quite a clip. Antonia sat on the bench and clung to her parcel as they flew along the coast road. After that conversation with Cicely, she had climbed once more to the attic and fumbled her way in the half-dark to the stack of paintings, choosing at random one of the more explicit works. Surely it was worth something? She wrapped it up in brown paper and string, covering up the full breasts and the naked flesh and hiding it at the back of her wardrobe. But how should she go about selling the painting, and to whom?

She had hoped that it hadn't been noticed, but the night before, when she had just come in from cutting some flowers for the dining table, Malcolm burst into her room.

"Antonia!" His hair was slightly tousled, and his shoulders were covered in dust.

"Whatever is the matter?" she said.

"I've been calling!" he said. Shouting, more like, she thought.

"Have you?"

"I've just been in the attic to look out my winter galoshes," he said. "You haven't been up there recently, have you?"

Antonia's palms bloomed with sweat. She didn't want him to know about the vase. Or the painting.

"Me? No," she said. "Why?"

He stood in silence for a moment as if wondering whether to speak.

"Nothing," he said. "Never mind."

Surely he hadn't noticed anything missing? It was highly unlikely. The attic was large and poorly lit. He could have spotted, however, that someone had shifted boxes and rooted through the tea chests, or that stacks of paintings had been straightened and, if he was keenly observant, he might have noticed that there were a couple of empty spaces in the mayhem. But what could he do about it? Maybe she should have told him. But she had promised Cicely. And there were some parts of her and her life that she didn't want him to know about. Henry Morris, for example.

A few days earlier she had sent Henry a postcard, asking if he could meet her on an urgent matter. As soon as the card had been sent, however, she had been filled with so much regret that she had half a mind to run after Bill, who had been dispatched to the post office, and take the card back. What would Henry think when he received it? How many years since they had last corresponded? Maybe he wasn't even resident at his address anymore. She half hoped he wasn't. She wished him away from Gourock, from Scotland—from Europe, even. She imagined him walking along the beach of a tropical island, beneath a sunset of brilliant reds and yellows, his feet bare, his skin golden brown. The next few hours were agony. Until, that is, she received his card, sent by return. Her eye ran over the familiar handwriting and the stamp stuck at a slight angle, the way he used to place it, a secret sign that his heart was constant. Now it was surely nothing more than a slip of the hand.

"Hunter's Quay," he had written. "11 am on Wednesday. Yours, H."

As she rode away from Balmarra, she realized that having an excuse to see Henry might be the tonic that she needed. Ever since Cicely's arrival she had felt as if a mirror had been held up to reveal a reflection of herself that she had not recognized, one that she did not like. She saw herself and what she had become clearly for the first time in years. How had she become so middle-aged, so old, so stuck? But now she felt a familiar lightness inside. She told herself that it was a business matter, that there was nothing more to it than that: She was doing it for her sister-in-law. But as she had put on her favorite day dress, which she kept for high days and holidays, and had tied the red cashmere scarf that Cicely had given her around her shoulders, she noticed that she was shaking. The thought of seeing Henry again after all this time was exhilarating—and terrifying.

The pony-and-trap slowed down as they approached Hunter's

Quay. She arrived at the pier at the same time as the ferry from Gourock, and there he was, disembarking, older now and slightly stooped
from the weight of secret troubles: Henry Morris, the painter.

"Miss Pick," he said when he reached her, and she didn't correct
him. At that particular moment she had no wish to be Mrs. Malcolm
McCulloch.

"Henry," she replied, for she had always addressed him by his first
name. "Thank you for coming at such short notice."

"Anything for a friend."

It was his eyes that struck her first. She had forgotten how blue
they were, a shade she would recall later as cerulean, the color of
shallow water over white sand. The rest of his face, however, had
grown craggy with age. And she saw now that his clothes were stiff
on him and were his best, kept for weddings and funerals; eventually,
she guessed, his own. On his left wrist his shirt was fastened with
one gold cuff link; on his right, a twisted paper clip did the job. And
she was suddenly sorry and wished she had not stolen that single
cuff link from him all those years ago.

They took coffee in the dining room of the Royal Marine Hotel.
At eleven in the morning they were the only customers.

"I was sorry to hear of your father's passing," Henry said once
they were seated. "He was a generous man."

"Kind of you to say," she replied, "although not strictly true."

The bartender brought a plate of shortbread and hovered next to
the door to the bar. She wanted him to leave. She wished they were
alone, on Karrasay again, Henry's easel propped in front of them,
the scene, like their future, still an unfinished sketch. A bell rang in
a distant room. The bartender left to attend to it. Henry picked up a
teaspoon and turned it over and over in his fingers. Like her, he was
unsure what to do with his hands.

"Such a pretty scarf," he said softly. "Suits you."

"It's the warmest thing I own," she began, automatically defusing
the compliment out of habit. "Anyway, it's been too long . . ."

She felt his eyes on her face, and so she took off her hat and smoothed down the felt. She had followed his career from a safe distance, spotting articles in the local paper that mentioned that his paintings had been accepted for group shows in the Royal Academy in London or the National Galleries in Edinburgh. He seemed to be doing well, or as well as could be expected for a man of his occupation. She had also kept an eye on the classified section, alert for any mention of a marriage. He had not, as far as she knew, been wed. She kept her left hand in her lap where he would not see her wedding ring.

"It's so nice to see you again, Miss Pick."

"Please. Call me Antonia."

"As you wish. So what can I help you with?" He smiled and waited expectantly.

Antonia drained her coffee cup and poured another. She would have to speak soon or he would get the wrong impression.

"I wanted to ask your advice. You see, I have one of my father's paintings that I'd like to sell, and I thought you might know of someone who might like to buy it."

He studied her.

"I am afraid I am not an art dealer," he said. "But I know a few people who I could ask."

"The thing is, I need to sell it rather quickly."

"When, exactly?"

"As soon as possible. Tomorrow?"

He laughed, and when she didn't, he stopped, then picked up his cup and set it down again without drinking.

"How can I put this without causing offense?" he said softly. "Antonia, is there anything the matter?"

"Oh no, it's not for me!" she said. "It's for my brother's expedition."

She told him about Cicely Pick's unexpected arrival from India, about the niece, and about her brother's life collecting rare and precious plants that needed urgent finance. She did not mention Malcolm once.

"It's all been rather chaotic, as I'm sure you can imagine," she said.

"Yes indeed," he said.

The painter was silent for a moment, and she suddenly saw a change in him that she hadn't noticed at first. All that ambition, that desire for success, the hubris that he had once radiated, was gone. If one was being unkind, one might say that he now seemed pickled in disappointment. And she remembered then that it had not been her who had cooled, who had stepped out of the ring, but him.

"Have you been busy?" she asked. "With commissions?"

He sighed and told her that he had not, that his style of painting seemed to be somewhat out of step with public taste.

"But they will catch up, surely?"

He nodded but she saw that he didn't quite believe it.

"I was thinking of going to France," he said. "To Paris."

Antonia suddenly found herself overcome with melancholy. For what? For a lack of opportunity. For the absence of choice. She would like to go to Paris, too, to paint. Or to go together with Henry Morris, although not the one who sat across from her smelling of cedar wardrobes and coal smoke; instead another, younger version, the one she had first known. But he had not wanted her. She swallowed, then stared at her hands in her lap. Her life seemed to telescope to the point where she realized that the moment when she could have run away with a painter, with Henry Morris, had probably long since passed. Even if he had wished it—and he hadn't—she never had the courage, the wherewithal, the nerve, and now it was too late.

"I have a friend who is a friend of a painter called Matisse," he said. "Have you heard of him?"

Antonia was pulled back to the moment and shook her head no. She drained her coffee cup once more and tried to pour another, but there was nothing left but a few bitter black drops. He watched, taking her in, reminded once again, she was certain, of her limitations, her failings, her naïveté, as clear as the willow pattern on the china cups.

"Let's see that painting, then," he said softly.

Antonia placed her parcel on the table and untied it. Henry Morris pulled back the brown paper, and his face froze for an instant.

"Not quite what I expected," he said.

"It seems my father had rather unorthodox taste."

His eye ran over the painting, taking in the details, looking for something to say other than the obvious.

"It could be a scene from Greek mythology," he finally said. "Venus or the Sirens."

She didn't voice what they were both thinking: Was this really art, or something else?

The bartender came in again to ask if they required lunch. Henry swiftly covered up the painting with the brown paper.

"We won't, thank you," he told the waiter.

Henry looked at his watch. The next ferry left in quarter of an hour.

"What do you think?" she asked.

"I can't promise anything," he said. "But I'll see what I can do."

"Good man," she said.

"I try to be," he replied. "Don't always succeed, mind."

He rose to his feet and pulled on his coat. While his back was turned, quick as you like, she pocketed a teaspoon.

11

Once Antonia had set off, Cicely put a bridle on the pony and rode him up into the hills behind the house again. From there she could look down at the finger of open water below, still as glass, and beyond, the clutter and sprawl of the sugar towns, Greenock, Gourock, and Port Glasgow. A tiny black train moved along the far bank heading east, trailing a veil of white steam and gray smoke. Closer, in the forests below, autumn was approaching, and clusters of leaves were already yellow or orange or blood red. Every time she rode through the estate, she discovered a part she had never seen before—a stream, a thicket of trees, or a bank of wildflowers untouched, or so it seemed, by anyone for years. She saw a movement, and her eye was drawn to a figure moving slowly but purposefully through the trees. It was old Mr. Baillie. What was he doing so far from the house? Perhaps she should mention it to Jacob.

It was late afternoon by the time she returned to the house. Malcolm's car was parked outside. The door to Kitty's room was ajar, but there was a change in the air, a thinning, an absence. Even without looking inside, Cicely knew she wasn't there. She looked in her own bedroom next door and in the nursery. She searched the house, then asked Dora and Cook, but they hadn't seen her. Be calm, she told herself. Kitty can't have gone far. She was aware that over the last few days she hadn't seen that much of her. She was always out in the garden, exploring the estate, playing games. But she always told her she was going; she never went without saying good-bye. And she always took the dog.

Outside it looked like rain.

"Kitty?" she called in the hallway. But there was no answer.

Malcolm was sitting in the drawing room with the paper in his lap.

"Can I have a word?" said Cicely.

"Now?" he said. "I was just about to do the crossword."

He looked up, saw her face, and closed his newspaper.

"Thank you, Malcolm."

It was the first time she had used his Christian name, and it felt foreign in her mouth, flat as a piece of slate.

"Well?" he said. "How may I be of service?"

"I've lost Kitty," she said. "Have you seen her?"

"In fact, I have. The little scamp was in the attic," he said, smiling as if it were all a joke. "Some rather precious items have gone missing. I don't know where they are or what she's done with them, but we'd rather like them back."

"Kitty?"

"Yes, Kitty. A precious vase and a painting. Of a rather pornographic nature. I'm sorry to tell you, but there it is."

He opened his newspaper again and started to read the puzzle clues.

"Kitty is only eight years old," she said.

"Mrs. Pick. Did you go up to the attic?"

"No."

"Well then," Malcolm said he as filled in a word.

"When exactly was this?"

"An hour or so ago. I asked her about the attic, and she denied it. And so I threatened to give her a good tanning if she didn't give them back."

"A what?"

"A pasting," he replied. "Of course I didn't actually do it."

She sought out his gaze, making him meet hers.

"Why would you want to do a thing like that to a little girl?"

"She'll have to get used to it once she starts school," Malcolm said.

"I won't allow that," she said. "Not here or at school."

"Won't you, indeed?"

He sighed theatrically.

"We should never have come here," she said.

The door was suddenly blown open. A rush of cold air filled the hallway. Malcolm was still writing out letters at the top of the page.

"Mrs. Pick," he said. "With the greatest respect. She's just a child."

He looked up at her with a bemused expression, as if he were not the only one watching, as if he had a crowd at his shoulder, a crowd of Malcolms all waiting for her to open her mouth and make a fool of herself.

"My point exactly!" she replied.

"And children get into mischief."

Take a deep breath, she told herself. There was much she could say that was probably expected: she should thank him for his hospitality, for his generosity, his bountiful munificence.

"Malcolm dear?" Antonia was standing in the doorway. How long had she been there? How much had she heard? "What's going on?"

He kept his voice steady.

"I was just explaining to your sister-in-law the rationale behind corporal punishment," he said.

"Why on earth would you do that?" Antonia asked.

Malcolm's face went red. He licked his lips, he scored out a word. The calm facade had fallen. Sweat was seeping out of his pores, making his skin shiny. And still he kept his voice level.

"I know you'll agree that children should be taught that stealing is wrong, my dear. That rooting through other people's belongings is wrong!"

"What are you talking about?" said Antonia.

"I told you! I was up in the attic looking out my galoshes. I noticed that some things were missing!"

Antonia's hand flew to her mouth.

"I'm so sorry," she said.

"Why are you sorry!" said her husband, his voice rising at last.

"It was me," Antonia said. "I was in the attic. I took a few things."

"A Sèvres vase?"

"Yes. And a painting."

For a moment there was silence. All Malcolm's swagger was suddenly gone. He frowned at Antonia, put down his newspaper, and placed the cap on his pen.

"Why didn't you say?" he said. "I asked you, and you said you hadn't set foot up there for months."

The grandfather clock ticked. Cicely pushed past Antonia, out of the room.

"What's wrong, Cicely?" Antonia called after her. "Has something happened?"

In the glass house the gardener's dog was asleep beside a heating pipe. So Kitty was alone.

Jacob was wheeling a load of coal toward the entrance.

"Is everything all right, Mrs. Pick?" he asked.

He tried to be reassuring, telling her she couldn't have gone far, that she was bound to be fine, that she would be back as soon as it started to rain.

"Will you help me look for her?"

He nodded, rousing his dog.

They searched the glass house and the vegetable gardens, the driveway and the stables. On the shore below the water crashed against the rocks, and the river was in full spate. Cicely saw it all and yet saw none of it, her eyes brimming with panic. She couldn't hold back the thought of Kitty in the water, Kitty caught by the current, her little hand stretching toward hers; Kitty crying out as she was pulled under. She had let her run wild, she had been too wrapped up in her own concerns. What if something unspeakable had happened?

"She's probably deep in her imaginary world and lost track of the time," the gardener said.

They spread out, they called her name, they searched the shore, the island, the woods, the hills, but she seemed to have vanished completely.

"Has she ever run off before?" Jacob asked.

"Never," she said.

"Maybe she walked to the road?" he suggested.

"She wouldn't have gone that far."

But maybe she had. Maybe Malcolm's threats had been enough to make her run away. Cicely covered her mouth with her hand as tears started to spill from her eyes. If Kitty was dead she would have no choice but to kill herself too. Coming to Scotland had been a huge mistake. She should never have left home. The whole trip was misjudged, disastrous. The daylight had started to seep away. It would be dark in a few hours.

"Let's look once more," the young gardener suggested. "I'll take the grounds if you take the glass house."

She walked around the outer path, looking behind wheelbarrows, water butts, towers of empty flowerpots; then she ran down the stairs to the boiler room. The vast furnace gave off a low rumble. The heat was oppressive, the walls, the floor, every surface, all covered with black soot.

"Kitty?" she called. "Kitty?"

She listened to the silence, to the slow dripping of a tap and the tick of the pipes. Nothing.

"Is there nowhere else to look?" she implored the gardener, back outside. "Surely there must be somewhere that we've missed."

"Wait a minute," he said, ducking back into the glass house. She had already looked there, she wanted to tell him, twice. He needed to go back down to the shore, to look along the riverbank, scour the beach. Why was he wasting time? As Dora talked about bringing in the farmer's lads to start searching the estate at daybreak, the dog started to bark. The door of the glass house swung open.

"Mrs. Pick," young Mr. Baillie called out. "I've found her!"

Never in all her life had Cicely felt such relief.

"I saw a movement," he explained as he led her to the center of the glass house.

She peered up into a palm tree and saw the quiver of green near the top.

"Kitty!"

"Mummy," she called down.

"Don't move," the gardener called. "I'll get a ladder."

"Leave me be!"

Cicely closed her eyes, suddenly exhausted. The branches groaned as Kitty moved farther up the trunk.

"Don't go too high," Jacob Baillie warned. "The branches won't support you."

"Kitty," she called out. "Stay where you are!"

With a sudden creak and snap, something broke. Kitty screamed as she tumbled, falling through the palm fronds, her arms and legs flailing, her mouth letting out several involuntary cries as she descended toward the cold hard earth.

"Kitty!" Cicely screamed.

She took a few steps, but the gardener was faster, cleaving the leaves of a tropical plant as he leaped forward. There was a grunt and then a small silence.

"It's all right," the gardener called out. "I caught her."

The leaves parted, and there they were. Cicely lifted her daughter from the gardener's arms, held her tight, and buried her face in Kitty's hair. Her breath was jagged, and her tears quickly soaked the fabric of Cicely's dress. Nothing mattered—not the house or the expedition or the money or her wounded pride—nothing but her daughter.

"I'll tell the others," said young Mr. Baillie. "Call off the search."

"Don't be angry with me," Kitty said once he had gone.

"I'm not," Cicely whispered. "Just glad you're safe. Don't ever do that again."

Cicely placed her on the ground and examined her. Kitty's arms and legs were covered in scratches, but apart from that she was fine.

"You know, I would never have let him hit you," Cicely whispered.

Kitty frowned.

"What are you talking about?"

"Antonia's husband."

"Oh, him? I'm not scared of Malcolm," she said with scorn. "He can threaten me all he likes."

Cicely took her shoulders in her hands.

"Then why?" she said. "Why did you hide? Have you any idea how worried I've been?"

Kitty stared at the ground. Tears started to run down her cheeks.

"I want it," she said.

"What are you talking about?"

"Don't be cross. Promise you won't be cross."

"What is it, Kitty. Has someone hurt you?"

"It was me," she said in a rush. "I took the letter you were looking for. I threw it in the fire. I'm so sorry."

Cicely let go of her. This was not the answer she had been expected. She swallowed down a flash of fury.

"But why would you do that?"

"I was angry with you for making me go to school when I wanted to stay with my ayah."

Kitty's eyes glittered in the moonlight. Her hair was tangled with sticks and torn leaves. Cicely loved her with a sudden fierceness. She took her in her arms and held her.

"And I know what you're going to do. Once you have Balmarra you're going to sell it, aren't you? To pay for my school. But I like it here. Daddy may not want this place, but I do. You can't do it. Please don't."

"Oh, Kitty," she whispered. "Why didn't you tell me?"

"You never listen to me."

"I will now, I promise," she said. "But there are some things I can't change."

"Of course you can. You can do anything if you set your mind to it, remember?"

The door of the glass house slammed, and Antonia burst in, breathless.

"I just heard," she said. "Thank goodness she's all right."

"She's fine," said Cicely. "Nothing that a hot bath and a cup of cocoa won't fix."

A card was propped up on the hall table when Antonia came down to breakfast the next morning. It was from Lorimer, a thank-you note for the vase. "There was no need," he wrote. "Accidents happen." He hadn't, however, returned it. She tore it up and threw it away before Malcolm could see. There was no word yet from Henry. Maybe she had asked too much from someone who owed her too little, if anything at all.

It was nine o'clock. Cicely and Kitty had not appeared downstairs for breakfast yet, and the house was silent but for a rhythmic thump from the kitchen below. Antonia hoped it was not pastry. Cook's touch was the same whether it was short crust or a roast that needed tenderizing: "Descended from a family of prizefighters," her father used to joke.

Cook was expecting Antonia in her overheated lair to discuss the household bills and the week's menus. It was a chore that she had undertaken ever since her mother's death, and it was one she loathed. A pound over, a rise in the price of milk, Cook would inform her with great concern, a sack of tatties sprouted. Well, can't be helped, Antonia would shrug, these things happen. And then it was on to food: Oxtail soup or chicken broth? Rice pudding or tapioca? Lamb chops or lemon sole? Anything you like, she was tempted to reply, as long as it's hot. Or cold. Or wet. Or whatever the recipe states. But she couldn't say that. She needed Cook on her side. Especially in the next few weeks.

"A what?" Malcolm had asked the night before.

"A social event," she had clarified.

"The one you proposed at Lorimer's? Surely you weren't serious?"

"I've given it some thought, and I think it might be rather fun."

Malcolm was silent, a sure sign of reluctance. It was almost eight, and they had both finished their evening nightcap—a whisky for him and a sloe gin for her. The measures were small, and it was more the routine Antonia relished than the alcohol consumption. They sat side by side on the divan as the fire burned down to embers.

"It would be a party for Cicely and Kitty," she went on. "They are relations, after all."

"They say they are."

"Don't start that again. We need to make it up to them, after what happened. So embarrassing."

"I didn't hit her," said Malcolm. "I simply said I would, which is not the same at all. What were you doing up there anyway?"

She turned and looked at her husband.

"Me?"

"You said you were up there. In the attic."

He waited for an explanation.

"You don't really think that Kitty would steal from us, do you?" she said. It was a poor attempt to change the subject.

"Antonia," he said. "What did you do with the vase? And the painting?"

There was no escape. For a second she thought she might tell him.

"Why do you care?" she asked.

"The vase is a Sèvres, very sought after and worth a thousand or so," he went on. "And as for the painting, I'm sure your father said it was a William Etty."

"Did he?"

Antonia felt her face turn pink. He had never told her he owned an Etty. The artist had fallen out of fashion, but his work must still be worth something. She rose, picked up the poker, and gave the glowing coals in the fireplace a prod. Could she ask Lorimer for the vase back? Hardly.

"You didn't do anything foolish, did you?" Malcolm asked.

Antonia rose, wiped her hands on her skirts, and turned.

"I took them," she said, "to get them valued. For insurance purposes."

That seemed to satisfy him.

"Why didn't you say so?"

She didn't answer and instead placed their glasses on a tray. As she was putting the bottles back into the drinks cabinet, she heard Malcolm rise and throw some more coal on the fire. So, she thought, the night wasn't over yet.

"Who did you ask?" he said. "To value the painting?"

Malcolm sat down again and folded his arms. There was something about his mouth she noticed, something provocative, which was unusual for him.

"Hmm?" she said as she rearranged the bottles. "Oh, an artist's gallery. I asked the one who painted the house—what was his name?—to make an inquiry."

It was as close to the truth as she could admit. She closed the glass door and turned. Once more, she decided, she would try and change the subject.

"Anyway, what *I* want to know is what possessed you to behave that way toward Kitty?"

Malcolm's face seemed to close in on itself.

"How was I to know?" he said.

"Best if we put it all behind us," she suggested softly.

She sat down beside him and laid a hand on his knee for a moment or two. It seemed to calm him a little. The fire crackled. The clock struck the hour.

"Anyway," she said, rising to her feet once more, "the party. I thought we could hold it in the glass house."

While he stared at the fire, she paced back and forth, describing her vision—the colored paper lanterns, the masks, the spicy food, the theme.

"You don't know anything about India," he interrupted. "You've never been."

"I've never been anywhere."

He leaned back on the divan and looked at her from beneath his brows.

"You're not that sort, Antonia," he said.

"What sort do you mean?"

"You know. Capricious, frivolous. Impulsive! A masked ball indeed!"

She rose, walked out of the room, slamming the door behind her.

"Antonia!" he called out after her for once. "Neither am I! As I said, we're a different type."

His words echoed in her head the next morning as Cook was reeling off her usual fare, milk puddings, cutlets and hashes, braised beef and potted hams. She'd made the same dishes for as long as Antonia remembered, and she still managed to burn or undercook, to dry out or curdle. Like her parents, Antonia did not want to offend her in case she took the hump and walked. Good, or at least adequate, staff were hard to find in these parts. She herself could barely boil an egg. Without a cook, they would have to live on toast. Not a bad thing, she sometimes thought when faced with a plate of glutinous mutton stew or leaden sponge pudding and lumpy custard.

"Couldn't we try something else?" she said, the words out of her mouth before she could stop them. "Some new dishes, perhaps."

"What was that?" said Cook, aghast.

"With some new flavors?" she added quickly with a small smile.

"No one has ever complained before," Cook said, slamming her book shut and sitting back in her chair.

"It's not a complaint, Just a suggestion. I was thinking of you, that you must be bored always cooking the same dishes."

"Bored?" Cook repeated.

Antonia swallowed. This was worse than she had imagined.

"You see, I have in mind an occasion," she said. "An event in the evening, a social event."

"Well, why didn't you say so?" Cook said before locating on a shelf an ancient book of recipes, held together with string.

"Savory jellies," she announced. "Pig's head in aspic. That's what you're imagining, I expect. I have all the recipes in here."

Antonia hadn't the heart to tell her that what she really had in mind did not involve a savory jelly. Instead she acquiesced, just to let Cook get used to the idea.

"Just the thing," she offered.

"And what about the week's menu? Is that all right for madam?"

Her words carried an accusatory undertone. How had they ended up here, Antonia wondered, with her, the mistress of the house, having to tread so carefully around Cook's feelings?

"Perfect," she said. "As usual. Thank you."

With a scrape of her chair, Cook stood up, took a ball of dough from a bowl, and started to knead vigorously.

What "sort," what "type," were they? The sort that stayed in one place, rooted, like a tree? George's words from all those years ago suddenly flooded back to her: "Seeing the world is the greatest thing a man can do." How unfortunate to be born with a timid disposition and of the wrong sex. She had taken off her glasses, and the world had blurred. Had she fumbled through her life like this, seeing nothing but the faint outlines of things? Mistaking one thing for another, a bed for a divan, indifference for love, an entente cordiale for a marriage?

"Actually," she said to Cook, "on second thought, could you hold off on the savory jellies? I have in mind a theme."

Cook frowned.

"A what?"

"An Indian theme. You know, curry and the like."

"Mrs. Pick," Cook began. "Let me give you a bit of advice."

"If you don't feel able to cope?"

Cook narrowed her eyes. She was a woman who prided herself on being able to deal with any adversity.

"I am perfectly capable," she said, her breath billowing up a small cloud of flour, "of mastering an exotic menu."

"I'll look out some recipes, then," said Antonia.

"No need," said Cook. "I have plenty."

She had done it. She had managed to get Cook on side. It was the first hurdle, and she had jumped it—inelegantly, it was true, but effectively. The food for the party would be Indian. Or an approximation. As she headed back up the stairs to the hall she heard the sound of bicycle tires on the gravel of the driveway, followed by the doorbell ringing. It was the postman. There was a parcel from India for Cicely, and a letter addressed to Antonia from Henry.

She took it upstairs to her bedroom, closed the door, sat at her dressing table, and opened it. It contained a promissory note for one hundred guineas and a card, a small sketch of the Clyde in pen and ink. She turned it over and read: "A, I found a buyer in Glasgow. Best of luck to your brother's venture, H." It was far less than she might have hoped, but at least it was something. The guest room door closed with a slam, and she heard the faint sibilance of voices as Cicely and Kitty headed to the breakfast room. Antonia rose to her feet, adjusted her spectacles, put the check in her cardigan pocket, and hurried downstairs to deliver the good news.

12

Wrapped in brown cotton that had been sewn along the seams, George's parcel smelled of sea salt and railway stations, of rotting vegetation and fresh growth. Cicely took a pair of scissors and cut it open. Inside were a sketchbook filled with botanical illustrations in George's hand, as well as a number of pressed leaves and petals flattened between tissue paper. The writing was tiny, lines and lines of explanation, of dates, of map locations. Much of it was almost illegible. There was a letter, too. Cicely laid it flat on the dressing table, the tiny copperplate looping and dashing in slanting lines across the page, the writing dense and spotted with blots, crossings-out, annotations, and corrections.

"My dear Cicely," George wrote:

> Here are the pressed samples from the plants I mentioned,
> including the early flowering Buddleia. Take them
> to Edinburgh to the Regius Keeper at the Botanics
> immediately for preliminary identification. I am sure
> I am onto something with a few of them. Later in the
> year I will go back for seeds. Speed is of the essence. I am
> not the only Scotsman in the area. Another plant hunter

by the name of Magnus Hayes has recently appeared.
At one point last week I could see his camp from ours,
I smelled roasting meat and heard laughter. He is, you see,
so much more well-equipped than we are.

This was what George had dreaded. This was why he had left so quickly. To get there first. But now he had competition.

We are presently staying in a small village next to a
river. The villagers talk of a valley, accessible only by
a threadbare rope bridge, that has been unexplored by
Westerners and which, they say, is full of flowers from
February to August. Once you have sent word from
Balfour, I will decide whether to wait here for autumn
and go and collect the seeds or to leave the mules and
carry on alone by foot, taking only the essentials, specimen
jars, cameras and basic supplies. I hope the situation at
Balmarra has been resolved. If my sister is dragging her
heels then I would consider hiring a lawyer to do our
bidding. I have found a coolie to take my post back to
Lhasa and wait for your next telegram.

A small knock sounded at her bedroom door. Antonia opened it and poked her head in.

"Can I have a quick word?"

She had managed to get some money, she said, one hundred guineas from the sale of a painting. Cicely tried to look pleased, but it was only a fraction of what they needed. It would barely pay for a term at Kitty's school. She would wire the whole amount to George. It would keep him afloat but not for long. Every day she waited for a letter from Mr. Drummond, the solicitor, but nothing came. The thought of going back to his office in Dunoon filled her with dread. There must be other ways, other means, surely?

"Is that parcel from George?" Antonia asked.

"It is," she replied. "I'm taking his specimens to the Botanics in Edinburgh tomorrow."

Antonia picked up the notebook and inhaled its cover.

"Years ago Father made a hefty donation to the Botanics," she said. "So maybe they'd be willing to support my brother's expedition in some way."

Would she be able to persuade the gardens to invest? If the specimens were impressive enough, there had to be a possibility?

"Thank you, Antonia."

The next morning Cicely and Kitty left at eight in the pony-and-trap and caught the eight-thirty ferry. It had been fair when they had woken up, but when the boat reached Gourock, it had started to rain. Kitty carried a leather satchel she had found hanging in the cloakroom and which she packed with a book, a pack of cards, and a couple of apples. Cicely took a day purse and George's specimens in a large brown-paper envelope.

"The envelope's getting wet," Kitty said. "Why don't you put it in my satchel to keep it dry?"

On the train Cicely rehearsed in her head what she would say, and imagined the Regius Keeper's reaction while Kitty stared out of the window. If he pledged enough, then maybe they wouldn't have to sell Balmarra. But what about school fees? It wasn't a perfect solution by any means, but it was better than nothing. By the time they were approaching Edinburgh, she had already concluded the deal in her head.

Arriving at Waverley Station felt like stepping back into the civilized world as she had left it. The door of the train swung open, and Cicely took a deep breath: steam and smoke, gray stone and freshly mown grass. Below it all was the sweet smell of freshly brewing coffee. How she longed for a cup. How tired she was of the pale-amber liquid that they drank at Balmarra that bore very little resemblance to the tea she was used to.

Princes Street was packed with people strolling through the Pleasure Grounds or along the wide streets, stopping to admire the Scott Monument, the Floral Clock, and the castle, set into its rock above. There was a tangible sense of leisure in the air, of time to waste and money to spend. The Royal Botanic Gardens was on the other side of the New Town, a five-minute ride in a taxicab or tram, a passerby informed them, or a fifteen-minute walk, recommended if the weather was fine. The sun shone as if on cue. Kitty's hand slipped into her own; all was right with the world. As they crossed George Street, however, Cicely wished she had not worn her tailored woolen coat. Summertime in Scotland was changeable, and they had dressed in layers.

Dundas Street was a very fine row, with art galleries and photographer's studios. One caught her eye, a studio with an image of a well-dressed couple on their wedding day in the window, the man looking at the woman with an expression that could not be read as anything other than complete infatuation.

"Can we?" Kitty begged, "Can we have a cabinet print taken to send to Daddy?"

The interior of the photographer's studio was dark after the brightness of the street. Once their eyes grew accustomed, she saw that the interior resembled a junk shop or the backstage of a theater, with its random props—a chair, a bench, a vase, and its drapes, velvet curtains, and painted backdrops of gardens, forests, or the seaside. The photographer was young and charming and offered them a special rate, even though they were of a mind to get a portrait taken anyway.

"What would you like?" he asked. "Portobello Beach? Falkirk Palace?"

The backdrop was Kitty's choice. Cicely posed in front of a wooden flat, painted to look like the door of a train. The words "First Class" were picked out above the words "Edinburgh to Glasgow." Kitty stood at the window above as if looking out of the carriage. Then the studio lights were illuminated, hot and yellow as the Indian sun, and the photographer pulled his black hood over his head and focused the lens.

"Hold still," he called out. "Don't move an inch while I count. Five, four, three—"

Her chin was raised, her breath held. Kitty's too.

"Two, one!"

The image was taken, their faces fixed on a plate of treated glass, and they could step down. They paid him two shillings and could pick up the prints next time they were passing.

The Regius Keeper was an elderly man called Isaac Balfour. He was the professor of botany at Edinburgh University and looked exactly as Cicely expected he would, with heavy, hooded eyes and neatly manicured whiskers. He was sitting at his office window in the Royal Botanic Gardens, staring out onto a square of perfect lawn, deep in thought. His desk was bare but for a pile of correspondence in a tray and a vase of asters. The door had been left ajar, but she knocked anyway.

"Enter!" said Professor Balfour.

"Cicely Pick," she said by way of introduction. "And this is my daughter, Kitty. I think you may be acquainted with my husband's work. His name is George Pick."

He rose to shake her hand and smiled.

"What a pleasant surprise," he said. "And you've come from—?"

"Darjeeling," she supplied. "We arrived in Scotland a few weeks ago."

"You're staying at Balmarra, I suppose? Please, do sit down."

"You know it?" she asked as they sat down in two large chairs before the desk.

"Oh, yes. And I knew your husband's late father, Edward, a man of—how shall I put it?—charming but uncompromising temperament. So what can I help you with today?"

She explained that she had received a parcel from her husband who was on an expedition in the Himalayas, collecting specimens.

"I have heard that the political situation in China has had consequences for the whole area."

"Correct. George was compelled to take advantage and leave as soon as he could."

"And he has a patron, I suppose?" said Professor Balfour. "A venture of this type is not inexpensive."

He was smiling broadly, but something in her hesitation made him blink.

"Hard to put in place in a hurry," he added.

"That was what I wanted to talk to you about," she said. "Is this something you ever consider?"

"It is," he said. "Although usually at an earlier stage. But I would be very interested to see what he has found so far."

This was, Cicely told herself, all going well. It was all going to turn out fine.

"I received his first package a few days ago," she said. "He sent a book of illustrations and a number of pressed specimens. My daughter has it."

But Kitty was staring straight ahead with a look of horror on her face. It was then Cicely noticed that she was not carrying the brown leather bag.

"Kitty?" she said softly. "Where is your satchel?"

"I think. . . ." she whispered. "I'm sorry, Mummy. I think I must have left it on the train."

Edinburgh blurred as they walked back up the hill to Queen Street. Balfour had invited her to come back and see him as soon as she located the specimens. And they both agreed that they were undoubtedly not lost but just misplaced. She had told Kitty several times that it wasn't her fault. It wasn't the end of the world. But she could tell by the turn of her daughter's mouth and the slant of her shoulders that she didn't believe it. They rode in silence most of the way back, all the joviality of the outward train journey gone.

The satchel was handed in to the stationmaster's office in Aberdeen.

It took a week before he sent it by rail to Greenock Station. It was another week before she was informed that it had arrived. A few days after that she stood once more in the Regius Keeper's office in Edinburgh. It was raining heavily outside, and she had not brought an umbrella.

"Would you like something to drink?" Balfour asked. "A cup of tea?"

"No, thank you," she replied as she pulled the brown envelope from her bag.

"I should warn you that shortly after your visit I received a package from an agent representing a man called Magnus Hayes."

Cicely sat down. Her hat dripped into her lap.

"He found some interesting new species in, I think, the same area as your husband was looking."

"But not these specific plants? I mean, they could be others?"

"I very much hope they are," he said. "If you leave this with me, I'll let you know as soon as I can."

She closed her eyes. Her head had begun to hurt.

"Are you sure you wouldn't like a cup of tea?" he asked.

All of Antonia's initial enthusiasm for the party had turned into a rising sense of dread. She woke up every morning with half a mind to cancel. But fifty invitations had been delivered and forty-two replies received, not a single one informing her that regretfully they could not attend. Also, the sundries had been ordered and her mask and evening gown, of a more modest cut and color this time, were in the finishing stages. And yet, what else could it be but a disaster? She had no experience as a hostess, no natural gift for wit or for grace on the dance floor. What had she done? What had she let herself in for? Not only the cost, which would be a good deal higher than her initial estimation, but also the inevitable public humiliation. The only reason people had accepted, she suspected, was to come and have a good laugh at their expense. And she rolled over in her single bed and tried to tell herself it was an ordeal that would soon be over.

After breakfast she walked down to the glass house and tried to see it as others might. An area next to the rose garden had been cleared and a small dance floor installed. With a band in the corner, the glazing capturing the last of the evening light and the sway of candles in lanterns hung in the trees, it might, she considered, look not too bad. But what if the guests, eager for a glimpse inside a house that few had ever set foot in before, noted the damp stains on the ceilings and the warp of the floorboards? She could already hear the whispers: seen better days, dilapidated, decrepit, deranged. No, she told herself, if she imagined disaster, she would be almost responsible if it came to pass. She must seize the proverbial nettle, screw her courage to the sticking place, and throw herself whole-heartedly into making Cicely's party, as she called it in her head, a success.

The masks would make the event exotic, colorful, avant-garde. She had bought, in a more positive mood, ten bolts of silk in lemon yellow, brilliant orange, vibrant green, and turquoise, that she intended to wind around the pillars or drape from the roof at the entrance to create an exotic effect. As for the food, it would be spicy—kedgeree, curry, and rice pilaf; the punch laced with cardamom and slices of bottled peaches. All they needed now, she told herself in attempt to lighten her mood, was an elephant.

But what of the party's special guest? Ever since she had given her the money for George, Cicely had been distracted, making several trips to Edinburgh and spending the rest of her time walking around the gardens or sitting in the library with a novel. When Antonia had tried to involve her in the planning, asking her opinion of the menu or the decorations, she had feigned interest but offered no view of her own.

"What will you wear?" Antonia had asked.

"I'm sure I have something," she replied.

Antonia had twice been on the point of offering to pay for a new outfit, for she suspected that Cicely's funds could be running low. But something in her sister-in-law's manner prevented her.

"I've ordered two masks," Antonia mentioned. "Maybe you would like one of them, your choice. But anyway, you wear clothes so well that it doesn't really matter what you wear. You would look beautiful in a potato sack!"

Cicely looked at her for a moment and then glanced away. Had she really, Antonia asked herself, just suggested that Cicely's clothes resembled bags for vegetables?

"The dressmakers in Darjeeling are clearly masterful," she went on in an attempt to cover up her faux pas. "And so inexpensive!"

Cicely started to laugh.

"Antonia," she said, "I know you don't mean to say the wrong thing, but somehow you always do."

Antonia felt a hot flush rise up in her face. She fought her first impulse to be offended. Cicely wasn't trying to hurt her feelings; she knew that now.

"It's a skill of mine," she said. "Honed over many years. Kick me if I start to say something inappropriate at the party."

"I'm sure that won't happen," said her sister-in-law.

Antonia was a silent for a moment, willing her to continue. But finally, when she was certain that no offer of help was forthcoming, it came.

"You don't need help with anything, do you?" asked Cicely.

"Actually," she replied, "I do. Any idea where we can get an elephant at short notice?"

She kept her face straight. Cicely frowned.

"That's a tall order," she replied. "Would it have its own suite of rooms?"

"Naturally."

"Ten bottles of champagne?"

"Let's make it twelve."

"Leave it with me," she said.

"I've never seen an elephant," said Antonia. "Maybe one day. Did the gardens agree?"

It was such a sudden change of subject that Cicely started.

"They will let me know," she replied.

"Really?" Antonia replied. "I would have thought, that under the circumstances—"

"He's not alone," she said. "There's someone else in the area."

"Oh," she said. "That's unfortunate."

In the low light from the window, Cicely looked so utterly defeated, so crushed, that Antonia was tempted to reach out to her with both arms. She held back; it would only be awkward, unreciprocated. An idea occurred: Instead of using the party to announce her presence on the social scene, she would use it to raise charitable donations for her brother, George.

13

The letter from the Regius Keeper arrived the day before the party. It was propped up on the hall table, a crisp white envelope with an embossed crest on the back and her name, or the name she went by, in copperplate writing: "Mrs. George Pick Esquire." For a moment she held it in her hand, measuring the weight of it, which was heavier than it looked. It was the kind of stationery that projected a certain authority, the sort used by registrars and magistrates, advocates and tax inspectors—thick and slightly rough under the fingertips. She slipped the envelope into her pocket and hoped no one else had seen it.

It was midmorning, and despite a chill breeze, the sky was blue and the light had the clarity of a high altitude. Outside Kitty was in the garden throwing sticks for Maisie, the gardener's dog. Antonia was fussing over the drinks, Pimm's or punch? Cicely had promised to help; there was still so much to do, so much to organize. But no one would miss her, she hoped, for a little while at least.

Cicely opened her bedroom window, lit a cigarette, took a long, slow draw and then exhaled, the smoke rising and curling into the air. She rarely smoked anymore unless she needed something to calm her. This was one of those occasions, and so she closed her eyes and imagined a white prayer flag, a *windhorse*, or *lungta*, as they were called. In the center was a drawing of a horse with three flaming jewels on its back. Her ayah had taught her what this meant: It was a prayer for transformation from bad to good fortune. She pictured the flag high up on a mountain path, rippling in the wind. She prayed to the gods, to the three flaming jewels that signified the Buddha, the Dharma, and the Sangha. Then she prayed to Saint Christopher, to the Virgin Mary, to God. Outside the wind blew and the trees whispered and settled. Her hands shook as she slit the envelope and extracted the folded letter. Finally she opened it.

Unfortunately, Isaac Balfour wrote, her husband's package had indeed come too late. The specimens collected were duplicates of Hayes's. Cicely closed her eyes. Her prayers hadn't been heard. Neither God nor the Buddha nor any other deity had been listening. She folded the letter and put it back in the envelope. How would she break the news to George; how could she tell him that all his effort, all his hard work, all his time, had so far come to nothing? But there were more plants, surely, and in the next batch there might be new specimens, new discoveries? But how could they afford for him to remain there? One hundred guineas wouldn't go far.

She heard Kitty's voice below. She was making up complex imaginary games with many characters. Cicely loved the way her daughter played, blocking out everything that was happening around her.

"Not here!" Kitty called out. "We must head to the hills!"

Without income from the sale of Balmarra, Goerge would have to abandon the expedition, Kitty's education would be canceled, and they would have to borrow the money for their passage home. George would become a tea planter, and her life would be over, quite literally. No, Cicely decided, she couldn't let that happen. She must stick to her original plan. Kitty would be disappointed, but she would get over it. It was the only way. There was a knock at the door. It was Antonia, wondering if she'd be able to help Cook get the flavoring right for a party dish.

"You mean now?" Cicely asked. "Right now?"

"What better time than the present?" Antonia said. "Are you all right? You look a little pale."

"I'm fine, thank you."

Cicely closed her door and followed Antonia down the back stairs to the kitchen.

"It smells delicious, don't you think?" she said. "It was hard to get Cook to agree. Between me and you, she could do with a challenge. She's a little stuck in her ways, I'd say."

A large pot was bubbling on the kitchen stove. Cook was stirring it crossly.

"I don't know how it's supposed to taste," she began immediately, as if answering an accusation neither of them had made. "I've never eaten anything from the Orient."

"What about kedgeree?" Antonia said. "That's an Indian dish, isn't it?"

Cook ignored her and kept on stirring as if trying to mash out lumps. Cicely peered into the pot and sniffed. It smelled like ordinary stew.

"What do you think?" Antonia said. "I want it to be authentic."

"Do you have spices?" Cicely asked Cook.

She nodded her head toward a small packet of curry powder that lay on the kitchen table.

"Had to get it sent from Glasgow," Cook complained. "They don't have the likes in Dunoon. Cost a pretty penny too, by the bye."

"Is this all you have?"

"How much do you need?" Cook asked in alarm.

"Well, our cook doesn't usually use powder. He uses fresh turmeric, coriander, and cumin seeds that he roasts and then grinds. But I don't suppose you have those here."

Cook looked at her as if she had suddenly started speaking another language.

"Perhaps you have some ginger?"

"Ginger?" repeated Cook. "We have ginger beer."

"No, that won't do."

Cicely tore open the packet and poured most of the golden-brown powder into the stew.

"What is she doing!" said Cook, her voice rising. "That's sixpence' worth!"

"Now taste it," said Cicely.

Cook raised the spoon to her mouth and tentatively licked it. Her eyes widened, her face flushed, and she rushed to the sink, poured herself a glass of water, and drank it down. Antonia seemed to be struggling not to laugh.

"Are you all right?" she managed.

Cook nodded but screwed up her face.

"Too hot for you?" Cicely asked.

"Don't know how people can eat that Oriental fare," Cook said eventually. "You can't beat a nice mutton stew. Why go and ruin it?"

Antonia, however, was delighted. She tried a mouthful and claimed it was delicious.

"It has to be the real thing," she said. "Not some great fakery or trick. I'd like your opinion on the decorations too. Malcolm hates them."

The glass house was festooned with garish fabric. In bright greens, pinks, and blues, long swaths were draped and looped to form an elongated tent shape.

"It's supposed to look like a harem," Antonia explained. "I'm going to cover the floor with cushions."

Cicely wondered if Antonia had any idea what a harem actually was.

"Well? What do you think?" she asked.

"It's certainly eye-catching," Cicely replied.

Antonia looked pleased at her response.

"I thought you'd like it."

Antonia remained in the glass house, draping and redraping the silk. Cicely passed Malcolm at the top of the stairs on the way back to her room. His face was ruddy, and his left eye twitched.

"She doesn't know," he said quietly. "Has no clue."

Cicely peered at Malcolm in the half-light of the hall.

"I'm sorry?" she said. "Know about what?"

Malcolm took a step closer, then glanced over his shoulder to check he wouldn't be overheard.

"Know why you're here."

Cicely opened her mouth to reply, to deny anything he could accuse her of. But then she swallowed. What was the point? Why deny it?

"But if you ask me, you have some cheek!" he went on.

She raised her chin.

"I'm sure," she said, "that we can sort something out."

He wasn't placated. Instead he almost laughed.

"If you think we can 'sort this out,' then you don't know the half of it—"

He would have gone on, she could tell by the look on his face, but he seemed to bite the words back, to swallow the urge to play a winning stroke.

"It's just not right," he said. "Turning up on our doorstep like that. I mean, did you really just expect that you could waltz in here and take everything from under our noses? Did you?"

She was silent. He went on; he couldn't help himself.

"Because there are other individuals involved, I'll have you know," he said. "It's not as simple as you might assume."

And with that, he gave her a look and headed down the stairs.

In her room Cicely looked out at the sea loch corrugating in the breeze. The woods were a confusion of color, as bright as a child's painting. It was hard to imagine what the hills would look like once the season had turned and the leaves had fallen. Why had Malcolm waited until now to confront her? Had he too paid a visit to the solicitor? And what did he mean, other people were involved? A feeling of unease crept through her. She would have to see the solicitor again after all as a matter of urgency.

The paddle steamer had just docked at the pier when Cicely arrived in Dunoon. The town was full of day-trippers from Glasgow: ladies with parasols, children in their Sunday best, and men in straw boaters and bow ties. A brass band was playing at the bandstand in the Pleasure Gardens, and blankets were being spread out on the grass for picnics or to lay down babies.

Unlike last time, Dunoon's post office was empty. Although there was a small crowd of young men in caps hanging around outside the billiard room across the road, it appeared that most local people planned their days in the summer according to the paddle-steamer schedule and absented themselves as soon as one docked. The man behind the counter looked pleased to have something to do and glanced over her words quickly, calculating the price of the telegram rather than reading.

"Since it's international it's four shillings," he said apologetically.

She paid, then wrote down the name of the telegraphic office in India that George wanted it sent to. Should she have cushioned the blow? She still hadn't forgiven him completely for what he had asked her to do, and part of her wanted him to experience something of her ordeal. And yet she felt a pang of guilt despite the fact that he would never have to know about the misplaced satchel.

"Is there any mail for me?" she said.

"Not today, Mrs. Pick."

This wasn't a town where a person went unnoticed or unremembered. Several people had greeted her already, giving her a nod of the head or a tip of the hat. She smiled in return even though she had no idea who they might be. Mr. Drummond, the solicitor, however, acted as if he had never seen her before.

"I hope you don't mind," she said once the secretary had shown her into his office.

He clearly did mind and gathered up a pile of paper as if she had caught him in the middle of something.

"You don't have an appointment, do you?" he asked.

"No. I was just passing by and was wondering how everything is progressing."

She hoped to keep her tone light; it didn't have the desired effect. The solicitor stood up, hurried around the desk, and tried to usher her toward the door.

"I'll write when there is news," he said. "Until then—"

"Mr. Drummond," she said, holding out her palm. "We need to know how long it will take. Last time you assured me that it would take no more than a week, or at most a month."

"I said no such thing," he replied, his eyes bulging just a little with affront. "I do not have a crystal ball, and I must say it doesn't do any good to come barging in like this. It's just not how we do things here."

For a tiny moment she considered tears. But that would only cement what he clearly already thought of her.

"At least tell me why it is being held up?" she tried. "There must be an explanation, surely?"

"I'm afraid that is strictly confidential," he said as he opened the office door. "All I can say is that my client's affairs are rather more complex than they first appeared."

What could be complex about Edward Pick, she thought as the solicitor closed his door behind her. He was an old man, in his eighties, by all appearances. But who were the individuals Antonia's husband mentioned? Had he said it just to throw her off or was there some truth in it? Her hand formed a fist, and for an instant she was tempted to pound on Mr. Drummond's door, to insist he explain. Everything depended on the will, the legacy, and yet the one element that George had assured her was solid, fixed, certain, was moving away from them, evaporating before her eyes.

"Can I help you?" Mr. Drummond's secretary, a small woman with a large folded umbrella in one hand, was standing behind her on the stairwell.

Cicely's hand dropped; she shook her head and pulled on her gloves.

"No," she said. "No thank you."

She started to head back down the stairs, but the woman had no doubt seen her desperation. At the bottom her ears strained to hear the solicitor and his secretary. But she could not make out the words through the door, just the tone, and it was disparaging.

Once she had straightened her hat and composed herself again, Cicely stepped out into the street, walking at twice the pace of the other pedestrians, past children staring at window displays and queues for ice cream. At the end of Argyll Street she looked up to check for traffic, and saw Antonia's husband mingling with the paddle-steamer crowd on the other side, his hat pulled low on his brow. She ducked into a shop that sold animals made of seashells and sugar mice, and pretended to look at the postcards. At Malcolm's elbow, her head bowed to listen to what he was saying, was a woman. She was no longer young but elegantly dressed in a white blouse and a wide gray hobble skirt. As Cicely watched from behind the rack, they entered the Argyll Hotel together. Before he let the door close behind him, Malcolm quickly surveyed the street as if to make sure he hadn't been spotted. Poor Antonia. It appeared that her husband wasn't quite as devoted to her as he liked to make out.

Antonia hovered in the entrance of the glass house, adjusting the drapes and checking her hair with her hand. Her dress was a heavy silk crepe in a caramel shade with gold-thread embroidery around the bodice, her shoes were made of matching silk, and her mask was decorated with beads and feathers. Despite the fact that Malcolm had refused to join in and had not visited his tailors to procure a new outfit or bought a mask as she had asked him to, everything had fallen into place. She had taken off her glasses and pinned up her hair, she would dance a polka or two and drink the rum punch, she would inhabit Pick's Palace as its owner, not its caretaker, for Balmarra, as her father had always promised, was hers.

The evening wind was light, and the candles in the paper lanterns that hung on strings along the driveway barely flickered. Every windowpane, every column, every iron grating of the glass house had been swept or washed and polished. Five tables had been pushed together at one side, and fifty places had been set. In the garden, the lawns had been mowed, the bushes cut back, and even the main gates had been repainted. There was wine from London, flowers from a nursery in Kent, plus stone fruit from glass houses in East Lothian. Everyone had pulled together, the Baillies, Dora, Cook, Bill, plus a couple of local girls brought in to help.

It was just after seven. The guests would be arriving soon. Cicely was still in the house getting ready, and Malcolm was at the drinks table supervising the creation of the rum punch. They had barely had a moment alone since the argument. It remained within her, a rolling boil of tension and disquiet that would not cool down no matter how much she ignored it.

"And you just gave it to Lorimer?!" Malcolm had shouted. "Without any consultation?! Without telling me?!"

"I knew how you would react!" she said. "Besides, I broke his vase."

"But how do you know his was of the same value? It was probably a copy!"

"Malcolm, I'm sure that if it was, he would have said."

"I wouldn't be too sure about that," he replied. "He's a wealthy man for a reason."

And he had shaken his head as if she were a badly behaved schoolgirl instead of a fully grown woman about to hold a sophisticated social event.

"Anyway," she had said, "maybe my father's was the copy."

They both knew that this was unlikely. The one thing that Edward Pick was a stickler for was authenticity. He was adept at spotting fakes and liked to boast of how often he had avoided being duped. After that, the subject had been dropped.

She had decided that she would tell him the truth eventually, that she had sold the Etty for George. What business was it of his? Weren't they hers to sell anyway? And then, on a whim, she had written a card—she had invited Henry. She doubted he would come. She wondered if she had seen the last of him. Was it merely sympathy that had brought him to Hunter's Quay a few weeks before? She hoped not; she hoped that he had come because he had wanted to see her again as much as she him.

The band, an accordion and a fiddle player, were in the kitchen drinking tea. She had wanted something more contemporary, but in Dunoon, there was only one kind of musician and that was traditional. And now she wondered if she should have pushed the proverbial boat out and hired a string quartet? She took a final look round the glass house. Maybe the colored drapes were a little over the top? Too late now, she told herself. It would all have to do.

The minutes inched by, ten, then twenty, then thirty minutes past the hour. Her anxiety rose. Maybe she should take ill, call it all off, send everyone home, blow out all the candles, close all the doors. It was sure to be nothing short of a disaster, one of her own making.

Finally she heard a car approaching followed by the slamming of its doors. She pulled her mask over her face. It was an old couple from Kilfinan who had been friends of her father's. They looked slightly aghast at the decorations and the masks, but Malcolm quickly engaged them in conversation about the shooting season. Antonia hovered near the door as another couple of motorcars arrived and then a pony-and-trap. By eight there were two dozen guests and the band had started to play their first set of three. Apart from the first couple, most people had risen to the challenge, Antonia was pleased to see, and wore masks decorated with beads, feathers, and glitter. Laughter mingled with the music, a faint breeze lifted the colored fabric, the punch bowl had been refilled twice. It was all right, Antonia told herself. It was going to be all right.

"Good evening, Antonia!"

Keir Lorimer was dressed in an evening suit with tails and a black satin mask. He had brought a magnum of French champagne, a spray of orange orchids, and a large wooden box tied up with a pink satin ribbon that he placed in a chair.

She untied the ribbon and lifted the wooden lid. It was a gramophone.

"This is just on loan," he clarified. "It arrived last week, and I'm quite in love with it."

Lorimer rushed outside and brought back a copper horn and a small stack of recordings.

"Couldn't carry everything all at once," he said as he attached the horn to the machine. "Much heavier than they look."

"How thoughtful of you," Antonia replied.

"There's some ragtime," he said as she sorted through the discs. "A turkey trot, a cakewalk, and a bunny hop."

"Maybe you could choose one, Mr. Lorimer?" she suggested.

But his gaze was fixed elsewhere.

Cicely Pick was standing, quite still, at the door. She was wearing an ivory silk dress, and her hair was pinned up and fastened with pearl-encrusted combs. Her mask, the more lavish of the two Antonia had ordered, was white and embossed with pearls. With her head slightly tilted to the left, she appeared to be waiting for the answer to a question, perhaps. Lorimer seemed to pull himself back to the moment, to Antonia.

"Anyway, lovely setup you have here!" he said.

But she had seen his eyes even behind his mask. It was a look she recognized. Best pretend she hadn't. That was the beauty of masks.

"Thank you," she replied. "We're so pleased you could come."

She placed a drink in his hand and was just about to introduce him to the nearest guests when he stopped her.

"I must pay my respects to Mrs. Pick," he said. "Excuse me."

Soon the paths and dance floor of the glass house thronged with peacock feathers and taffeta, diamanté and satin. All the doors had to be opened to let in some cool air. When the band took a break, Antonia wound up the gramophone, and the glass house filled with the heady blast of trumpets and the trombones. At first no one danced. But then a few of the younger guests, people who spent time regularly in London or Paris and knew about the craze for animal dances, took the floor and demonstrated the steps. Soon everyone had their hands raised into claws as they danced the grizzly bear.

At nine-thirty Dora rang the bell for dinner. A large table had been set with plates, cutlery, food, and wine so that the guests could serve themselves. And yet the dishes that had sounded so exotic in the kitchen only a few days earlier were less impressive in reality. Although it was flavorsome, Cook had not mastered the intricacies of a rice pilaf. It was so overcooked that the rice had the consistency of a pudding, and the raisins were either bloated or burned. Nevertheless that didn't stop the guests loading their plates and sitting down at one of the tables.

"Indian fare!" Malcolm said as he took a place opposite Cicely. "You must feel quite at home?"

"Actually we rarely eat curry at home," Cicely replied. "Our chef cooks in the French style."

Lorimer, who was sitting a few chairs along from her, let out a laugh. No one ate much of the mutton. A few people persevered, gulping down water in huge quantities, but most complained that it was just too spicy. Antonia's mouth burned as she forced down a forkful, purely to make a point. They would be eating it for days, she joked. But maybe it didn't matter. She drank a glass of punch and then another.

"We should do this again," said Malcolm. "Maybe at Christmas. If one celebrates Christmas in Bengal?"

Antonia looked at him. Was he serious? He had been so against the idea. His face was flushed, and his eyes blinked a little too often. And then she saw he was staring at Cicely.

"You could advise Cook in the matter of French cuisine," he said. "If you're still here, that is."

It was poised as an innocent remark, a joke even. And yet it wasn't.

"Malcolm!" she warned with a smile.

"I've actually grown rather fond of the place," Cicely replied. "Dunoon is rather gay when the paddle steamer docks. Even on a Friday afternoon, wouldn't you say?"

And then the most peculiar thing happened. Malcolm stared at her openmouthed and started to choke so badly that Lorimer had to whack him on the back with the flat of his hand. Antonia wasn't a fool. Something had been revealed, something that Malcolm didn't want anyone to know—especially, she supposed, her. And then she remembered the hotel receipt she had found. Port and lemon. Lemon and port. He might have taken a lady client out for a drink. It could have been perfectly innocent. But another narrative spun out in her head like a reel of thread that had been dropped. A woman drunk on port, the taste of lemon on her lips, the lace of her underwear transparent in the afternoon sun. She glanced at her husband's hands, at his short, thick fingers folding his napkin into a smaller and smaller square. He was opaque, his heart invisible in his chest. He could do whatever he liked, and she would never guess.

A breeze rattled the glass, and it started to rain so heavily that buckets were deployed to catch the drips from the leaks in the roof. Rather than detract from the atmosphere, the storm added to it, the guests shrieking as they dodged streams of water or were suddenly soaked. The masks made it impossible to read a face, and so people laughed more loudly, gestured more expressively, walked and danced and moved like players on a stage. The party was going better than she had hoped. And yet Antonia was suffused with disappointment.

The plates had just been collected when they all heard the sound of the front door slamming. The man who appeared was wet through. His suit was badly fitting, and his wet shoes left prints on the iron grating. He wasn't, all the other guests noticed, wearing a mask.

"Can I help you?" Malcolm said, standing up.

"So sorry I'm late," he said, handing his hat to Dora. "I walked from Hunter's Quay."

"You came!" Antonia said, leaping up from her seat to shake Henry Morris's hand in welcome. "I'm so, so glad."

14

Cicely was sitting at the other end of the dining table from Lorimer, but even so she was aware of him, had her ear tuned to his conversations to pick up the odd word. When the late guest arrived, they all shifted to make room, and this brought Lorimer a little closer. His eyes were liquid through the slits in his black satin mask. In a sea of badly cut wool, he looked elegant and relaxed. His suit was a perfect fit. A lick of his dark hair fell forward, and he kept sweeping it back with his hand. He noticed her looking at him and looked right back. Cicely blushed beneath her mask. No one saw, no one knew—no one but him.

The food was finished, and the band was about to begin a second set. Antonia was deep in conversation with the late guest and hadn't noticed. Malcolm was still in a fizz after her comment. She hadn't meant to say anything, but he had put her on the spot. Lorimer leaned forward and seemed to be about to engage her in conversation. There were two options open to her: she could ignore him, which would be awkward for both of them, or she could initiate her own: She decided on the latter. The band called the Dashing White Sergeant. The dancers took their positions.

"Mr. Lorimer, will you join me?" Cicely asked.

"Keir, please," he corrected. "And I'm sorry, but I don't know any of these dances."

"Then I'll teach you," she replied.

He hesitated but then relented. On the dance floor she took his hand and showed him the steps.

"It's really very simple," she said.

"Where did you learn to dance?" he asked.

"At school," she replied.

"I didn't go to that sort of school."

"What sort of school did you go to?"

He didn't answer. The dance began, but he was always on the wrong foot, two steps behind, confused, out of time.

"Sorry," he said. "So sorry."

The next dance was Strip the Willow. It was far simpler. The women danced with all the men, one after another, first Lorimer, then the doctor, then eventually Henry Morris, whose damp clothes still gently steamed on his body. At the end Cicely came back to Lorimer, who held her a little tighter than before. The next dance was about to begin. Lorimer suggested they go out for a breath of fresh air to cool down a little.

The rain had stopped, and the darkness was dense as velvet. The glass house had steamed up with condensation, and the colors of the paper lanterns, red and orange and green, and the flicker of candles blurred through the windowpanes. Cicely shivered. Lorimer offered his jacket, and she was glad of its many layers of silk and wool.

"Smoke?" he asked, pulling off his mask. He lit two cigarettes and passed her one. She inhaled, then blew a pale stream into the air and watched as it rose up and drifted away. A burst of laughter came from inside the glass house. Someone was doing an impression of Prime Minister Asquith. "Malcolm was right," Lorimer said. "You should do this again, here in the glass house."

"Maybe," she said.

Maybe the new owners would hold parties? Or maybe they would demolish it?

"But your father-in-law is probably spinning in his grave," Lorimer continued. "All these people having a nice time among his precious plants."

"Or he might have enjoyed it?"

"Did you ever meet Edward Pick?"

She shook her head no.

"He wasn't one for social occasions," he said. "Although I'm sure there was a side to him, another side. He did love his exotic blooms. I'm sure he would approve of the collection."

"What collection?"

Keir didn't explain.

"Why don't you take off your mask?" he continued softly. "Or is that breaking the rules?"

She took her mask off, feeling suddenly exposed.

"That's better," he said. "I can see you now."

She watched as the smoke from her cigarette mingled with his. Her mind started to turn; if her father hadn't met George in that bar in Darjeeling, if she hadn't been taken on that very first hunt for plants, if she had not skipped all those lessons in piano and dancing, if she had not made all those choices, then where would she be? But she couldn't regret any of it. If it hadn't happened, she would not have had Kitty.

"I never replied to your card," she said.

"I know."

He was standing close, so close she could smell his cologne and beneath it something else, the giddy hint of adrenaline that matched her own. Was it the dancing that made his breathing a little rapid? His jaw was clenched, his head bowed, and she felt a dissonance of contradictory impulses that made the air around them seemed to tremble. Why not go for a ride in his plane? In her place George wouldn't have hesitated.

"So," she said, "is the offer still open?"

"How about tomorrow morning?" he asked. "The forecast's good. I'll send a car for you."

The door closed behind them with a crash, making them both jump.

"Have either of you seen Antonia?" Malcolm asked.

Cicely shook her head, then pulled her mask back on.

"If you do, please tell her that I'm looking for her."

The door slammed again. For a moment they stood perfectly still. The storm had passed, and yet Cicely could hear the rain pounding against the glass, like applause. Suddenly the door flew open and Antonia appeared.

"Here you are!" she said. "Cicely, I have a surprise."

Inside the glass house the guests were clapping—it wasn't rain— standing in a semicircle, looking at her with an expression that she could read only as pity. Antonia explained that she had orchestrated a collection for George's expedition. As she went on to explain his plant-hunting trip in detail, Cicely stopped listening. She felt physically ill. It was like a whip-round—a charity collection.

"I need to check on Kitty," she said.

"But you're coming back?" Antonia said.

She gave a small nod, even though she had already decided that wild horses would not drag her back.

Henry wore a frock coat and starched wingtip collar of a style popular in the 1890s. But then, he wasn't the only one. Folded-down collars and knotted neckties of the type worn by Lorimer were still a something of a novelty outside Glasgow and Edinburgh. Maybe it had something to do with the way that time slid by so slowly in these parts that it almost felt as if you were standing still, caught in the amber of a moment where nothing changed. It was an illusion, of course. Everything was changing faster by the day. Motorcars were replacing ponies and traps, ships were sailing across the Atlantic at record speeds; the skies were filled with airships and airplanes. No wonder Antonia had the impression that she had been left behind.

"Was I last to arrive?" asked Henry.

Antonia waved her hand.

"Last but not least," she said.

She had taken off her mask in solidarity with Henry, and it now dangled from her wrist by a cord and felt vaguely ridiculous. Henry seemed nervous. He complimented her dress, her hair, the decorations, the food—in fact everything thing he laid eyes on.

"I must introduce you. . . ." she said but she didn't clarify to whom. Her eye fell on Malcolm, who was sitting on a bench on his own. A tiny frown gave her away; Henry looked from Antonia to Malcolm and knew. His face registered sympathy, disappointment, concern. Yes, she had married the red-haired lawyer, who laughed too loudly and who did not care for painting or flowers or the distant slant of sun across a moorland. But then again, why not? Henry had not wanted her.

The accordionist caught her eye. She had paid them to play until ten, and it was already a quarter to. How could time have passed so quickly? With a crush of the accordion, the fiddle player announced the final reel of the night.

"Shall we dance?" Henry asked. The very last thing on earth Antonia felt like doing was dancing. She was, she knew, not talented in that art. Henry was still looking at her expectantly.

"Why not?" she said.

He held out his hand, and they moved, not without grace, around the floor.

"It's been years since I've been here," Henry said. "I can't remember the last time."

But Antonia could. It was the day he had promised to deliver the finished painting to her father. She had been waiting, hovering near the front door. The hours slipped by, and the daylight turned to dusk. When she finally went to dinner, there was the painting, hanging in the hallway.

"Why didn't you let me know he was here?" she asked her father. "Didn't he ask to see me?"

"The man was only here for ten minutes or so," her father had told her. "Came in through the servants' entrance. He was in a rush to get back. Didn't want to keep him."

He had looked at her strangely then, a look that she had tried to replay in her mind many times.

"What do you think of my painting?" her father had asked.

At that point she was ambivalent. She shrugged.

"It's what you wanted, isn't it?" she had said.

"Exactly so," he had replied.

She had written to Henry once, twice, three times, each letter a little less hopeful of a response, each one indicating possible reasons why he might not reply, such as, "You're probably in Paris," or "I imagine you have a show."

Weeks passed and then months, until finally she accepted that the excuses she herself had suggested had long since expired and he had not responded because he didn't want to. She put away her paints and brushes. It would be a year and a half before she could look at a tube of burnt sienna and not feel bereft.

And now he was here again, and her father was gone. She glanced at the painter's face, his chin, strong beneath the whiskers, his ear, his mouth. Why had he forsaken her?

"Can I tell you something?" he asked.

She nodded.

"All those years ago, I wanted to see you again. I wanted to, but—"

She lost count of her steps. She tripped over her feet.

"What are you trying to say?" she said. "Could it be that maybe you shouldn't?"

He paused, he sighed. He clearly could not contain it. And so he told her.

The room spun, a haze of blues and reds and greens. And suddenly she saw Edward Pick making his point with a wave of the hand and a good-bye where he never had the good manners to make eye contact. Henry had not known the paintings and sketchbooks her father had showed him were hers. He had been led on, encouraged, provoked. But then again, maybe he could have guessed.

Antonia's feet stopped. She stood still.

"You mean it was you?" she said. "You were my father's expert?"

Henry stared at the string of paper lights as if trying to read a message.

"You told him that I had no artistic talent?" she continued.

He turned to her, and he looked as if he might be about to weep.

"It wasn't true, you know," he whispered.

Why hadn't it occurred to her before? Because it was not such a stretch of the imagination to regard herself as unworthy.

A sensation returned that she had buried deep, a moment from long ago: Henry's hand on her shoulder as he pointed out something on the horizon—a bird, a boat, she couldn't remember what—and the way it lingered there like the physical manifestation of an intention. He had been so close that she could feel his breath, the rise and fall of it, the buzzing hum of him only inches away. It was unmistakable, she saw that now, but somehow she had convinced herself it was paternal, platonic.

"For a time I thought we might have eloped," Henry said and looked her straight in the eye.

A flash of anger sparked, then just as suddenly subsided. Would she have gone, abandoned all she had if he had asked her to? Would she have had the courage? She hadn't had much of it then, not enough even to question her father or defy the so-called professional opinion.

"We'd have ended up in limbo," she said softly, "in some god-awful place like Eastbourne or Calais."

The last song finished with a sigh. Coats were collected, cigarettes put out, drinks downed. Cicely had not come back from checking on Kitty. And then it was a round of good-byes and thank-you-for-comings as the bucket at the door filled up with donations for George's expedition. The band packed up their instruments and gave Henry a lift to the ferry. By a quarter past ten, everyone had gone, everyone but Malcolm, standing below an orange tree, finishing off a glass of wine.

"You know why everyone came, don't you?" he said.

Antonia decided that would not rise to the bait, she would not react. But it didn't matter what she did or said: He was going to tell her anyway.

"It's your sister-in-law," he continued.

"What about her?"

"Can't you see?"

"Whatever are you talking about, Malcolm?"

"Her color," he said. "They all want to see it for themselves."

Antonia remembered Lorimer's party with a lurch. The tiny triumph she had felt when she had revealed Cicely's mixed blood seemed pathetic now. She was sure it hadn't taken long for the news to spread; George's wife was part Hindustani.

"What color are you talking about?" she asked, knowing all too well.

"Dark," he whispered theatrically. "Mixed race, half-caste, a sambo. Her ancestors were not all white, that's clear. Same goes for your niece. And then you top it off by asking for a handout on her behalf."

"Not for her, for George."

"Same difference. Making her look like a charity case."

"Surely she wouldn't think that?"

"Why do you think she rushed off and didn't come back?"

Malcolm seemed on the brink of saying more. His red hair seemed to stand on end, his fingers seemed to curl in on themselves, his teeth clenched. She would not agree, acquiesce, or submit to him this time.

"You know," she said lightly. "I don't really care why people came, but the fact is that they did. And I, for one, had a wonderful time."

15

Cicely woke in the gray light of dawn, her mind going over and over the same facts, her body twisted up in the sheets, too hot, too restless, to sleep. Images of the night before came unbidden into sharp focus—the glass house from outside all lit up in the dark, the table of untouched food, Lorimer's face in the half-dark, the humiliation of Antonia's collection.

She opened her eyes, rose, dressed quickly, and crept into Kitty's room. Kitty was still sound asleep, her breathing steady, a small smile on her face. She had no idea how fragile the world was, how close it was to falling apart. Once Cicely had kissed her gently on the forehead, she tiptoed down the stairs, along the hall, closed the front door quietly behind her, and headed up one of the paths that led to the glen. She had to be outside, to feel the cold, clean air in her chest, to clear her head, to pick over the confusion she felt, to try to make sense of the night before.

The ground was damp with dew, and a fine mist hung in the air. Everything was more intense than her memory of it—the vivid orange bracken, the evergreen trees, and the deep dank smell of the earth. She'd had only one glass of punch the night before, but even so her head hurt, her hands trembled, her heart wouldn't stop churning.

A light sweat bloomed at her hairline and around her neck, but the skin immediately cooled.

When she finally looked up she found herself in a small clearing. A makeshift shelter of sticks had been built against a bank. It was a child's den, with a small doorway just large enough to duck through. Kitty must have built it. Cicely ducked inside, where there was a log to sit on and a biscuit tin very like one she had seen in the kitchen. Was she intruding? Kitty need never know. She pried the tin open. It contained a collection of dried petals and a pair of secateurs, a couple of stale biscuits, and a penknife. She imagined her daughter playing at plant hunting, collecting, and harvesting just like her father. A knot formed in her chest, a tangle of pride and love and sadness. George would have been proud of her if he had been there. But George wasn't there. In truth, he hadn't been a part of their lives for a long time.

The glass house had been swept and tidied, but some of the detritus of the party remained. Lorimer had left his gramophone and all the records. No doubt his coachman would come and pick them up in the next few days. She picked up a disc at random, placed it on the velvet-covered turntable, and gave the handle a few cranks. Then, carefully, as Lorimer had, she placed the needle in a groove. The music blared out, louder than she expected, wheezy with brass. The sound bounced around the huge glass house, drowning out the dripping pipes and the rumble of the boiler, and just for a moment she imaged herself transported to another place, another country, another life. All she had was this one, however, and she had to find a way to make it work out.

"Mrs. Pick?" a voice rang out above the music.

Young Mr. Baillie was standing a few feet away. His shirt was un-buttoned at the throat. She lifted the needle from the black celluloid.

"Sorry. Did I startle you?" he said.

"A little," she replied. "Isn't this a wonderful contraption?"

He nodded. Cicely suddenly felt foolish, listening to Lorimer's gramophone alone and so early in the morning.

"I was wondering," she said. "Did you lend Kitty some gardening tools?"

"I did," Baillie replied. "She's started collecting specimens with a passion. She takes after her father."

Carefully Cicely placed the disc back in its paper sleeve. She didn't want to scratch or damage it.

"The seeds are doing well," he added. "Whatever it is, it's not native. I've looked everywhere, and the closest I can find is *Davidia Involucrata,* but the leaves are a slightly different shape."

What was he talking about? She had a vague memory of another conversation with him, earlier that summer, but couldn't summon the details. A car was approaching along the driveway.

"What time is it?" she asked.

"Around nine," young Mr. Baillie replied. "Are you expecting anyone?"

"Heavens, I forgot!" she said. "Yes, I am."

Keir Lorimer's driver held the back door open as she climbed inside. The early-morning mist had burned off, and patches of blue sky appeared above. The wind was light and the air was crisp. And yet Cicely barely saw or felt any of it. Was she properly prepared? Was this a good idea? All the certainty she had felt the night before had now evaporated.

The airfield was exactly that, a field with a mown strip down the middle and a covered shed at one end. Lorimer was waiting for her beside his biplane, a wood-and-canvas construction with two cubbyholes for a pilot and passenger. In his hand he held a spare pair of goggles and a leather flying cap.

"I missed you last night," Lorimer said. "When you didn't come back."

Cicely smiled but didn't respond. She wanted to put the memory of the previous night behind her—lock it in a box and throw the key away.

"Anyway, here she is," he said. "I call her Baby."

The plane looked as fragile as a child's toy. Cicely was suddenly apprehensive. The newspapers were full of stories of planes crashing and aviators being killed.

"It is safe?" she asked.

"I'm a much better pilot than I am a dancer," he said.

He smiled at her, and she had no doubt that this was true.

"Hand me the glasses," she said.

"The goggles," he corrected. "I'll lend you a warm jacket. And push your hair into the cap. It can get a little windy up there."

She pulled the flying cap over her head, then the goggles, and put the jacket on. It was so big the sleeves covered her hands. Lorimer helped her up into the passenger seat, then climbed into the seat behind. The engine roared to life, loud, much louder than the car. They jerked forward and headed to the top of the field.

"Ready?" Lorimer shouted. "It'll be a bit rough until takeoff."

As they raced across the bumpy ground of the field, the plane rattled so violently that she was sure it was going to fall apart. And then, just when she was about to beg him to slow down, to stop, they lifted into the air. The field, the road, the land all fell away. Below, the loch stretched out blue and black beneath the ruffled surface. The coastline, a crinkled edge frayed with weed. As they passed above Dunoon people stopped in the street to look up and watch them. Children waved hello. They flew over Lorimer's place, then Balmarra and Karrasay, then skimmed the green-and-purple velvet hills behind, sending deer in all directions, the white of their tails flashing against the bracken. Eventually they turned, a great looping semicircle, and flew west, over nameless peninsulas, islands, headlands, and lighthouses to the open sea. Here there were fishing boats and gulls, tiny islands and a score of black shags, and then only the scud of the surf and a vast swell of blue.

High, high above the world, she felt every inch of herself tingle.

She was aware of Lorimer's eyes on the back of her neck, of his body behind her. Both were strapped in tight to this construction of leather and wood, paper and steel: they were part of it, two living souls against the mechanical whir of the motor, the propeller chopping the air into a silver blur. If only they could remain here, now, in this moment.

They made another turn; the sun was in her eyes, her throat narrowed, and she was glad he could not read her face. The landscape became familiar, and she recognized the Clyde and their rippling shadow on its surface. And then the peninsula, the town, the airfield. Landing was worse than taking off. She closed her eyes and couldn't look; she wasn't expecting the jolt and jar as the wheels hit the ground, and let out a scream. They were going so fast that for a moment she was sure they would crash or catch fire or hit the fence at the edge of the field.

"It's all right!" Lorimer yelled from behind. "We made it!"

Once the engine was switched off and the propeller whirred to a standstill, the silence seemed louder than ever. Lorimer helped her down and lifted the goggles from her eyes.

"Well?" he said. "Glad you came?"

"I don't think I'll ever see the world in quite the same way again," she said. "Thank you for showing me."

"Now you see why I'm addicted," he said. "It's like nothing else."

The wind blew across the field and seemed to stroke the unmown parts like a hand over a pelt. Two shafts of sunlight fell from the clouds into the loch, turning the water to molten silver. With the wind, the sun, the silence, the moment seemed to slow down, to frame itself.

"It's beautiful down here too," she said.

"But everyone can see this," he replied.

"Not everyone does," she replied.

Lorimer took a deep breath and let it out. She pulled off the flying cap, handed it to him, and shook out her hair. He took it, and for a fraction of a second before letting go, she felt the current from his hand, through the cap, to hers.

"It must be beautiful in the Himalayas too," he said. "All those remote valleys."

What was he suggesting? She had a sudden desire to tell him everything, about her broken marriage, about George.

"Keir—"

"Tell me," he interrupted. "Have you heard of the Snow Tree? It grows out there, in the middle of nowhere, in the Himalayas. In the breeze its white leaves look like a snowstorm."

"I suppose you want it for your garden," she said.

"Everyone wants the Snow Tree," he replied.

He was staring out at the fields. The clouds had closed over, and the light was gone.

"Keir?"

"I have a man out there," he continued. "Looking for it, amongst other things."

"A man?"

"His name's Magnus Hayes. You know him? Or perhaps your husband does? He was recommended."

Cicely's vision suddenly pricked with spots of light. She placed her hand on the car to steady herself.

"Are you all right?" said Lorimer. "Mrs. Pick?"

"I'm feeling a little faint," she replied. "Actually, could you drive me home?"

Antonia had taken down all her journals and sketchbooks from the top shelf and was looking through them one by one. Illuminated by the morning sun that streamed through the library window were pages and pages of watercolors, drawings in ink and pencil, of the hills, of flowers, of trees, of heathers and hedgerows, years and years of work. What might she have become if she had gone to art school and been tutored? What direction might her work have taken? Her father had conspired to keep her close, to instill such a lack of confidence in her that she had never left him. And despite the fact that she had loved him, she suddenly saw him for what he was: a vain and selfish man. She felt the singe of sadness. What was the point of all his wealth, his land, his gardens, his good fortune, if he could not use them to nurture others?

There was a light knock on the door. Kitty was standing on the threshold.

"Can I come in?" she asked.

"Of course."

Kitty glanced down at the sketchbooks, picked one up, and carefully began turning the pages.

"Who did these?" she asked.

"I did," Antonia replied.

"They're very good," she said.

"You think so?

The letterbox banged shut as the post arrived. Dora brought up two letters both addressed to her. One was a bill from the dressmaker. The other was from the India Office in London. It could be a circular, a plea for charitable donation, or something else equally benign, and yet Antonia felt something plummet within her. Kitty seemed to sense it.

"What is it?" she asked.

"Oh, nothing, just a bill."

"Can I borrow some of these, Aunt Antonia?"

She started, unused to being addressed thus.

"Sorry, yes, as many as you'd like," she said.

Once Kitty was gone, she sat down, inhaled deeply, and then let the breath go. Then she slipped her thumb underneath the flap and opened the letter. It seemed that George, her brother, had gone missing. Some belongings identified as his had been found in a remote valley. The India Office would write again as soon as there was more news. They had attempted to inform his wife, but their letters had been returned. Could she pass on the news?

16

Cicely woke up in the late afternoon. The light outside was a flat solid gray that seemed to press down on her head like granite. She was lying on her bed still fully dressed. She could barely remember the drive home. A fever had plastered her hair in damp strands around her face, and her skin was covered with a film of sweat. She sat up, nudged her legs over the edge of the bed, and tried to stand. A wave of nausea hit her. She was going to be sick. She placed both feet on the floor and slowly rose. If only she could get to the bathroom she might be all right. But the bathroom at the end of the corridor suddenly seemed so far away, farther than she could possibly walk. She launched herself across the floor, each step taking a Herculean effort. What was wrong with her? Had it been the plane ride? That terrible conversation with Keir? Her limbs were as heavy as stone, she couldn't catch her breath, the carpet was treacherously far below.

Dora found her on her knees in the hallway. She gathered her up, took her back to her room, helped her undress, and put her to bed. Then she brought a damp cloth and a bowl full of cool, clean water. A note was immediately sent to the doctor, and he was there within the hour.

"I'm sorry to tell you that it looks like malaria," he said once he had examined her. "Easy to become infected on the Indian subcontinent, but it can take weeks, sometimes, to flare up."

Cicely remembered the long hot journey across the plains from Darjeeling. She remembered the chug and rattle of the train as they passed through rice fields and across low-lying water. A signal changed, and they had stopped next to a stagnant pond at dusk, the sky reflecting like a disk of light in the dark, for some time. The air had been gray with clouds of mosquitoes that shifted and bloomed like smoke. Kitty had been curled up in her lap asleep. Cicely knew that she should have closed the window, but she didn't want to wake her daughter—she looked so peaceful, so serene, the smooth skin of her cheek warm and soft—and instead covered her up with a scarf. Later, she recalled, Cicely tried not to scratch the raised angry red welts of dozens of bites on her arms and ankles while Kitty, thankfully, had none.

Dora helped her sit up as the doctor gave a spoonful of medicine to deal with the fever. Within a few minutes her eyelids were so heavy that she had to close them. When she opened them again, the doctor was gone. How long had she slept? It felt like minutes but could have been hours. Time seemed to slip, to skip and jump. It was the dead of night and then the morning again; the doctor was there in a different suit urging her to swallow more medicine. But still her muscles ached, and her head spun. One moment she was so hot that her skin ran with sweat and salt; the next she was chilled right through, her teeth chattering. The light hurt her eyes, and so the curtains were closed all the time. Days lost their shape. At one point everything seemed to shrink until all she was conscious of was the spoonful of liquid, the bitter taste it left in her mouth once, twice, multiple times. Her heart wasn't keeping time anymore, but losing it; her head felt leaden, her hands huge, and she couldn't distinguish between dreams and consciousness.

Sometimes she woke to find Nani, her Indian grandmother, sitting beside the bed, draped in a sari rather than the dress she usually wore. The rattle of her glass bangles and the smell of her perfume, jasmine and cloves, filled the room. Once she took Cicely's face in her hands, her rings cold against her cheek, and comforted her, whispering words in her ear that she didn't understand. But Nani had been dead for years.

"Hush now," said an unfamiliar voice. She opened her eyes. It was not Nani but Antonia. How long had she been there? It was dark outside, the middle of the night. Antonia was in her nightdress. Had she cried out in her sleep and woken her?

"How are you feeling?" asked Antonia.

"Strange," Cicely replied.

"You must rest. It will take a while, the doctor said. You've been very ill."

Cicely licked her lips and found them cracked. Her head was too heavy to lift off the pillow.

"My grandmother was here," she said. "In this room."

Antonia's mouth fixed, and she started to plump her pillows and straighten the sheets.

"You've been dreaming," she replied.

It was no use; she didn't have the strength to argue.

"If I die—" Cicely began.

"It hasn't come to that," she interrupted.

Cicely swallowed and gathered all her strength.

"If I do," she said. "Will you look after Kitty for me?"

Antonia blinked, and tears formed in her eyes.

"Of course," she replied, then took her hand and held it tight. "But that won't happen, I promise."

Antonia sat beside Cicely until she fell asleep again. A fire had been kept burning in the grate, and the windows were closed. The heat was oppressive and made Antonia feel light-headed. The truth was that the doctor hadn't been that optimistic. Malaria was a serious illness. Complications were common: organ failure, fluid on the lungs, or swelling of the blood vessels in the brain. Cicely's face was pale, and one arm lay above the covers, folded across her body as if it were a corpse. Antonia fought down a rise of panic. How would she get word to her brother if Cicely died? And where *was* her brother? He had probably gone off alone—it wouldn't be the first time he had shed most of his belongings and continued on with just a rucksack. But what if he had had an accident, his body lying at the bottom of a ravine or in an unreachable valley? How would she face Kitty? The girl would be an orphan. It was just too awful to contemplate. And why had she promised something she had no power to influence? Antonia felt an absence in the room already, a stillness to the air. She listened to Cicely breathe, in and out, in and out, as regular as the tide. Was that a rattle? She hoped not. Please get better, she silently prayed: Don't leave us.

"We'll just have to send the girl back to India," said Malcolm over breakfast the next morning.

"By herself?" Antonia replied. "Out of the question!"

"What have you told her?"

"Kitty? I haven't told her anything."

"Do you think she knows?"

Antonia shook her head. How would a child that age know?

"Well, we can't keep her here indefinitely," Malcolm said. "She must have relatives."

"We're her relatives," she replied.

Why couldn't they adopt her, if it came to that? Kitty was her niece, after all. And who else did she have?

"We must do for her what her mother wanted," she replied and rose from the table. "I'll check on her now."

Kitty was sitting on the nursery window seat, staring out. It had been raining all night, and the garden paths were muddy. Since Cicely had been ill, Antonia had been spending more time with her niece, first at mealtimes and then in the afternoon when Malcolm was at work. They played jackstraws, worked jigsaws, and Antonia pulled out some of her favorite books, *Treasure Island* and *Heidi*, and promised to read them aloud to her.

"Good morning," Antonia said brightly. "What are your plans for today?"

The girl shrugged.

"It's so wet outside. And my boots are still damp from yesterday."

Antonia sat down beside Kitty, who leaned back so her body was resting against her. It was such a trusting gesture, so instinctive, that Antonia had to resist the urge to hug her tight, to comfort her as a parent would. But, she reasoned, it might be the wrong thing to do; Kitty might object, push her away. She had never been around children, did not know what they wanted.

"How is Mummy today?" Kitty asked.

"She's sleeping," she replied.

"She's *always* sleeping."

"It's the body's way of getting better," Antonia replied.

For a moment they were both silent.

"Is that true?" Kitty asked.

"What do you mean?"

"Is she going to get better?" Kitty's voice broke. "I mean, it's been ages."

Without thinking, Antonia pulled Kitty into her shoulder as she started to cry in big gulping breaths.

"She's going to be fine," she whispered. "I promise."

"Are you sure?"

"I'm sure," she replied.

Now she had made two promises, neither of which she was confident she could keep. Once Kitty's sobs had subsided, she laid her cheek against Antonia's shoulder for a moment before pulling away, wiping her face with her sleeve and then staring out of the window again.

"I wish it would stop raining," she said.

"You must be bored here," Antonia said. "With no one to play with."

"I was supposed to go to school," she replied.

"You still can. In fact, you must."

Kitty pulled back and looked at her.

"And leave Mummy?"

"You can still come home at the weekends and see her. It's what she would want."

"Really?"

"Absolutely."

Kitty cocked her head to one side.

"I suppose I could," she said.

"We'll need to buy you a uniform. There's a shop in Glasgow we'll need to go to get you kitted out. And I'll write to the school today and let them know the situation and find out the dates. How does that sound?"

Kitty nodded. Antonia stood up. It was good to do something, to have a plan.

"As long as you're sure Mummy wouldn't mind."

"I'm sure. I know she wouldn't."

"Thank you, Aunt Antonia."

Antonia nodded; she couldn't speak. A lump had risen up in her throat. The poor girl, one parent at death's door and the other God knows where.

"Whatever happens," she whispered, "you have me. You know that, don't you?"

17

Cicely was dreaming of snow, a blizzard of white that softened and blurred. How easy it would be for it to envelope her. She heard voices in the hallway speaking first her name, then George's. Was it the minister come to pray by her bedside for recovery, for mercy? Or was it the undertaker come to measure her for a casket? Then an echo in her ear, a voice.

"Mummy," said her daughter. "Don't leave me."

And then, as if being dropped into the moment from a very great height, she woke up. The world seemed to stop spinning, to fix itself. There was no one in the room, no snow. She was alone.

"Kitty!" she called. The light hurt her eyes, and she covered her face with her arms. She climbed out of bed, surprised at how weak she felt. Her bare feet on the wooden floorboards sensed every groove, every splinter. Carefully, tentatively, she walked toward her daughter's bedroom. The connecting door had been left ajar, as she always insisted. Her daughter's bed was made, but the room was empty.

"Kitty!" she called again. "Kitty?"

She didn't care who she woke or what time it was. Anxiety filled her chest like air. Where was her girl?

"Get back into bed!" It was Dora, her hair in a loose plait, wearing her nightclothes.

"Kitty's not here," Cicely said.

Dora wouldn't meet her eye as she propelled her back to her room.

"Where is she?" she insisted. "Dora!"

"I'll tell you in a minute, but first let's get you sorted."

Once Cicely was back in bed, the sheets and blankets shaken, the covers tucked, Dora sat down on the chair beside her.

"School," she said. "She's gone to boarding school."

"But she doesn't start until September."

"It's already September," Dora explained. "We've all been worried about you, Mrs. Pick."

"I need to go to her, to make sure she's all right."

"But it's six in the morning. You can't go anywhere. Not now, at least."

Cicely took a deep breath and let it out slowly. How could so much time have passed? How could so much have happened and she not be aware of any of it?

"How are you feeling?" Dora asked.

"I'm not sure. I don't remember anything," she said.

"The doctor gave you medicine. He said it might cause memory loss. I'll make us both a cup of tea, shall I?"

Cicely did feel as if something had changed—a slip, a blur, the world not quite what it had once been. She glanced around the room. Two huge vases full of flowers stood on the dressing table, and a fire was burning in the grate. There was a small pile of books next to the bed that she didn't recognize. She closed her eyes for a second, and when she woke again it was midmorning. A cup of stone-cold tea sat on her bedside table. Someone was knocking at her door.

"Come in!" she called.

"I heard you'd woken up," Antonia said. "If you sit up I'll fix your pillows."

"Where did all the flowers come from?" Cicely asked as Antonia fussed with the bedding.

"Lorimer's been sending them every week," she replied. "We've practically run out of vases. And I suppose you heard from Dora that Kitty's started school?"

"How can that be? I haven't paid the school fees, Antonia," she said. "Or bought the uniform."

Cicely's eyes filled with tears. Antonia sat on the bed, took off her glasses, and started to polish them.

"That's all been dealt with," she said. "She'll be home at the weekend to see you. She spent hours sitting at your bedside, you know."

Cicely lay back on the pillow. She didn't have the energy to object. She closed her eyes.

"I'm so tired," she said.

"Just work on getting better."

"Any word from my husband?" she asked.

"From George? No," she said.

When she woke again it was dark outside. The house was silent; everyone was asleep. She climbed out of bed, pulled on her robe and slipped her feet into a pair of shoes, took the lamp and, pausing frequently to catch her breath, crept downstairs and out the front door. The night air was chill on her bare skin, but at least there was no wind. Inside, the glass house was warm and damp. There was something comforting about the smell of earth, the steady roar of the subterranean boiler, and the rattle of the iron pipes. And there, in a square of moonlight, was a small seedling with tiny white leaves.

Antonia arranged the roses, taking one out at a time and returning it to the vase in a slightly different position. They were tea-scented Chinas, pale pink and vibrant yellow, with full heads that drooped if you weren't careful, like overtired debutantes at a dance. She paused and listened for movement from Cicely's room. The house was quiet.

Nothing moved but the curtains that occasionally swirled in a draft. It was best to keep everything calm, she had decided, to wait until her sister-in-law was sufficiently recovered before giving her the news about George.

Antonia suddenly missed Kitty. She missed her laughter, even missed her slamming of doors and the crash of her boots on the stairs. At first the violence of the girl's presence had horrified her. Petals would fall before they should, their heads snapped off by a jostling shoulder or a careless arm; her flowers would literally wilt, the buds die without opening, the leaves crisp and turn brown, as Kitty passed by. Over the weeks, however, she had become accustomed to listening for her voice and the funny little songs that she sang. They had grown close, shared jokes, and admitted a common love for Peter, the goatherd from *Heidi*, even though he was only a character in a novel.

And now Kitty's absence rang out like the peal of a bell. Antonia had begun to see Balmarra through the girl's eyes, to see it as a place to be explored, to be claimed through games and treks, through adventures and crusades. Now the estate had reverted to what it had been before, beautiful but isolating.

The clock struck the hour, eleven, and then fell silent again. The moment stalled, as if waiting for something to happen. Nothing did. She ran her finger down the stem of one of the roses, the prick of a thorn sharp. A bead of blood appeared on her skin. The triumph she had felt after the party had been short-lived. She had raised sixty-two pounds for George's trip, not much in the overall scheme of things. Maybe the offense she had inadvertently caused was greater than the value of the gesture. Likewise, as time passed she began to question her original intentions. Yes, she could play the part of landed gentry, she could roll her hair and carry off a silk gown; she could dance a waltz and entertain the gin set. But she was still stuck in the same skin, the same body, the same life. Her father had cheated her, taken the one element that could have bloomed and snipped it off like a bud. Hearing that he had used Henry to do it only made it worse.

Cicely's arrival, however, had forced her to change; she had felt braver, stronger, more determined. Although she hadn't yet told Malcolm that she was paying Kitty's school fees, she would when the right moment arose. They would have to make savings somehow. But where? Cook would complain if she cut the household budget— she was always hinting that she needed more, that she was having to scrimp and save, use tea leaves twice and buy cheaper cuts of meat. Maybe they could all wear an extra cardigan, heat one room, and save money that way? The coal bill was a huge expenditure. She suddenly saw herself at fifty, wrapped up in chrysalis of woolens.

A door closed upstairs, and the rush of air made the rose petals shiver just a little. Someone was coming down the staircase slowly, one step at a time, like a child. Cicely appeared at the doorway dressed in her coat and hat, so thin and angular that the eye was drawn immediately to her wrists and her cheekbones.

"Should you be out of bed?" Antonia asked. "So soon?"

Cicely seemed to sway slightly in her boots.

"I'm going to Edinburgh," she said.

"What? Why?"

"Because I need to," she said. "I need to see the Regius Keeper at the Botanics urgently. Could you arrange the pony-and-trap to take me to the ferry?"

Antonia shook her head.

"You're not going anywhere," she said. "You've been very ill."

Cicely, however, was adamant.

"If I can't use the pony-and-trap, I'll walk."

Buttoning up her coat, her sister-in-law began to head toward the front door. Her skin was pale as chalk. Antonia had no doubt at all that she would do as she proposed.

"Cicely," she said. "Wait. Wait a minute."

Cicely turned, sensing something in her tone of voice, something ominous.

"What is it?" Cicely said, her eyes searching her face for an answer. "What's happened?"

Antonia was sure that Cicely could read her expression like a newspaper headline. She should tell her about George. It wasn't fair to keep it from her. But her courage deserted her; her mouth would not form the words, her mind blanked. She would tell Cicely tomorrow. Or the day after. A few days would make no difference.

"Nothing's happened. I'll ask Bill to hitch up the trap," said Antonia. "In fact, I'll take you to Gourock on the ferry, and perhaps I'll come to Edinburgh myself."

Cicely closed her eyes for a second, relief written all over her face. Then she gave a small nod.

"Thank you," she said. "Gourock would be perfect."

"Are you sure? It'll be almost a day out," she said. "I think I shall rather enjoy it."

"I would rather go to Edinburgh alone, if you don't mind."

"Very well, but the offer's there."

Cicely glanced down at the bowl of roses.

"You grow the loveliest of flowers," she said softly.

Antonia plucked a rose from the arrangement, a yellow damask, its petals jeweled with dew, the flower tightly budded but just on the brink of opening, and threaded it through Cicely's buttonhole.

"Here," she said. "For my dearest sister-in-law. You had us scared for a while."

18

Cicely stared out of the window as the train sped through the Scottish countryside, the roads at right angles to the tracks like lengths of silver ribbon, the fields crowned with haystacks. Winter was coming, and she could taste it in the air, the sweetness of woodsmoke and leaf mold. Before she boarded, Antonia had suggested once more that she might come to Edinburgh too, but Cicely had used all her energy to insist that she didn't, that Gourock was far enough. Now she felt drained, exhausted, as if she had no reserve left to draw on, and she wondered if she'd made the right decision in coming alone. Several times she felt the rise of fever in her blood, and she had to wipe her brow with her handkerchief and breathe deeply until it receded. A few of the other passengers looked at her for a second longer than was polite, but there were others on the train who were more noteworthy than she—a man with a parrot in a cage in the next compartment and a young woman who spent the whole journey sobbing into her sleeve.

After finding the seedling in the glass house she knew she would not be able to sleep anymore. She had crept into the library and lit a lamp. By breakfast time she had not only found an account of the French priest's discovery and loss of the Snow Tree, she had come upon a beautifully painted illustration in a notebook. She took the leaf and seed sample and compared them. Unless she was mistaken they were the same. Where had they come from? This must have been what Jacob was trying to tell her, the seeds he had been growing from the envelope she had dropped all those weeks ago in the glass house. She could only guess that they had belonged to Edward Pick, a specimen brought back by a plant hunter, and he hadn't realized what the envelope contained.

By the time the train arrived in Edinburgh, her body felt weak, unconnected, vague. The seedling in its pot grew heavier by the minute. She had felt so tired on the walk to the Botanics that she had to grab a railing and hold it for a moment or two to catch her breath. Once she had regained her composure she saw that she had stopped in a familiar place. It was Dundas Street, the photographer's studio just a few doors down. And there they were in the display window: a girl staring out of a railway carriage while a woman stood in front of the door. Cicely barely recognized herself. She looked happy, elegant, and—compared with all the other subjects—several shades darker. In India, where people were all shades from white to dark brown, they were on the paler end of the spectrum. Here they were brewed tea amongst a sea of faces as white as milk.

A man was standing at the doorway, watching her. It wasn't the same photographer as before. This one was older.

"Looking for something more specialized?" He gave her a wink. "Something Continental?"

"I'm sorry?"

"I can do you a Mata Hari," he said, raising an eyebrow.

She forgot the prints, turned away, and rejoined the throng on Dundas Street, pulling her hat lower. Was that how she appeared to the world here? As an exotic dancer? A courtesan?

Isaac Balfour was out for lunch and wasn't due to return until three. She should have written to arrange an appointment, his secretary scolded; she shouldn't have come all that way without one.

She knew this was true, but when she had woken up that morning feeling better, she knew she must take advantage. And besides, time was of the essence.

Outside, a rush of wind ruffled the trees. The sun came out, filling Balfour's office window with color, brilliant green against the ache of blue. What would George say? It was not his discovery. Did it matter? If she was right she could make an arrangement with Lorimer. He would pay handsomely for it. Maybe the money would be enough for Antonia and Malcolm, and eventually Kitty, to keep Balmarra.

"Mrs. Pick?"

She opened her eyes. Isaac Balfour was standing in front of her, a faint smile fixed on his face. Had she fallen asleep?

"You wanted to see me?"

"I did," she said and rose to her feet. "I have a plant I would like you to look at."

As she explained that her gardener had grown it in the glass house, Balfour examined the seedling. Then he glanced up at her from beneath unruly eyebrows. Cicely was suddenly nervous. Had she been mistaken? Maybe Baillie had been wrong, and it was just a common species?

"The leaves have a very distinctive shape and color," the Regius Keeper said. "I would have to check the records, but if my memory serves me right it appears to be the same shape as that known as the Snow Tree collected by Père Armand David in the 1860s. He described it in detail in his journals, but the seeds were lost. But you know that, I expect."

"I do," she said.

He smiled. At last.

"Pass on my congratulations to your husband," he said.

The wave of relief was so strong that she felt almost as if all her strings had been cut.

"I'll write and tell him today," she said.

"The first of many discoveries, I hope," he said. "Where exactly did he find it?"

Cicely hesitated. She hadn't prepared an answer.

"I'm sure he won't give away its exact location to anyone," Balfour said with another smile. "I know some collectors would pay a pretty penny for a Snow Tree."

After she had seen Cicely off on the train, Antonia wondered what she might do with herself rather than head straight home. Even if she had wanted to see Malcolm, he didn't like being disturbed while he was working. Instead she walked along the coastal road, all the way to the Customs House in Greenock, and then she found herself heading toward the old sugar refinery.

The redbrick wall of Pick's refinery was still intact. It was too high to see over and loomed above the cobbled streets the way it always had, with a seam of weeds at the bottom and the peeling remnants of paper notices stuck all the way along. Antonia glanced at them as she passed: a circus, a flying show, a church fete, a meeting for suffragists. The gate was locked, but the chain was rusty and gave way when Antonia pushed it. She stepped through and pulled the gate shut behind her. It wasn't trespassing, was it, if the lot was still unoccupied? After the fire, her father had put it on the market but no one, so far as she knew, had come forward to take it over: There were six other refineries in the town already.

The factory looked almost the same as she remembered apart from the soot around the windows and the scatter of broken glass on the ground. Two parallel silver wagon tracks looked almost polished, despite the fact that the cars were piled up in a shed, wheelless and broken. The drying rooms with their huge ovens were still intact, but the rest of the refinery, where dark brown muscovado sugar from the West Indies had been boiled and purified before being transformed into cones of white sugar, was skeletal—a blackened framework of charred wood and twisted metal.

Was it just her imagination that she could still smell sweetness in the air? As a girl she had loved this place, the crystals she had been given to suck as a treat, the rough dark stickiness of the raw sugar in its sacks and the polished surfaces of the white cones before they were wrapped in blue paper and packed. She had not known then—it had simply never occurred to her—that not everyone had servants or an estate. The rude awakening came when she was a little older and was taken by her father to pay their respects to the families who had lost members in a refinery fire—there were always fires. She remembered the scratch of her Sunday clothes against her skin at the church service that seemed to last for hours, and then the walk along narrow dark streets, delivering toys to bereaved children, followed by the slow realization that whole families lived in houses smaller than a single stable and that some of the children were not wearing shoes even though it was cold enough for boots. It was then that she saw that her papa had two faces, one for family and one for the rest of the world. She barely recognized the latter, and it scared her. Over the next few years it came in small parcels of insight, each one more dreadful than the last: Pick's Sugar employed hundreds of people, most of whom lived in abject poverty. The fact that cones of clean white sugar were produced from the filthy sacks of brown was an almost perfect illustration of the way that their wealth had been created from squalor.

Everything her family had was the result of alchemy, of trans-formation; that you could take one thing and produce another. Her great-grandfather had sailed to Jamaica as a cabin boy, and his son had come back thirty years later with a fortune. When she had asked her father about those days, however, he had been reticent. And yet it had some long-lasting effect on him. She remembered a time when her father had crossed a busy road in Glasgow rather than pass a black man. Was it guilt, shame, remorse, or a mixture of all three? And who was the black woman whose portrait he had stashed away in the attic?

The sun came out as she entered the old boiling house. The fire had gutted the office, and a thin ash dust still hung in the air. A few things had been left on a shelf, and she lifted each in turn; a clay sugar mold, a pair of metal nippers, and a tin with "Pick's Sugar" embossed on the top. Should she tell Cicely about George? Was there any point? It was just like him to disappear. He would return; he always did. And then she thought about Malcolm. Even before Cicely and Kitty had arrived, love had become a habit rather than a choice. Could their marriage recover? Maybe she should look for a solicitor and start the process of divorce? And yet the idea of being a social outcast, a divorcée, alone, unloved, did not appeal. And what of her husband himself? She had thought him a good man once. Could she feel the same way again? The clay mold fell from the shelf and shattered on the floor, making her jump. She moved a few broken fragments with the toe of her boot.

A paddle steamer blew its horn on the river. An omnibus passed by on the road on the other side of the wall. A bird sang in what was left of the rafters in the roofless refinery. Life went on despite everything. She already knew what she would do next. She had decided days if not weeks before. She brushed the dust from her skirts, smoothed her hair, and bit her lips to make them rosy. Then she headed back out the refinery gate.

19

The hall was crowded with children, ranging in age from around three, Cicely guessed, up to about twelve. While a string of them played tag, some of the older ones carried the youngest on their hips, shoulders, and backs. Their voices rose up to the vaulted ceiling and echoed across the polished marble floor like birdsong.

It had taken Cicely several days to recover from the Edinburgh trip. As soon as she felt stronger, however, Cicely had arranged a meeting with Lorimer at his office at the mill, taken the ferry, then the train to Paisley, and walked along the river Cart. And now here she sat, on a wooden bench beneath a large framed advertisement for sewing cotton, as the daylight fell in great shafts from the windows and the dust mites danced.

The sheer scale of Lorimer's business was so much larger than she had expected: There were twisting mills and dyeworks, a counting house and a spooling shop. There were hundreds if not thousands of workers, and the clatter and noise from the machinery and the smoke from the chimney stacks and the smell of caustic soda were overpowering. And now this: a room full of children when Lorimer had none.

A small group of women stood by the window, shushing the children or picking one by name to scold.

"John Mackenzie. You've been telt already! Helen Bain. I'm watching you!"

Although it was a cold clear morning, Cicely noticed that many of the smaller children were barefoot. In general, the others' clothes were too big or too small, sleeves falling over hands and trousers ending above ankles. But they didn't seem to notice or care. What were they doing there, she wondered, bringing so much life to such an industrial space? Finally a door opened to a room at the far end of the hallway, and the children were ushered inside. Within moments the great hall fell silent.

After she had checked that her hair was tucked into its comb, she looked at her face in a small compact mirror, smoothing out the lines below her eyes. She wore her brown coat with the rabbit-fur trim— her best—and had spent some time applying kohl and lipstick, face powder and cologne. Although the effect was what she had intended, she suspected that there was something in her face that could not be hidden or blotted by rouge.

"You're here!" a voice called out.

Lorimer stood in a doorway at the far end of the hall. The door was large, and he looked very small. She stood up.

"Yes," she said. "I want to thank you for seeing me at such short notice—"

"It's been a busy day," he said, walking toward her. "I hope you haven't had to wait too long."

"Not long," she said.

"You see, once a year we distribute boots, stockings, and shoes," he explained. "To children who need them."

"That's very generous."

He shrugged his shoulders in acknowledgment.

"It's a small gesture," he admitted.

Lorimer's office looked out across the river to a glade of trees on the other side. The absence of red brick and chimney stacks, of any sign of the mill, made it feel as if it were turning its back on the works, on all the ugliness and sprawl. There wasn't much there; a desk, two chairs, and a large wooden filing cabinet.

"You look well," he replied. "Are you fully recovered?"

"Almost," she said. "But this disease has a habit of relapsing. I'm not sure one is ever completely recovered."

"Then you must take care," he said, pulling out a chair. "Please. Sit down."

She sat, then waited until he was seated opposite. The pale light fell slanted on his face, his shoulders, the angles of his hands.

"Mrs. Pick," he said. "How may I help you?"

"I'll get straight to the point," she said. "What would you say, Mr. Lorimer, if I could give you what you wanted?"

He stared at her and then started to arrange his pens on his ledger.

"It depends what you mean?" he said.

She was suddenly sorry for her choice of words, for what she was about to say. It made it seem as if all that came before was merely a preamble to a business transaction. And yet the anxiety she had lived with since she had arrived in Scotland had finally eased. If this business turned out the way she hoped, Antonia could keep the estate, Kitty could attend school, George's expedition would be properly financed, and she would be able to go home and resume her life in Darjeeling. A shadow briefly crossed her heart.

"Mrs. Pick?" he said, bringing her back to the moment.

"The Snow Tree," she said. "We have found the Snow Tree."

He leaned forward. He closed his eyes, then smiled.

"That's second on my list," he said. "But please, do go on."

Although that sentence would echo in her head for days afterward, all she could hear at the time were her own words, the ones she had rehearsed for days beforehand.

"We have grown a specimen from seed, and I have had it verified by the Regius Keeper at the Botanic Gardens in Edinburgh," she said. "The botanical nomenclature, if you wanted, could include your name."

"Your husband would give me that?"

"You can have both," she replied. "The seedling and the name."

His mouth tightened, and he sat back in his chair. Noise from the factory spilled into the room, the regular boom of a machine, the yell of a foreman, the spin of the bobbins.

"And it's the only one, you say, the only one that's been successfully grown here?"

"According to the Regius Keeper, yes."

"How much were you thinking?" he asked.

"Maybe you could offer what you think it's worth?" she replied.

He named a figure, much higher than she had imagined.

"I'll send Mr. Baillie over with the seedling," she said. "And thank you."

It was as they were saying good-bye, as they stood beside the door, not yet open. Maybe it was the sense of gratitude she felt, the intense relief. He was standing close, so close that she could hear his breath, in and out, she could feel the rapid beat of his heart in his chest and sense the pull of him, the tug of every nerve in her body. Or maybe it was the fever that remained in her blood, the race of mortality in her veins, but something made her hesitate and linger on the threshold. As a telephone rang in an office somewhere and was not answered, as the machinery clattered and rumbled in the spooling shop, as the waterwheel churned on the river, it seemed for one vivid moment that something passed between them, the recognition of an impulse that couldn't be articulated.

Lorimer raised his right hand, he moved it toward her, and for a second she thought he was going to touch her. Instead he reached down and pulled a loose thread from her coat. She imagined that he could pull and pull and her coat, her dress, her slip would fall apart. She would literally be undone.

"It grew from a seed," she said.

"It did," he replied.

A knock sounded on the door. It was opened by a clerk.

"Mr. Lorimer," he said. "You're needed on the telephone urgently."

"Maybe it's better," she said softly, "if we conduct the rest of our business by letter."

"Better for whom?" he asked.

Henry's house was modest, a two-up two-down a couple of streets back from the Esplanade. An old bicycle was propped up outside. Antonia ran her fingers over the rusted steel of the frame and the wicker of the basket before she took a deep breath and knocked. It was clear that even though it was already ten, Henry had been sleeping. It was also clear that he had not expected that she would ever visit. In fact he looked downright horrified. She considered making her excuses and leaving, but as soon as she opened her mouth to begin to suggest it, he ushered her inside, as quick as you like, before the landlady saw.

"Will she start a scandal?" Antonia joked. It was easier to make fun of the situation than to show how awkward she felt.

"No, she will start a conversation," he replied. "Which is far worse in my experience."

It was only once that she was inside that she realized that he did not live in the whole house but had just a bed-sitting room. He closed the door and looked around for somewhere for her to sit. Almost every surface—tables, the mantelpiece, the bed, the chairs, and most of the floor—was covered with books, newspapers, paint tubes, palettes, canvases, letters, and empty coffee cups. An open suitcase lay on the floor. A cat was curled up on a cushion on the only armchair, so he cleared a wooden seat at a table and offered it to her.

"I'm sorry—" he began.

"Don't be," she replied. "I really shouldn't have dropped in on you like this, without warning. It was most impolite."

He made a pot of tea and poured them both a cup.

"Going somewhere?" she asked, indicating the suitcase.

"Actually, yes," he replied. "Paris."

"For good?"

He gave a decisive nod. She felt momentarily pleased for him.

"Well," he said, finally sitting down. "Is there anything else I can do for you or is this a social call?"

She sipped the tea, then inhaled deeply.

"Either way," he added, "it's lovely to see you again."

She found she was staring at Henry, at his unwashed hair and unlaundered collar. And despite the fact that either one would make any other man undesirable, on Henry they had the opposite effect. Or was it because he was leaving? Did that fact make him more attractive? He picked a spot of bright blue paint from the palm of his left hand.

"Henry," she said softly.

He didn't answer. The milkman's cart clattered by outside; a young girl skipped past the window, singing softly to herself; a factory whistle blew a few streets away. And then there was silence, a silence that seemed to grow deafening. The moment had passed, she saw now, years earlier. Antonia collected her thoughts, her gloves, and drained the cup of tea.

"I must be getting home," she said and rose to her feet. "Thank you so much for the tea."

Tears were approaching, like a cold front. Without another word, she rushed to the door, let herself out, and then knocked over the bicycle with a clatter.

"Antonia?" He was at his door, frowning, his eyes bluer than ever in the morning sunlight.

"Sorry," she said as she tried to lift the bike back up again. "If only I weren't so clumsy."

He flinched as he took the handlebars from her.

"Come back inside," he said softly. "I have something to show you."

It was a painting, but like no other painting Antonia had ever seen. A woman holding a box. But the figure was broken up into a series of painted planes. The box contained an assortment of objects, so abstracted it was hard to work out at first what they were.

"It's called *Heirlooms*," Henry said. "You've seen cubist paintings before, I expect, by Braque or Gleizes?"

She shook her head no.

"Is that a ring?" she asked, pointing out a gold elongated shape.

"A ring? No," he said. "It's a cuff link."

Her heart began to thump, her head to throb. The painting was a portrait of her, all fractured and contradictory, with a box of stolen things weighing down her lap. How did he know?

"I was going to try and exhibit it," he said. "But now I think I would like you to have it."

"That's very kind," she said, referring to the painting. "But really, you shouldn't give your work away. I shall buy it instead. At your next exhibition."

Henry didn't put up a fight, he didn't plead or beg or coerce. In fact he let it go quite easily. They both stared at the painting for a moment, and then he turned to her. The light from the window revealed the crags and crevices, the slow slide of age. His eyes sought hers. No one knew she was here, no one was watching, no one would ever know what intimacies passed between them. His hand reached across and took hers, the skin soft and warm.

"Antonia?" he said. "Why don't you come with me?"

"Where to?" she whispered as if someone were listening.

"Paris," he said.

"Paris?" she repeated. The word filled her mouth with hot breath and thrill. She saw it all; a small flat in the city with a view of the tower, the smell of linseed oil and varnish, the taste of red wine in her mouth. How would it be to run away, to bolt, to escape her marriage, her responsibility, her situation? To leave everything behind, to start again? She was breathing faster, her hand trembling in his.

"It's just a thought," he said, and she could already sense his growing hesitation.

"An excellent thought," she replied.

He smiled, then raised her hand to his mouth and kissed it. She could feel the heat of his breath on her skin and bit her lip to try to stop the giddy spin of her heart. She moved closer, she closed her eyes, her mouth sought his and found it.

Henry's body was unlike Malcolm's in every way. The hair on his arms and chest was curly and dark, his torso was hard and lean. His fingers were beautiful, long and elegant; if only she had a pencil. And the strangest thing of all: They seemed to fit, his mouth on hers, her shoulder in the crook of his arm, the length of her back into the curve of his chest and belly. She felt then, as she lay on his single bed, that she had never been truly naked before.

The ferry blew its horn, and its bass note reverberated deep within her. Henry stood on the quay, raised his hand, and gave her a single salute. As she watched, he grew smaller and smaller until she couldn't make him out anymore. The lights of Gourock were coming on, specks of brilliant orange against the dark of the approaching night. Where had the day gone? One moment it was morning, the next late afternoon. She could still taste his skin: peppercorns and cedar shavings. Why shouldn't she go to Paris? The idea was terrifying, fantastic, wonderful. Why not? For a moment she watched the soar of a gull overhead and felt the same weightless glide. Then she turned and faced forward, watching the peninsula rise up, black against the torn colors of the setting sun.

With the dusk came doubts. What would become of Balmarra? How would Malcolm cope? And Cicely and Kitty? The heady burst of elation she had felt was already starting to dissipate. She couldn't just bolt, at least not now. Even before they docked, she had changed her mind. She suspected that Henry knew she would. He hadn't, after all, made any firm arrangements. Maybe he saw what she couldn't, that her cage was of her own design.

It was night by the time Antonia returned to Balmarra. As she climbed the steps she could see Malcolm in the drawing room filling out the crossword, the evening unfolding like all the others that had been and those that were still to come. She was suddenly angry, furious in fact, with Malcom and with Edward Pick and his burdensome legacy, and so she turned on her heel and headed back down the steps, down the driveway to the glass house. Inside, her eyes took a minute or two to adjust. An orange had been left on a small table in the optimistic hope it would ripen. She picked it up and held it in her palm. It was as small and hard as a golf ball and would never turn from sour to sweet. Then she heard a flapping sound far above. A small bird was trapped in the apex of the house, its wings in a blur as it banged the glass.

First she took the pole hook and opened all the windows; then she filled a bucket with cold water from the tap. The thought passed through her mind that some of the plants were rare and therefore could be valuable, but there was no time to go down that route. Getting them ready to sell might take months to orchestrate, and she would have to keep the boiler stoked and pay the coal man in the meantime.

The first bucket released a huge cloud of steam and the smell of hot metal and soot, the second just the hiss of smoking coal as the fire in the boiler went out. The third covered the heap of coal in the cellar with a sheen of moisture. It was done. She wiped the tears from her eyes as she replaced the bucket next to the water butt; for years this had been her world. As she walked past her roses she felt like a murderer. How long would her plants last without heat? Not long, she suspected. And yet there were other, hardier roses that they could plant outside.

The money she saved from heating the glass house would pay for Kitty's school fees. And for a young woman, an education was more important than a rose garden, wasn't it? She paused at the door and listened. The flapping had stopped; the bird had found an open window and flown away.

20

Cicely stayed in bed late, not rising to get dressed until noon. She had barely slept all night. What had happened, or not happened, with Lorimer kept her awake, and she replayed the scene in her head, looking for another possible interpretation. But there was none. She rolled over in her bed and covered her face with her sheet. She was a married woman, a mother. What had she been thinking?

Now that Lorimer had made an offer for the Snow Tree, she could start making plans to return to Darjeeling, to her husband. She tried to summon up George's face, his voice, his laugh, but the images, the memories, the affection, were becoming blurred around the edges. How long had it been since he had written? Two months? Did he ever think of her? She must write and tell him her news. But how could she explain where the Snow Tree came from when she didn't know the answer herself? And Lorimer's generosity? He might suspect. He certainly wouldn't be happy about it. In her defense, she had found a solution that suited everyone: George would have enough money to continue the expedition, and even though he would legally own it, his sister could remain at Balmarra for as long as she wanted. If Antonia could pay Kitty's school fees until they could afford to do so, then Kitty could stay at school. All was well.

And yet, back in India, life would be so empty without her daughter. Maybe they would move back to town? Or maybe they would move away, to Simla or Kiarighat, where no one knew them and they knew no one. But how long would it be before the next expedition, before the money ran out again? They had lurched from one crisis to the next for years. Now that she knew about Jane Fintry, she wondered if her marriage would ever be the same. An image of Lorimer's face came unbidden into her mind. No, she told herself, she must leave this place as quickly as possible before she did something she might regret.

The house was quiet—it seemed everyone was out. The night before there had been a hard hoarfrost, and even though the fires were lit, it was so cold you could see your breath inside. She would not miss the cold, the damp. It was then she noticed that something had changed in the air—an absence, a silence. Cicely pulled on her coat and headed out to the glass house to check on the seedling. The door to the glass house was lying open. Young Mr. Baillie was standing at the far end, his head hanging forward. Inside, instead of condensation, sheets of ice misted the glass. The gardener turned when he heard her approach, but his face revealed nothing.

"Why is it so cold?" she asked.

"The furnace," he explained. "It must have been out all night."

"What?! How can that be?"

He flinched slightly. He was angrier than she first realized.

"I stoked it up around six last night. Someone's been in after and thrown water on it. Come and see."

Sure enough, at the bottom of the stairs the boiler sat in a pool of dirty water. The fire was out.

"Couldn't you light it again?"

"Have to wait for the coal to dry first," he said. "It will take days."

"Where's the seedling?"

He led her back up the stairs to a low table at the back of the glass house. Her breath rose in white clouds; her cheeks stung pink. The seedling looked scorched and brown. All the bright new life, the tiny white leaves, was gone.

"The frost got it," he said.

"Can you rescue it?" she asked.

He sighed, then shook his head.

"Nothing I can do, I'm afraid."

"Aren't there any more seeds?"

"I planted them all. Only one germinated. I'm sorry."

Cicely let out a small involuntary cry. She closed her eyes. If only she could open them again to a world where all was right. This was her divine punishment, clearly, the price of her impulsive thoughts. Now once again she was back where they started.

Antonia sat on the bench at the top of a small col. She not been back since they had shown Cicely the spot just after she and her daughter had arrived. A paddle steamer puffed its way up the loch below, leaving two frills of foam in its wake. The woodlands across the water looked like a painting, each tree a daub of color. The trees were their most glorious at this time of year, their leaves gold and copper and terra-cotta, a brief precious show before the winds blew them all away and winter came.

That morning a parcel had arrived from the India Office. It held, she suspected, George's things. What if he was dead? What if her optimism had been misplaced? She had stashed it in the hall cupboard beneath a blanket. Now she shivered and pulled her red cashmere scarf a little tighter around her shoulders. There was a metallic taste in the air; there would be rain or possibly snow before dusk. Someone was coming up the path, her husband, she could tell by the heavy intent of his footfall, not quite a walk but a stomp.

"Where have you been?" he asked.

"Why?" she replied.

"The hothouse boiler's been sabotaged," said Malcolm. "I've a good mind to call the local constable."

"Please don't do that."

"And why not?" he asked.

She sighed.

"Because I did it," she replied.

He shook his head.

"My dear Antonia, what is wrong with you?"

"Me?" she replied. "Nothing. And you? Anything you'd like to tell me?"

"I don't know what you're talking about!"

It was all becoming absurd, Antonia thought. Did he really want her to spell it out? It seemed so.

"Have you been seeing another woman?" she asked. What was the point of tiptoeing around?

"It's not what you think," he replied. "I know that sounds like a cliché, but in this case it's true."

He hadn't denied it. That, in a sense, was a relief. She didn't want to argue when all she had as evidence was a receipt for a drink in a hotel. And yet the moral high ground, she discovered, did not give her any sense of triumph at all.

"Actually, on second thought," she said, "I'd rather not know."

Malcolm's mouth was turned down at the corners. He sat down beside her.

"The thing is, I had the whole thing in hand," he said softly.

"What are you talking about?"

He pulled a letter from his pocket and handed it to her.

"It's from your father's solicitor," he said.

"Really? I thought his affairs were all sorted out."

"Sadly not," said Malcolm. "As I've told you already, why did you think George's wife came here?"

She turned on the bench to face him.

"But he left it to me," she replied. "Balmarra is mine, isn't it?"

"I have no idea anymore," he replied.

21

Antonia stormed into the guest bedroom without knocking. She had mud on her boots, and her hair was springing out of its pins. Cicely was standing in her undergarments.

"Is it true?" she demanded. "You only came here to claim the estate for my brother?"

Cicely pulled her day dress over her slip and faced the mirror. She had been expecting this moment for weeks, and now, finally, here it was. Remain calm, she told herself, don't react. Antonia noticed the letter from the solicitor that was propped up on her sister-in-law's bedside table, snatched it up, checked the sender's details, and then threw it down again.

"I had grown"—Antonia said, then swallowed—"to like you. I had thought of you less as a sister-in-law and more as a friend. I gave you and your daughter everything I possibly could."

"I know," she replied.

"I put the boiler out to save on coal, to use the money to pay the school fees."

So Antonia had killed the seedling. Cicely smiled. How ridiculous it seemed, one action that ruined the next.

"It's not funny!" Antonia yelled.

Tears were welling up in her sister-in-law's eyes. Cicely laid a hand on her forearm. She shook it off.

"What are you planning to do with Balmarra?" Antonia asked. "Sell it, I suppose. I can't imagine George wants to live here."

Antonia had answered her own question. Now, Cicely realized, she could go home. Springtime in the mountains was beautiful, snow on the high peaks, crocuses and primroses in the forests. She would ride through the foothills again, through the orange groves and tea plantations, breathing the fragrant mist that rose up from the valleys. It would look, feel, smell the same as always. It would be she who had changed.

"Have you heard from my brother recently?" Antonia asked.

"Not recently, no," she replied. "I'm sure we will soon, though."

There had been no telegrams from George for some time now. And yet she wasn't worried. Out in the field, communication was difficult.

The day before she had decided to send a telegram. As usual, there was a queue in the post office. It had seemed a good idea at the time, but once she had a pen in her hand and a blank sheet in front of her she had no idea what to say. Words came into her head, but they were all the wrong ones. "Where on earth are you?" or "How could you do this to us? Stop."

"Mrs. Pick?" the clerk asked. "Are you all right?"

She didn't want to break down, not there in a place where customers were buying stamps and postal orders.

"Perfectly," she said, pulling her face into a smile. "Good day."

She hadn't sent a telegram.

"You know George," Antonia said. "It's what he does! He'll turn up again soon. But you know, I'll never forgive him for this. Never."

And then, with a slam of the door that made the whole house

reverberate, she was gone, the red cashmere scarf discarded in a heap on Cicely's bed.

The storm came in the middle of the night, the wind howling around the gable end and shrieking down the chimneys. By morning it hadn't subsided; several trees were blown over before lunch. The winds hit the Clyde Estuary hard; the tide was so high it damaged the boats in the shipbuilders' yards and blew over a couple of cranes. The esplanade at Fairlie was washed away, while at Port Glasgow the river burst its banks and flooded the town. At Balmarra, huge waves crashed around Karrasay, making it an island once more. The driveway was strewn with branches and leaves that had been ripped from the woodlands.

Despite the storm, the meeting was in the Argyll Hotel at eleven. Malcolm would take Antonia in his motorcar; Cicely would ride with young Mr. Baillie in the pony-and-trap. Cicely had the decency to wait until Antonia and Malcolm had eaten breakfast before coming downstairs and eating her own. Once she was dressed, Antonia stood at her bedroom window and stared out across the loch. The water was almost black and flaked with white. For how much longer would this view be hers? Everything she had thought solid was now air—her home, her marriage, her future. She thought briefly about her brother, about how he sent his wife rather than come himself. She hadn't opened the parcel yet. And then she thought about Malcolm. Was he still having an affair? Maybe she couldn't blame him.

A knock sounded on the door, and then it opened. Cicely Pick stood there in the clothes she had arrived in, her brown coat with the rabbit fur at the collar and wrists.

"Will you come for a walk with me?" she asked.

"With you? Now?"

"There are some things I want to tell you," she said.

The glass house was as cold as a morgue. The leaves of the palms and the fruit trees were brown at the edges. The iron pipes were silent, but another bird that had flown in, a blackbird, and it sang loud and clear high up in the roof of the dome before finding an open window and flying away.

"I just wanted to say that I tried," Cicely said. "And I was almost there."

Cicely told her about the envelope in the book, about the seeds and the illustration, about the Snow Tree and how Jacob had grown one single plant there in the hothouse.

"Mr. Lorimer wanted to purchase the Snow Tree seedling," she said. "For his collection. He was willing to pay a great deal of money for it. And so you see I thought I had found another way that would suit everyone."

Antonia inhaled sharply. She remembered the clouds of steam and slow hiss of cooling metal.

"Why didn't you tell me?" she said. "That you needed money?"

Cicely smiled and shook her head.

"I did," she said. "And you were very generous. But it wasn't enough."

"And where did the seeds come from?" Antonia asked. "And the illustration?"

"Well, therein lies the mystery," she said. "They fell out of a book. The one you gave me from the library."

"Really! But what were they doing there?"

Cicely shook her head.

"I was hoping you might have an answer to that," she said.

A car horn blew: Malcolm was ready to go.

22

The room the solicitor had booked at the Argyll Hotel faced the
street. It was, Cicely guessed, a private dining room—a large oak
table took up most of the space. Cicely sat at one side of the table
and Antonia and Malcolm at the other. A coal merchant's horse-
and-cart passed by outside. The long low blast of the paddle steamer
sounded as it approached the harbor. A clock ticked. A tray of tea sat
in the middle of the table, but nobody touched it. The door opened
and they all turned at once. They had been expecting the solicitor,
but it was a woman, the same woman Cicely had seen with Malcolm.
Close up she was older than she had first appeared, but she was undeniably well-preserved. She nodded to Malcolm, then took a seat at
the foot of the table. All the color drained from Antonia's face. She
stood up and started pouring tea into cups.

"Would you like one?" she asked the woman.

"Yes, please," she said as she removed her gloves. "Wild weather
we've been having."

Once Antonia had handed it out, however, the tea sat in its cups.
Cicely glanced at Malcolm. He was staring straight ahead. What
was going on? Who was this woman, and why was she here? Finally,

at quarter past the hour, Mr. Drummond, the solicitor, bustled in, papers escaping from his clutch.

"Sorry to keep you waiting," he said, even though he did not seem remotely sorry or provide an explanation as to the cause.

"Now," he said, once he had poured himself a cup of tea, stirred in two sugar lumps, and taken a large gulp. "We are here to discuss the last will and testament of Edward Pick. As you may or may not know, he changed his will often, but I have the latest, one that he drew up in May 1911, only a week or two before he passed. As his executor it has fallen upon me to make sure that, without prejudice, his estate is distributed according to Scottish law."

Cicely's mind started to drift; she hadn't slept well the night before, and the lawyer's voice droned on in a monotone. She closed her eyes and pictured George on a distant mountainside, Kitty at school, the view from her bedroom window in Darjeeling.

"Mrs. Pick?" said the solicitor. She came back to the moment. Everyone was staring at her.

"Edward Pick left his estate to your husband and his descendants."

She took a deep breath and let it out. She knew this already; it had been in the letter. But finally it was confirmed. She would instruct Mr. Drummond to deal with all the legal issues and find a buyer. Maybe she would even take a room here at the hotel until she had a passage booked.

"On one condition," he went on.

Cicely cocked her head. No condition had been mentioned before.

"Here's where it gets a little awkward," the solicitor said, pushing his glasses to the bridge of his nose. "My client was a man of certain views, views that many of us do not share in Scotland. He was an industrialist, a sugar man. Refining was in his blood. Mrs. Pick, I'm sorry to place you in this position but I need an honest answer. Are you or are you not . . ."

He stopped and swallowed.

"Am I what?" she asked.

"Pure," he replied.

"Pure?" she repeated.

"I need clarification that you are British, that you have no tarnish," he clarified.

"Tarnish?" Cicely couldn't quite believe what she was hearing. "Could you explain?"

Mr. Drummond turned beet red, and his voice took on an angry tone.

"We all know what I mean," he said. "Do I have to spell it out?"

"I'm afraid you do," said Cicely.

Antonia sat forward in her seat.

"This is ridiculous," she said. "Cicely, don't admit anything."

"You're asking me if I am . . . white?"

"That's right," he said. "As in, not black, not one drop of native contamination. Your word will be good enough."

Antonia stood up.

"Let me see that," she demanded.

The solicitor handed over the typed page. There was a split second when Cicely was tempted. It would be so easy. Who could prove it otherwise? It was nothing more than a lie, a little white lie, to be specific.

"Well," said the solicitor. "Mrs. Pick?"

She hesitated. A valve opened in her heart, and a rush of pressure was released.

"I am most certainly not," she said.

"Not?" said the solicitor.

Cicely swung her legs to the side and stood up. She couldn't do it, not for George or for Kitty. She could not deny everything she was, and they would have to live with the consequences. Edward Pick must have guessed this would happen. But what kind of man takes such animosity to his grave? What had made him so bitter, so vindictive toward someone he had never met? She would send George a telegram and let him know it was over. But first she needed a drink, a gin, perhaps. And a cigarette.

Once Cicely had left, the room suddenly felt cold. And it was not just the draft that came from the open front door of the hotel. Antonia turned to Malcolm. He was staring straight ahead, but under the table his knee was bouncing up and down.

"Did you know about this?" she whispered.

"Let's talk about it later," he said.

Antonia's mind was reeling. How could she continue to live in the house, knowing what her father was? What would Cicely do now? Antonia was the one who had put out the boiler. It was her fault that the seedling had died. A waitress came into the room to refresh the tea.

"Let's talk now," Antonia insisted. "Because if you knew, why did you keep it to yourself?"

"Antonia," Malcolm scolded.

Once the maid had finished, Mr. Drummond whispered something to her. She gave a small nod and left the room. The solicitor cleared his throat; he was staring at Antonia over his spectacles.

"My client, in anticipation of this outcome, had other beneficiaries in mind."

The door opened, and she jumped. Jacob was standing there with his cap in his hand.

"Oh, no," Antonia said. "We're not finished yet."

Mr. Drummond, however, ignored her.

"Do come in, Mr. Baillie," he said. "And sit down."

"Hello, son," said the woman.

Son? Malcolm leaned his head forward just an inch or two. What on earth was going on?

"And so," said the solicitor. "It is my duty to inform you that there are two main beneficiaries of Edward Pick's estate: Mrs. McCulloch and Mr. Baillie. The house and all its contents go to the former, and the gardens to the latter."

Jacob's mother clapped her hands over her mouth, and tears welled up in her eyes. He, however, didn't respond at first. And then he shook his head and mumbled something.

"What was that?" said Drummond. "Speak up, man."

Jacob Baillie stood up and put down his cup.

"I didn't know about this," he said to Antonia. "And to be honest I don't think I can accept it."

"It's legally yours," said the solicitor. "To do with as you wish."

He looked at her with some concern in his eyes. He wasn't a bad person. This wasn't his fault; it was her father's. Did he think it was funny? Was he laughing somewhere?

"Mr. Baillie. Jacob," said Antonia. "It seemed he wanted you to have it. You should accept."

Jacob frowned, then turned and walked out of the room with a slam of the door.

"Jacob!" His mother rose to her feet. "I'll be right back."

After she left, Mr. Drummond considered his papers.

"Why did he leave it to Jacob Baillie?" Antonia asked.

Mr. Drummond's face closed.

"Really," he said, "that is none of my concern."

"Malcolm?" she asked.

But her husband's gaze was fixed on the rim of his teacup, and he would not speak.

23

After she put out her cigarette, Cicely sat and stared out at the loch.
The waves were crashing against the pier, great explosions of froth
that rose up and fell back on themselves until they were absorbed
by the swell and undercurrent of the next wave. She had finished
her second gin and placed the glass back on the table. How would
it feel to surrender to the tug of the tide, to let go of everything, to
submit to the deep dark blue? As she watched, she saw a section of
seawall suddenly crumble away, leaving exposed earth and broken
stone. Another wave came and then another.

"What you did—"

She started. Antonia was standing at her elbow.

"Took real courage," her sister-in-law continued. "I'm so sorry."

Cicely sipped from her glass even though there was nothing left
but icewater and lemon.

"At least Balmarra is officially yours now."

"Only the house. He gave the gardens to Jacob Baillie. It seems
my father had some connection with his mother."

They sat and watched the rain fall onto the sea in great gusts and
squalls. Cicely remembered Malcolm and the woman that summer
afternoon when the town was full of day-trippers. It must have been

hard to keep a secret like that in a small town. Maybe Antonia was the only one who didn't know.

Antonia paused—her whole body, her hands, still—her eyes cast down. Was there something else she wanted to say?

"Cicely, I meant to tell you this before. But I didn't want to worry you unduly."

"Worry me?" repeated Cicely.

"It's George. The India Office wrote to me. They think he might have gone missing. Some of his belongings were found abandoned. But as you say, he's done it before. I'm sure he's absolutely fine. But then a parcel came. I couldn't open it. I'm sure . . . however . . . you know George. Against the odds and all that."

Cicely closed her eyes.

"How long have you known?"

"Only a couple of weeks."

"You should have told me," Cicely said.

Antonia gave her a look.

"I could say the same to you," she replied.

It was strange to arrive back at Balmarra in the knowledge that part of it would soon belong to someone else. Malcolm had been silent for the entire drive home. They passed old Mr. Baillie on the driveway pushing a wheelbarrow filled with debris from the storm. As they parked the car they heard a whirring from above. A small biplane passed by overhead, almost skimming the treetops. Lorimer was out for a spin again. Life went on. George had done it once again: He had disappeared just at the point where his presence was most necessary. Poor Cicely. Poor Kitty. As she was about to get out of the car, Malcolm reached for her hand.

"Antonia," he said. "He wasn't a bad man, your father."

"Wasn't he?" she said. "I mean, why would he leave the estate to the gardener?"

"He must have had his reasons," he replied.

Her mind spun with reasons: illicit affairs, illegitimate children.

"He's not my brother, is he? Jacob Baillie, I mean?"

"No," said Malcolm. "He's not."

Antonia let herself out and slammed the door behind her. Was it sinful to be ashamed of one's family? Of one's husband?

"How can you be so sure?" she said. "You lied to me."

"Not exactly lied," he replied.

"Surely I should be the judge of that."

Malcolm turned in his seat. He adjusted his driving gloves.

"Can we talk about this later?" he said. "I have to go to work."

"Now? You're going now?"

"Some things never change," he said. "We can't live on air, Antonia."

The hint of blame in his words, the suggestion that she did nothing all day, riled her. He glanced over, waiting for her to react. She suddenly felt defeated, as if all the air had been pumped out of her. She did not have the energy to argue.

"Whatever you say."

Malcolm swung the car around to face the opposite direction and drove back toward Dunoon.

Antonia had a headache. Her mouth was parched. She needed a glass of cold water. She took the back stairs, the servants' entrance. In the kitchen Cook was bashing something in a bowl and Dora was chopping onions. Antonia stood at the sink, poured herself a glass from the tap, and drank it down. She could feel them exchanging glances.

"Will you make time later to do the week's accounts?" Cook asked.

"Not today," Antonia replied. "Tomorrow?"

Cook's gaze dropped to whatever she was pummeling in the bowl. She hit it with more force than before.

"As you wish," she replied. "The pennies don't count themselves."

"I'm fully aware of that," Antonia snapped. "But one *day*? Does one day really matter?"

Dora stopped what she was doing, and Cook paused for a fraction of a second, then resumed.

"Anyway," Antonia continued. "I'll be in the drawing room if anyone's looking for me."

"We'll be here until five," Cook said. "It's a cold supper tonight, seeing as it's Thursday."

It was their evening off. She had forgotten that.

Antonia sat in her mother's favorite chair and stared at the unlit fire. The clock ticked, then struck five. The kitchen door slammed. She heard Cook's and Dora's voices receding as they walked down the driveway. Malcolm wouldn't be back until much later, and she had no idea when Cicely would return. Would she come back at all? She thought of Henry. He had changed the color of her, like a shade on a lamp. Was he in Paris yet? Nothing had changed, and yet everything had. Well, she could make changes too. She would start by clearing out the attic, throwing away all the useless things, the rubbish and detritus held on to for purely sentimental reasons. She would let it all go. And then she would turn to her marriage and do the same thing. It was about time.

The attic was pitch-black. The gas lamp in her hand lit up the tea chests and the stack of oil paintings but little else. Had she really seen a portrait of a black woman, and if so, who was she? The painting was still there, just as she remembered it. This time she examined the back of the canvas. It was labeled, the script faint but legible. She read it once and then read it again just to make sure.

This moment. She wanted to mark this moment, to take a small pause, to stop her mind from racing. Her father had kept a box of cigars and cigarettes for guests in the drinks cabinet in the drawing room. It was full—proof, should it be needed, that his guests were either nonsmokers or nonexistent. She picked a cigarette at random, placed it in her mouth, and lit it with a match as she had seen Cicely do. The first puff caught in her throat, and she had a small coughing fit. The second went down more smoothly and filled her with a sense of calm. She closed her eyes. She was suddenly more tired than she had ever been.

Antonia awoke feeling deliciously warm. The room was bathed in flickering light. And then the taste of burning filled her mouth. She leaped up. The carpet was on fire, the curtains too, in great licks of yellow and orange. She ran to the curtains, to a swath that was not on aflame, and pulled. It came down with a crash of sparks and embers on top of the divan, and within moments the divan was on fire too.

"No, oh no!" she said over and over.

Next she ran to the bathroom, emptied out a potted plant into the bath and began to fill it from the tap. It was pitifully small. When it was full she ran back to the drawing room. She had unfortunately left the door open, and the lintel was ablaze. She threw the water, but it had barely any effect. The flames were already leaping toward the banister above. At the top of the stairs, in the library, were all her journals, her sketchbooks, her life's—such as it was—work. In her head she could hear Malcolm's voice telling her not to be so stupid; nevertheless she took the stairs two by two. There was time. Time enough.

There were too many journals to carry. An old suitcase was stowed in one of the cupboards. She opened it and crammed them in. She took one last look at her beloved library and then ran down the stairs. Part of the carpet near the bottom was on fire. She was going to be burned alive. A headline suddenly appeared in her mind: AR-SONIST DIES IN COUNTRY HOUSE FIRE. She threw the suitcase to the bottom of the stairs, bundled her skirts into one hand, took a deep breath, and jumped. She landed on the wooden floor on the palms of her hands and her knees, skinning both. She barely felt it. She picked up the suitcase; she didn't look back. At the door she hesitated: Henry's painting hung on the wall. She could carry one more thing. And then she remembered the parcel from the India Office. It was in the hall cupboard beneath the blanket where she had left it. Just one more thing.

24

There came a point when Cicely knew she must stop drinking. She lit her last cigarette and tried to empty her mind of everything and everyone: the will, George, Antonia, Lorimer, the Baillies. She had come to Scotland believing that the whole process would be quick and easy. How could she have been so naive? And now everything that once was solid had evaporated into thin air. She exhaled the last of the smoke in one long stream, then put out the cigarette. The smell of burning remained.

The day had dimmed, the clouds silver, but thick black smoke was billowing from the north. She rose and headed to the main door of the hotel. A crowd had gathered on the pavement outside, staring at something in the distance. Someone mentioned Balmarra. At that moment she saw Jacob and the horse-and-cart approaching at full speed along the street. She stepped out, her arms waving. He pulled to a stop and helped her climb up.

Cicely could see the flickering light above the trees and heard the clanging bells of the fire truck ahead. When they reached Balmarra, the air in the driveway was full of falling embers, like burning snow.

They could feel the heat from one hundred yards away. Some of the panes of the glass house had cracked and turned black. Jacob was already providing buckets, and the firemen had formed a human chain to the river. But they could all see that it was too late: The fire had taken hold, and there was no stopping it. The house was a blackened frame lit up from within. Flames rose from the roof in a golden crown until there was a great crash and there was no roof anymore.

Malcolm arrived in his motorcar and came running.

"Have you seen Antonia?" he asked, looking around wildly. "Has anyone seen my wife?" Tears were streaming down his face. Cicely took his hand and held it. "My wife?" he repeated.

But no one had.

Antonia had been expecting help to arrive any minute. It was lucky that it was the servants' day off; they would be safe. And then she remembered old Mr. Baillie. Embers from the house were coming down on the roof of his cottage. It might catch, too. She pounded on his door, but no one answered. Then she shouldered the door once, twice, three times, until, with a splintering of wood, it opened. The gardener was in his bed in the attic, fast asleep. He was a little put out to see her standing in his bedroom.

"Mr. Baillie, there's a fire in the main house!" she yelled. "You must get out!"

"Where's Tom?" he asked.

"You mean Jacob? I'm sure he's on his way," she replied.

Antonia took a couple of blankets, helped him down the ladder, and led him outside. The fire brigade had finally arrived, and they were doing what they could.

"Antonia!" It was Malcolm. His face was red, his eyes narrowed. He was clearly furious. But then he took her in his arms and held her.

"Thank goodness," he whispered.

All they could do was watch the fire run its course. Luckily the Baillies' cottage did not catch. Everyone was speculating about what had happened: a gas leak, a fire in the kitchen, a faulty electric connection? A confession was on the tip of Antonia's tongue, but somehow she couldn't actually voice it.

"No one was killed," Malcom said more than once. "And at least we're insured."

She tried to remember if she had paid the last premium. So much had been going on, what with Cicely arriving and the party. Malcolm read her face.

"Don't say it," he said. "Don't tell me we're not?"

"I'm sure we are," she replied. But the more she thought about it, the more she was convinced that they weren't.

At least she had her journals. It was as she was brewing tea—these occasions always seemed to demand endless pots of tea—that she noticed old Mr. Baillie staring at the suitcase where she had stashed them. He picked it up and was about to head toward the kitchen table with it.

"Excuse me," she said. "What are you doing with my suitcase?"

He stopped and turned.

"I'm sorry. My Tom had one just like it."

It was a cheap old thing made of brown cardboard that was supposed to look like leather. Inside the lining was torn and the pocket ripped. Now that the house was gone, however, it was the only suitcase she had. And then she realized that apart from the journals, she had nothing left to pack. Everything she owned—her clothes, her books, her art materials, her childhood toys, her family heirlooms—was ash. The thought left her breathless, weightless, and to her surprise, ever so slightly exhilarated.

"You're welcome to have it," she said. "Once we get ourselves sorted."

"I took them, you know," old Mr. Baillie said. "And threw them away. Up the glen."

"Threw what away?" she said.

How old was the man now? she wondered. He should have retired years ago. He tapped his nose, then passed the suitcase back to her. It was empty. Surely he hadn't thrown away her journals? But no, there they were, stacked on the sideboard beside the parcel from the India Office.

At that point the front door opened and a crowd of people came in, Cicely and Malcolm followed by the firemen and Jacob. There weren't enough cups or chairs for everyone, and some had to make do with bowls and stand. She almost offered to nip up to the house and get some more until she remembered that she did not have a house; there were no more cups or chairs.

It was dawn by the time everyone left. Antonia, Malcolm, and Cicely slept in one of the former servants' cottages, the two women in the bedroom and Malcolm downstairs in an armchair.

"What a day," Antonia whispered.

"Indeed," said Cicely.

"I think I know why," she continued. "Why my father did what he did."

She turned to face Cicely. In the half-light she could see that her eyes were open. And then she told her about the painting in the attic of the black lady in blue and the inscription she had found on the back.

"Her name was Isabella," she said. "Isabella Pick. She was my great-grandmother. If you want my opinion, I bet half of Glasgow has an Isabella in their past."

"Does George know?" Cicely asked.

Antonia shook her head.

"I don't know. Actually, there's something else I need to tell you. A parcel arrived from the India Office. I saved it from the fire."

"Did you open it?"

"I think you'd better do that," she replied.

Antonia found Malcolm in the kitchen flicking through her journals. He looked up when he saw her.

"You're very good," he said. "I had no idea."

She took the journals out of his hands and began to shove them back into the suitcase.

"How long have you been painting?" he went on.

"Malcolm!" she said. He was no doubt humoring her.

"Listen to me," he said. "The reason I met Jacob Baillie's mother was to give her a monthly allowance. It was what your father wanted."

"What for?"

"I have no idea. There was nothing untoward going on. For a start, she must be in her fifties."

He was gazing at her, his pale lashes fluttering like moths' wings. But it was too late: The train, as it were, had left the station.

"What's that?" Malcolm leaned across and pulled a piece of paper from the torn lining of the suitcase.

25

Cicely sat on a bench in the ruined glass house. She needed to do this alone. The parcel smelled of waiting rooms, of dust and sweat. This was it, the moment she had been dreading. If these things were George's, they would have to wait for the discovery of a body. They could wait years and never find him at all. What would she tell Kitty? That her father was probably dead, but there would be no confirmation, no coffin, no burial.

She took a deep breath, then released it. Carefully she slipped the paper knife along the seam of brown paper and ripped it open. Inside were a few things: a pipe, a notebook with an address inside—Balmarra, Argyll—and a pocket watch, a name engraved on the back.

Antonia rose to her feet as Cicely entered the Baillies' cottage. She had been making toast on the range.

"Are you all right?" she asked.

Cicely nodded her head and walked across to Jacob, who was rinsing cups at the sink.

"Jacob, was your father called Tom?" she asked.

He put down the cup in his hand and folded the tea towel.

"He was," he said. "Why?"

"I'm so sorry," she said, and handed him the parcel.

Tom Baillie had disappeared twenty-one years earlier. There had been dozens of rumors—he had run off with another woman, he was in prison, he had changed his name and was living in Inverness. Someone claimed they had seen him once on the Northern Line of London Underground.

In fact for the last twenty-one years his belongings had been lying in a remote valley in the Himalayas. Edward Pick had sent his gardener's son on a secret trip to find rare specimens for his garden. No wonder he was so against his own son's vocation. Did he feel increasingly guilty? In his last few months was he filled with remorse?

The Snow Tree must have been collected by Tom Baillie. The envelope containing seeds and a specimen that Cicely found in the library must have been sent to Edward Pick. Why hadn't he registered it at the Botanic Garden? Why hadn't he planted them? It made no sense.

Old Mr. Baillie wept when he saw his nephew's belongings.

"I knew he was gone," he said.

A boy arrived later with two telegrams for Cicely.

"Need funds," the first demanded. "Send money now. Stop. G."

"Coming home in a week. Stop," said the second. "Love Kitty."

In retrospect the previous six months had been the hardest but most exhilarating of Antonia's life—Cicely and Kitty's arrival, George's disappearance, Henry, and the loss of Balmarra. But now she had been left with nothing, nothing but Malcolm. When she had floated the idea of the trip and he had thought she was joking, she was sure that her marriage would be the next part of her life to crumble.

In January she had been standing on the pier at Hunter's Quay, her suitcase packed, waiting for the steamer, when she heard her name. Everyone turned and stared. Only she kept her eye fixed on the distant white speck that was plowing its way across the firth toward her.

"Antonia!" Malcolm called again. "Didn't you hear me?"

He stood at her side, panting slightly.

"I'm not joking," she said without looking at him. "I'm not changing my mind."

Falling in love with a man, she had decided, was a gradual process. When they initially met, Malcolm had not struck her as someone she could care about, but slowly, week by week, she had found aspects of him to admire—the clear blue crinkle of his eyes, the curve of his calf, the unself-conscious joy he took in seemingly mundane things like a car engine, a shot of malt in a crystal glass, finding a penny on the street. It was his interest in her, however, the way he said her name, the small unsuitable gifts that made her laugh—a book on sheep husbandry, a pair of glove stretchers—but most of all his absolute certainty in the viability of the whole affair, that really cemented her feelings. To be chosen was intoxicating. By the time they were married, her head was turned. She was besotted, charmed, and in good faith, she had given him all of herself, she had opened up to him. And yet married life was not what she expected. No one, especially not Malcolm, could keep up such an intensity of feeling.

Falling out of love, she had discovered, was an altogether faster process. While the heart took time to soften, it could harden like a ground frost practically overnight. It was the little things, hair in the sink, the crumple of a shirt discarded on the floor for someone else to pick up, a sarcastic tone of voice. The vision he had of her, of which she had been unaware during their courtship, was as a woman who was inept, clumsy, indecisive, unsure of her own mind. And if she had remained, she could see herself shrinking into Malcolm's version of herself: a woman without color, without shape, without merit.

The steamer grew bigger, and passengers began to lift their bags in anticipation of boarding. Malcolm's face was white, tight, like the knuckles of a clenched fist.

"You have no idea about where you're going," he said. "You've never been there."

"I've never been anywhere," she said. "Malcolm, find someone else. Forget about me."

In her pocket she had a map, Tom Baillie's map, which she had found in his suitcase lining. Who knew, maybe she would also find her brother? If he was still there. Which was unlikely.

Malcolm took a deep breath, as if winded. And just for a moment she felt for him. People were glancing across at them, children's faces turned away by mothers' hands. The steamer was about to dock, and the crowd began to shift forward on the jetty. She picked up her cases and joined them.

"Antonia!" he said. "I won't allow it!"

It was the proverbial cherry on the cake, a comment that summed up everything that was wrong with her, with him, with their relationship. She didn't wait for more but started to walk up the gangplank. He would find out later that, with Mr. Drummond and the bank manager's help, she had taken exactly half their savings.

The train to London was about to depart from Glasgow Central. Her luggage was stowed, her hat in her lap. She had made a reservation for luncheon in the restaurant car once they had departed from Carlisle, but in truth she had no appetite. The door drew open, and for just a fraction of second, she imagined it was Malcolm, come to bring her back.

"Is this Number 14?" an elderly man asked. "We have a reservation."

"Where's the ticket?" his wife demanded. "You'll have to check."

It was compartment 14, and they did have two seats booked all the way to Crewe. They settled into the compartment, fluttering tickets, newspapers, handkerchiefs, and a box of toffees that they kept on offering and she kept on declining. The whistle blew, and the finality of the situation suddenly hit her.

"Where are you heading?" said the elderly woman.

"India," she had replied. "Or thereabouts. Have you heard of the Rong Chu? It's a river. I'm going to find the Snow Tree."

The woman's eyes widened a little as she unwrapped a toffee and started to chew.

26

The new year had arrived, and with it the heaviest snowfall they'd seen in the Peninsula in years. The hills, the gardens, the trees, were covered with a muffle of white. Old Mr. Baillie passed away in his sleep. It was a blessing, everyone said. He was ninety-two. On Jacob Baillie's instructions, the glass house was gone, dismantled and shipped by barge to Glasgow to be erected in the Botanic Gardens in the West End. The ring and clank of metal falling on metal had sounded out across the estate for three days as each pane of glass was wrapped in newspaper and labeled, each iron frame or pillar carefully cataloged. A barge was tethered in the water in front of the house, and using a small rowing boat that went back and forth maybe a hundred times, the glass house was loaded up and then sailed away. In the snow you could still make out its huge footprint and see the steps down to the boiler room, which was locked up now. Weeds would soon sprout in the cold damp earth. It could be planted anew with fragrant azaleas and flowering hydrangeas, or maybe it would be left to grow wild, to return to its natural state with foxgloves, primroses, and bluebells.

Cicely had moved into one of the former servants' cottages on the estate. Once the chimneys had been swept and the fires lit, it was much warmer than Balmarra had ever been. She had become interested in studying law, like Christabel Pankhurst, and planned on applying to the University of Glasgow. Maybe that way she could become self-sufficient? Antonia had gone on a trip and asked her to take care of her journals while she was gone. Cicely had seen the journals before—they had been in the library. She had no idea that Antonia had painted them. The botanical illustrations were extremely accomplished.

"And if I don't come back, give them to Kitty," she had said.

Kitty had arrived back from school for Christmas, looked at the blackened pile of rubble that had been Balmarra, and been philosophical.

"We could always rebuild it," she said. "Or maybe not. Maybe it's the garden that I really love."

Nobody was sure what was going to happen to the garden. Jacob Baillie didn't have the funds to run it. There was a rumor circulating that Keir Lorimer might make an offer, but there was another that he had proposed to an eligible young lady and was all set to move to Edinburgh.

One day in February, Cicely received a card from Lorimer asking if he could call. Although she'd seen his plane a few times, they hadn't spoken since that day she had called on him in his office six months earlier. So much had happened since then, so much had changed.

Lorimer arrived in a new car with a large bunch of hothouse flowers. She invited him in, but even though he sat by the fire Lorimer didn't take off his coat.

"Will you stay on at Balmarra?" he asked.

"For a little while. I want to be near Kitty."

"And your husband? If you don't mind me asking."

"We have decided to live separately," she replied. "The last thing

I heard is that he's living in Calcutta, trying to raise money for his next expedition."

What did Lorimer think of her now? she wondered. She offered him tea. He declined. Maybe all he had been attracted to was the thrill of the illicit. Cicely picked up the flowers.

"They're lovely," she said. "I'll put them in water."

"Wait!" he said.

Lorimer was on his feet.

"It seems to me that secrets have a corrosive quality," he said. "What's the point if you take them to your grave? Life is so very short."

She frowned. What was he talking about?

"Put your coat on," he went on. "I want to show you something."

The ground was covered in snow as thick as felt. A flurry fell from a branch; a crow rasped in a tree. They walked up the glen and then turned to the right. The path had been covered, and so Lorimer guessed the way, often taking them through thickets or pockets of deep snow.

"I wish you would tell me where we're going," she said.

"I saw something," he replied. "From my plane. It had been all covered up, but the winter storms exposed it."

It began to snow again, thick and fast, covering the tops of their hats, their shoulders, the backs of their legs. They stopped under the canopy of a tree. Was he lost? She most certainly was: She had never been to this part of the estate before.

"Cold?" he asked.

She shook her head no. He blinked once, twice, three times, his eyelashes full of snow. She reached up and brushed a single speck from his cheek. He swallowed, and then, in a single movement, he took her head in his hands, gently pulled her toward him, and kissed her on the mouth. It was audacious and glorious.

"I found it," he whispered. "It was here all the time. Look up."

Cicely glanced up at the swirl of snowflakes coming down from the sky, at the leaves of the tree above. It was hard to tell one from the other. Both, she now saw, were white.

It was unfortunate, Antonia repeated, that the mule carrying all their supplies had been bitten by a snake, panicked, and thrown itself down a ravine. Malcolm looked at his breakfast, stewed yak that was about to go bad, poked it around with his fork but didn't eat any. It was March, and they had been trekking for two weeks now, give or take a day. Their feet were blistered, and their bellies ached with hunger and an appetite for anything but yak. Malcolm had never looked so disheveled, his nose burned by the sun and a pale orange stubble covering his chin. It was growing light, and the early-morning sun made him look haggard. She was sure she looked equally terrible—her skin burned, her clothes torn and stiff with sweat and the reek of mule. At least they had porters, six local men and their beasts, who looked at the map and nodded their heads. They knew where they wanted to go.

"How long now?" she asked the lead man, who had a little English.

He smiled a toothless smile and pointed north.

"Two hours," he said.

Antonia swept back her hair and felt her spirits rise. They were almost there.

Back in the railway carriage, after she had bragged to the lady with the toffees, as the train was about to pull out of Glasgow, she saw the way the woman was looking at her. She was suddenly gripped with terror. What was she doing? Had she gone mad? She would be ripped apart by wild animals or be eaten by crocodiles. She got to her feet and made for the door, pulling, tugging, yanking it open. She had to get off. A breeze rushed down the corridor and caught the back of her throat. As the train started to move, she hurried along the carriage, faster as the train's pace increased. The door must be open, she realized, as she could hear the screech of the wheels on the tracks. There was a commotion up ahead: a shouting, a thunder of feet and effort and weight. She reached the end of the compartment, where the conductor was standing over the heaving slump of a man.

"You could have been killed!" the conductor was saying. "We take no responsibility . . ."

Her only exit was blocked. Antonia looked out as the city sped by. Maybe she should throw herself out. That would be a fine end, a crumpled mess at the side of the tracks. Someone would have to clean it up, and she wouldn't wish that job on anyone. Her eyes blinked with moisture. And then she became aware of a presence at her elbow. Where was her ticket? Surely she hadn't lost it already. Surely not. But it wasn't the conductor.

"I took the liberty," said her husband, "of flinging myself onto your train."

His trousers were torn at the knee. There was soot on his hands and left ear.

"I'll climb off at the next stop," he said, "if you want me to. But otherwise, I'd very much like to come on your trip after all."

He was looking at her in a way he never had before.

"But you have a job—"

"Bugger the job," he said.

"I'm going to the back of beyond," she went on. "To a place no one has really heard of."

He nodded.

"I'm in."

She shook her head no.

"Please," he said, taking a half step closer. "There was never— could never be—anyone else. But you."

As the train hurtled south, as they thundered through a tunnel and out the other side again, as the world was softened by smoke and steam and the heartbeat of the iron rails beneath the wheels, she saw that he was on the brink, just as she had been only minutes before.

"Look at you," she said, straightening his collar.

He took her hand and held it to his mouth.

"There probably won't be room for you at luncheon," she said. "We'll have to eat from the buffet car."

The idea of a hot dinner, even from a train buffet car, was heavenly to her now. As she lay awake beneath her blanket on the remote mountainside, the cold seeping up from below, Antonia couldn't stop thinking about food, mashed-potato-and-fish pie, cream cakes, and Irish coffee. She even longed for a crumb of Cook's pastry.

Breakfast the next morning was a lump of stale bread washed down with coffee so weak it was the color of tea. As usual they had risen before dawn and aimed to set off before it got too hot. The mountains here were higher than any Antonia had ever seen, their peaks covered in snow. They were aiming for a dip in the middle, a pass.

The climb was steep, the path rocky underfoot, and twice Antonia slipped and almost fell. But she made it, she reached the top of the pass. As they caught their breath, the lead porter pointed. On the other side was a narrow valley filled with forest. They were almost there. Down, down, down they went, their pace quickening until they reached a small fast-flowing river. There they decided to leave the mules and the porters on one side and wade across, their bags on their heads.

For the first time in her adult life, she felt close to George. Had he been here, had he felt this ice-cold stream rush around his thighs, had he looked up to see eagles soaring above? No wonder he had returned again and again. At the far side Malcolm held out his hand and hauled her up.

"If the map is right," he said, "the Snow Tree should be—"

"I know," she said.

They walked up a small rise and looked out across the valley. It was beautiful, the most beautiful view she'd ever seen. Malcolm walked ahead, then paused and looked back. Ever since he had appeared on her train, he had listened to what she had to say, asked her opinion, done what she asked, and although it was fair to say that it was often not without discussion, their roles had fundamentally shifted.

"Antonia?" Malcolm called out. There was a catch in his voice that she couldn't quite decipher.

She followed him over the rise. In her head she had visualized the Snow Tree exactly, its profusion of white leaves that looked like snowflakes. Instead of the tree, however, there was just a stump and an abandoned wooden hut. The wind rushed down from the mountains, and the sky clouded over. She closed her eyes and opened them again, hoping, she supposed, that it was all some terrible dream. But she was not dreaming. The tree had been cut down and been used to build the hut. She ran her hand through her hair and turned away. They had come all this way, spent weeks on boats, days on trains, then walked on foot for miles, eaten only yak for days—for what? For *this*? It started to rain, to thunder down in sheets and gusts that quickly soaked her clothes, her hair, even her boots. Could it get any worse? Malcolm's shoulders were shaking. He came over, and she saw he was not crying but laughing. He was in hysterics. It was impossible to remain upset. Her mouth began to curl up at the corners. As the rain poured, as the sky lowered and the day darkened, they sank onto the grass and laughed until they ached.

They spent the night in the hut and built a small fire to dry their clothes. Later, huddling together to keep warm, they found each other in a way they never had before.

The next day, when they returned to the river, all the mules and porters had gone, leaving just a single object: Antonia's suitcase. It wasn't quite so funny then. Without transport, tents, enough food—although they did discover a packet of stale digestive biscuits in the suitcase—or any idea where they were going, they tried to trace their way back. Antonia walked in front, Malcolm, still carrying the suitcase, close behind. They followed the path until it petered out; they drank from streams and slept entwined together under their jackets against the chill of the mountain night. The mountains seemed to stretch endlessly in all directions.

On the third day they climbed to the top of a ridge to try to get their bearings. They looked out across a valley and there, on the horizon, was a pale haze, like a riot of falling snow, a whole forest of trees with leaves as delicate and perfect as ice crystals.

"Is that . . . ?" she asked.

Malcolm stared. He frowned, he smiled; he hooked his arm around her waist and pulled her to him.

"We've found it," he whispered.

About the Author

Swordfish Photography

BEATRICE COLIN was a novelist based in Glasgow, Scotland. She was the author of *To Capture What We Cannot Keep* and *The Glimmer Palace* as well as radio plays and adaptations for BBC Radio 4.

Recommend *The Glass House* for your next book club!

Reading Group Guide available at

www.readinggroupgold.com